I0672581

WINTERVENTION

A Jamie Austen Thriller

TERRY TOLER

OTHER BOOKS BY TERRY TOLER

Thank you for purchasing this novel from best-selling author Terry Toler. As an additional thank you, Terry wants to give you a free gift.

Sign up for:

Updates
New Releases
Announcements

At terrytoler.com

We'll send you an eBook, *The Book Club*, a Cliff Hangers novella, free of charge. The one that started the Cliff Ford mysteries.

Sixty-three percent of Indigenous women in Canada have experienced physical or sexual assault.

An average of three a week go missing or are murdered.

1

He was the biggest man I'd ever seen.

Standing a dozen or so feet from me. In his size twenty shoes. At least that was my best guess.

I thought Alex was big. Alex was roughly six foot five. Two hundred pounds plus a couple of touchdowns. Maybe two hundred and twenty pounds.

This man dwarfed Alex. He had to be seven feet tall. Probably weighed four hundred and fifty pounds. Maybe five hundred. His fists were as big as my head. His thighs were the size of tree trunks. Or it seemed like it anyway.

I couldn't get any closer to him until I had a plan to take him down. Without getting hit. Or worse. I could picture myself in a bear hug. Him squeezing the life out of me. I'd like my chances better with a boa constrictor.

I could kill him easily enough. Even without my weapon. The bigger they are the harder they fall, Curly used to say.

Getting away shouldn't be a problem either. As a last resort, I had elusiveness on my side. He'd have a hard time getting close to me if I didn't want him to. But that couldn't be the plan. I had to fight him.

Which was problematic. I couldn't kill him. I needed him alive. He had information. That meant interrogating him. Assuming I could figure out how to get him to talk.

He kept looking at me with a silly confident grin on his face. Like he wasn't worried about me at all. He didn't know I was Jamie Austen. CIA assassin. I doubt he'd be that impressed even if he knew. To him I looked like a tree branch he could snap in two.

I could disable him. The easiest way to do that would be a swift kick to the shin. Strategically executed, that'd separate the tibia from the kneecap. Especially if all his upper body weight was moving toward me. That'd wipe the smug look off his face.

A sharp elbow would knock out what was left of his teeth. I'd get some satisfaction from that.

He'd fall to the ground like an axed tree.

That's what I was afraid of.

If he fell, I didn't know how I would drag him out of the building, through the snow, to the cabin.

Not possible. He had to get there under his own power.

Not only was the big galoot big, but he was ugly. I resisted the urge to say anything. I'd rather he be smug than angry.

Maybe if I had a gun, I'd like my odds better. Mine was buried in a snowdrift. From a couple of minutes before, when I fell and lost it.

He didn't have a weapon either. Ugly Guy probably didn't think he needed one. His rifle was back in his cabin. A few hundred yards from there. He didn't think it necessary to carry it with him to the barn. The only threat he faced in that area was a pack of wolves or a polar bear. And me. But he didn't know I was coming or why I was there.

It gave me an idea. The rifle would come in handy if I had it in my hands. Although having a gun can be a detriment, if you can't use it.

I did the only thing I knew to do.

Run.

Toward the cabin.

And hope he followed.

He did.

I exited the barn-like structure with precision. Giving him enough time to get close, but not too close. The door led to a snow-covered yard. The bitter cold hit my face immediately. Momentarily taking my breath away. The high today was supposed to be minus three degrees.

It was snowing again. I hadn't counted on that. The trail back to the cabin was icing over from the salt Ugly Guy had laid down earlier that day. I could envision falling on my backside. Hitting my head. Then the Willy Mammoth crushing what was left of my concussed brain between his hands.

Not a good plan.

So I decided to run across the yard. A mistake.

Evident the moment my shoe buried in the heavy snowdrifts.

The thinking had been sound. It was the most direct route to the cabin. Leading him through the snow would slow him down. Maybe it did. It slowed me down more. He was used to it. I had to hop like a bunny rabbit. Lift my leg high. Lunge forward. Catch myself in the snow without falling down.

Use up all my energy.

It felt like I was running with hundred-pound weights on my shoes. Running through a morass. Every time I took a step I sunk deeper in the snow. The wind whipped my face. Like razor blades cutting into my cheeks.

I could hear Ugly Guy breathing heavily as well. Which panicked me. If I could hear him breathing, it meant he was close. I didn't dare look back. That'd only slow me down more. I could feel his presence. He was only a few yards behind. If that.

The cabin was about twenty yards away. I could be up the steps and inside in a few seconds. I was so close I could feel the warmth inside. There I'd have the advantage. I could brandish the shotgun. Force him to give me information.

Try the shin kick. Then he'd be helpless to resist. He'd be in the cabin. Where I wanted him. I wouldn't have to drag him anywhere.

The cabin might as well have been a football field away. He was right behind me. I let out a yelp for no one's benefit other than my own. As if a scream would force me to run faster. Getting away was futile.

So I stopped to turn and face him once I realized the inevitable. Prepared a body shot with a closed fist.

It glanced off his side. Did more damage to my fist than to him.

Ugly Guy laughed. Maniacally. He was toying with me. Like a cat playing with a mouse. He reached for my coat and grabbed my hood when I turned around to start running again.

The second scream had more fear behind it. As I tried with utter futility to pull away.

Fortunately, the coat wasn't zipped, and I left him holding it.

He let out an expletive and threw the coat to the side. In the snow drift. Buried somewhere near my gun.

The winter elements bombarded my body. I still wasn't used to it even though I'd been there for two weeks.

I considered running in a different direction, away from the cabin. I couldn't escape without my coat. Hypothermia would set in within thirty seconds to a minute. The wind chill was somewhere around minus twenty.

The cabin was still my best option.

I tried to serpentine. He would get close, reach out, find nothing but air, curse, then try to change directions to match me.

I had an opening. For a moment, it looked like I was going to make it to the cabin. I was near the steps.

It felt like I was hit from behind by a Mack truck.

I did a nosedive, a faceplant, right into the snow.

Ugly Guy was on me within seconds. Sitting on my back. Weighing me down. Pushing my head in the snow and holding it there. My eyes were forced closed.

He was suffocating me. My lungs already burned from the exertion. I tried to breathe in, but my mouth filled with snow.

Was this how I was going to die?

All I could think about was Lily. My daughter. Her image flashed into my mind. It gave me the impetus to resist.

If we were on the ground, I might've been able to maneuver in a way to neutralize him. Instead, he had the advantage. His weight crushed my lungs expelling any remaining air.

I flailed my arms and legs.

To no avail.

I was going in and out of consciousness. If I didn't do something quick, I was dead. The strength left me. I could no longer resist.

All I could do was lie there and wait.

A calm came upon me. I'd read about drowning victims. How right before they died, an unbelievable calm and peace came over them.

That's how it felt now.

What would happen to Lily? It felt like I had several minutes to think about it. It could have only been a few seconds.

Alex would never meet her. Never even know she existed.

I felt tears form in my eyes, then freeze on my eyelids.

Right before everything went black.

2

CIA Headquarters
Four weeks earlier

Brad was enjoying toying with me. My CIA handler liked to make me guess where he was sending me on my next mission. I'd already guessed twelve different countries. His response each time was "cold." That's all he said.

Usually after four or five tries, he got bored and told me where I was going. For whatever reason, he was relishing watching me struggle to find the answer. Evident by the uncharacteristic smirk on his face.

Brad was normally all business. The consummate professional. He was one of the best analysts in the CIA. He had the ability to quickly assimilate facts and determine a course of action in a short period of time. His analytical mind didn't usually venture into the arena of practical jokes.

I didn't mind playing along. Seeing this side of him was refreshing. Maybe he was mellowing in his old age. Old was relative. He'd be turning fifty soon which was old for an operative but young for an analyst.

Brad had risen to the rank of Assistant Director of the CIA. Second in command. While he'd probably never become director, his skills were highly valued in CIA circles.

No one had to tell me. He'd been invaluable to me. He'd managed my entire career. Suffered through all my successes and failures. Every life and death moment. Almost like he lived vicariously through me. The tension filled dynamic brought out the best in both of us.

Which was why I enjoyed this brief interlude of levity.

"Topeka, Kansas," I blurted out playfully.

He frowned.

"No Jamie. This is an official CIA mission. You haven't been gone that long. The CIA still can't operate in the U.S."

The words warmed my heart. It felt good to be back with the CIA in an official capacity. In sort of a hybrid position. All my credentials were restored, but I could also freelance and run my own missions through AJAX.

AJAX was an art distribution company my husband Alex and I started as a cover for our CIA activities. AJAX being a combination of our names Alex and Jamie. We bought and sold expensive art. I minored in art history in college, so the cover was perfect for me. I got to do two things I loved. Rescue girls from sex trafficking and immerse myself in the art industry as a major player. I literally bought and sold tens of millions of dollars of paintings every year.

"I hope you don't send me somewhere cold," I said.

"You're the Winter Olympics Biathlon Champion. I thought you loved the cold."

"I didn't mind it when I was younger."

"Like you are so old now," he said jokingly.

I was returned to favor with the CIA because Israel finally resolved the issue with the missing Olympic Biathlon Champion. Meaning me. I'd been there working undercover for Mossad. Posing as an Olympic athlete. Competing in one of the events. The mission was a success, but the plan hadn't been for me to win the event.

After I won the gold medal, my face was plastered all over the world. Of course, I had to disappear. The acting CIA Director, Ryan Coldclaw, didn't think I could work undercover anymore.

As time passed, that became less of an issue in my mind. I'd only been recognized a handful of times and each time I dismissed it by saying I only looked like the woman. I never got any push back and thought Ryan was being too careful. My argument being, if it increased the risk in the field, I was the one being shot at. It seemed like my risk to take.

When the Israeli Prime Minister announced to the world that the missing gold medalist was killed by an avalanche while skiing alone in the Alps three days after the Olympics, the problem was solved. Along with the ongoing mystery that had captivated the nation.

It felt weird watching my own funeral which was televised to the entire nation of Israel. With much fanfare. I'd become a national hero there. Even though they didn't know who I was.

Since it was no longer an issue, I was back in business. Which meant I couldn't operate in the United States for the CIA but could run missions anywhere else in the world.

The file on Brad's desk intended for me had my curiosity piqued. I couldn't imagine where he might be sending me. I'd guessed the most obvious places. Thailand. The Philippines. Central America. Russia. Belarus. All places I'd been and were known as hotbeds for sex trafficking.

"Australia," I said as my next guess.

"Cold."

I let out a huge sigh. I usually said Australia first but didn't this time. It's somewhere I'd never been. On vacation or on a mission. A bucket list country. Someplace he'd never send me. It wasn't in his jurisdiction.

I always said Australia as a joke. For a moment, I thought maybe I should've led with it and got my hopes up. I should've known better.

Maybe cold was a clue since he kept saying it with emphasis.

"Antarctica," I said, kiddingly.

Brad laughed, then surprised me with his response. "Cold, but warm."

That didn't make sense.

"How could I be cold and warm at the same time?" I said.

"You'll understand when I tell you."

I let out another noticeable sigh. This one with a twinge of frustration behind it.

"There are a hundred and twenty countries in the world," I said. "Do I have to name all of them?"

"There are a hundred and ninety-five countries," he corrected.

"My point exactly. Go ahead and tell me."

"Guess. You were on the right track with Antarctica. And with the cold. Where you're going is cold."

"What's near Antarctica that is cold? Australia is near Antarctica. But you said that was wrong."

"It's summer in Australia right now," Brad said.

We were in the dead of winter in Virginia. It took me nearly an hour to get to Langley even though it's normally a twenty-minute drive. It had started snowing earlier that morning and traffic was slowed since the roads hadn't been plowed yet.

"What's the temperature in Australia?" I asked.

Brad picked up his phone sitting on the corner of his desk. Typed in something. Waited, then answered. It's ninety-five degrees in Sydney today. They're having a heat wave."

"Send me there."

"Maybe someday."

"Just tell me."

"You'll never guess."

"Then why are you putting me through this?"

"You always say I need to lighten up some. That's what I'm trying to do."

"I'm done playing."

"Nunavut."

I'd never heard of it.

"Where in the world is that?" I asked.

"The Arctic Circle. Near the North Pole."

I let out a cross between a gasp and a screech. That's the last thing I expected to hear. He was right. I never would've guessed it. At first, I thought he was kidding. His face said he wasn't.

"You can't be serious."

"Serious as a bull chasing a heifer."

I ignored the comment which to some might've seemed inappropriate.

"Is there a problem with female reindeer being sex trafficked that I didn't know about? Should I be looking into Santa Claus as my main suspect?"

"Inuits."

"Eskimos?"

"The Inuits would be considered Eskimos. Although the natives find that term offensive. I've heard anyway. So don't use it."

"You *are* serious. You're really sending me to the North Pole."

"Yep. Close to it."

"Is sex trafficking a problem in that region?"

Brad handed me the file. I opened it and found it filled with background information. Shy on actual mission objectives. Suspects and the like.

My mouth flew open when I saw the highlighted statistic.

"I thought that would get your attention," Brad said.

A report had been prepared several years before. Brad took the courtesy of bullet pointing it for me.

"This says they estimate thirty percent of all young girls in the region ages fourteen to eighteen are victims of sex trafficking," I said.

"Hard to believe, isn't it?"

My mouth was still gaped open.

"How many people live in the area?" I asked.

I leafed through the file looking for the information, even though I knew Brad had it memorized.

"Thirty-nine thousand. Roughly."

I did quick calculations in my head. Half of those were women. Half would be girls. Maybe a quarter of the girls were in the fourteen to eighteen age group. The primary age for trafficking in the region.

"That's over a thousand girls," I said.

"I know. That's why I'm sending you there."

The total numbers were higher in places like Thailand. The official estimate was more than two and half million people were being held in sex slavery around the world. I thought the number was at least three to four times that, but no one could prove it one way or the other.

The number in Nunavut was astounding if looked at as a percentage of the population.

I'd never heard of such a thing.

"Why don't the Canadian authorities do something about it?" I asked.

"They don't own it. The land was turned over to the Inuit people years ago. They are autonomous. With their own government and police force. Judges and court system. It's up to them to police themselves."

"It says here that a number of politicians are involved in the sex trade," I said, reading from the report.

"Sickening, isn't it?"

"That would explain why nothing is being done about it."

Brad nodded.

"Until now," I said. "I intend to do something about it."

"The report says that families are being offered $15,000 to $25,000 dollars for their daughters," Brad said.

"No way! Who has that kind of money in that area?"

"That's what you have to find out. I want you to start in one village, Yura Lake. It's on Baffin Island."

"Why Yura Lake?"

"Over the last ten years, the tiny town has exploded in growth. An anomaly for the region. The village is suddenly prosperous. That's suspicious to me."

I held the file in the air. "That's it. That's all the information you have for me. It's not much."

Usually, I had the names of individuals or organizations to go after. Most sex trafficking was considered organized crime. It took a number of people to manage that big an operation.

"The area is isolated," Brad explained. "Information is hard to come by. It's never been on the CIA's radar. I doubt we've ever run a mission up there. The island is cut off from the rest of the world during the winter months."

"What's the primary source of income?" I asked. "Could they be getting it from legitimate means? It says here that mining for gold, diamonds, and some oil and gas was enriching the area."

"It's possible. The region has vast resources. Tourism is also big. Three months out of the year anyway. Cruise ships go there. There's also hunting and fishing. There's no manufacturing industry to speak of. For obvious reasons."

"How do I even get there?"

"You'll have to fly. There are no roads from Canada into the region. From anywhere for that matter."

"No roads?"

"The land is boggy. Mostly islands. That also makes it hard to travel around. This time of year, you're driving on ice. Ferries between the islands don't operate during the winter months. Even in the summer, they have to deal with the ice and waves from storms. You'll fly to Ottawa. Then catch a flight to Iqaluit. I don't know how you get to Yura Lake. Probably by snowmobile or dog sled or something."

He was grinning like he was kidding, but I wasn't sure he was. Not if there were no roads.

"I can see why it'd be easy to run a sex trafficking operation there."

"The traffickers are able to operate with impunity. It's the most isolated place on the earth. Who's going to stop them?"

"Me."

"That's the spirit."

"I feel bad for the girls. They're trapped. They have no way to escape."

"That's part of the problem. Women are largely discriminated against in that region."

"They're discriminated against in this office," I said, roughly.

Brad's eyes widened.

"Why do you say that?"

"You sent Alex to the Cayman Islands."

Alex was there to track money hidden by bad actors. Terrorists and the like.

"I'm sending you to an island as well," he said, chuckling. "Baffin Island."

I rolled my eyes.

"What's the temperature in Cayman?" I asked.

Brad still had the phone in his hand. He looked it up. "Eighty-nine degrees."

I let out a groan.

"What's the temperature in Yura Lake? I'm almost afraid to ask."

Brad typed something on his phone. Then grimaced telling me everything I needed to know.

"Today's high is minus ten," he said, smiling from ear to ear.

"Be sure and send me a postcard," he said as I abruptly stood and stormed out of the office with the file in my hand.

3

The Arctic Circle

The nervousness in the pilot's voice told me all I needed to know. His words only confirmed it.

"Brace yourself for a rough landing," he said. "This turbulence is some of the worst I've ever seen."

We were making our approach into Iqaluit, the capital of Nunavut. In the Arctic Circle. I'd read all about the troubles getting in and out. Especially in the wintertime. By plane was the only way in. Flights landed during what they called windows. Breaks in the winter storms. I'd been stranded in Ottawa for five days waiting for one of those windows to manifest itself.

I'd tried to hire a private plane, but every pilot basically laughed at me. One actually said, "You couldn't pay me enough money to fly into that God-forsaken place."

There's no place on earth that's God forsaken. God cares about all of his creation. But I didn't argue with him. The pilot's point was well taken. Now that I was experiencing it first-hand. Flying there in the winter was crazy.

From my vantage point in the cabin, I could see out the window on both sides of the plane. When flying commercial, I always sat in the back. In an aisle seat. So no one could sneak up on me from behind. Not that I observed any threats on this particular flight. Still there were dozens of people and organizations in the world who'd love to see me dead and would pay great sums of money to make it happen.

Curly taught me to always take every precaution no matter how unnecessary they may seem. He was my trainer at the CIA. My mentor. May he rest in peace. His advice had saved my life more times than I could count, and I wasn't about to ignore it now.

Although I felt a little foolish being on this flight to begin with. This seemed like an ill-conceived mission. Flying into the Arctic Circle in the dead of winter to hunt for a sex trafficking ring all by myself.

The danger of the unknown aside, the weather was problematic. The expected high today in Iqaluit was minus one. The expected low was twenty below. Forty below wind chill. This part of the world experienced darkness all but one hour a day this time of year. I preferred working in the dead of night, but not when it was forty below zero.

I wondered if forty below really felt much different than twenty. I shivered at the thought even though the cabin was toasty. I'd worn layers for when we landed and was burning up on the plane.

I couldn't wait to get off for other reasons. The entire flight felt like I was on a ride at Disney World. One of those computerized 3D theater-like rides that jerked you around while you watched a big screen. Images that simulated danger. I didn't ride those anymore. I saw too much of it in real life to waste my entertainment dollars and time on it.

Same with video games. The last thing I wanted to do was get shot at by a terrorist on a television set.

Actually, the last thing I wanted to do was die in a plane crash on a mission. An operative's worst fear. Being killed from nonaction. Invest all your time training and die in an accident. Fall sick from eating or drinking the wrong thing. Or a literal fall. That'd be the worst. Hitting your head on the shower or tub. Slipping on a trail and tumbling over a cliff.

Getting hit by a bus.

With all the precautions I took, it'd be a shame to have nature get me. Especially when it was out of my control. I had zero confidence the pilot could land the plane in this weather.

Whatever they were paying him was not enough.

While in Ottawa, I had plenty of time to research Nunavut. What I found was surprising. A gallon of milk cost fifteen dollars. A jar of peanut butter, twelve dollars. A pound of bananas could run over five dollars. A twelve-ounce bottle of soda would set you back five bucks.

I thought things were expensive in the D.C. area. And they were. Nevertheless, I could get a pound of bananas for thirty to forty cents on sale at the grocery store.

It made sense why it cost so much in Iqaluit. When you considered what it took to get supplies there. They obviously couldn't grow produce or raise livestock. Everything had to be imported. The supply chain had to cost a fortune to develop and maintain.

The plane tickets were outrageous. More than two thousand each way. Maybe not so outrageous now that I was experiencing it. The only way to get there in winter was by plane. Coming in July would certainly make more sense.

Then I could come by cruise, although that ticket costs an average of a hundred and twenty thousand dollars per person.

The flight was surprisingly full. While the population of Iqaluit was around 7900 people, the demand for travel in and out was still there. I understood why people wanted to leave. But why did they want to go back this time of year?

Most flights were according to the flight attendant who seemed concerned by the excess turbulence. That made me even more concerned.

A jolt sent my stomach to the back of my throat. Or maybe my throat to the bottom of my stomach. We were in a small craft which also explained why we were being tossed around like clothes in the dryer.

Thirty souls were on board. I could hear the news headlines reporting the crash.

THIRTY-THREE DEAD INCLUDING THE CREW.

Curly would be mad at me for thinking those thoughts. He said to always keep a positive attitude. I would if my heart wasn't being jilted like a scorned lover's.

I wished A-Rad or Colonel were flying me. I trusted them. When I met them, they were flying missions into hurricanes. To gather weather measurements. I'd flown with them into the eye of a hurricane once. On a mission to Cuba.

That's what this felt like.

The lurching.

The wave pool-like motions.

Up and down. The high-tech aircraft we were in when we flew into the hurricane was built to withstand the stress. This plane felt like it could be snapped in two at any time.

A bang startled me.

Either something in the overhead bin or something in the cargo hold. I hoped it wasn't my bag full of weapons.

The pilot accelerated as we approached. Usually, we slowed down. We were coming in fast. The only way he could protect us from the windshear and hold it steady. I presumed.

For a moment, things stabilized.

The wheels of the plane banged into the runway. He didn't brake as expected. Instead, he accelerated again. Lifted off. A collective scream went through the cabin as the pilot tried to lift the plane back in the air quickly. On a steep rise.

The turbulence started again with a vengeance.

We banked to the left. Taking us back over Frobisher Bay. I couldn't actually see the water. Only the ice covering it. We were in the one-hour window of sunlight.

The airport was behind us now. A guide was supposed to be there to meet me. To drive me across the frozen bay to Yura Lake.

"I apologize," the pilot came on the intercom and said. "It wasn't safe to land. We're going to make one more approach. If we can't land safely, we'll have to turn around and go back to Ottawa."

A groan went up from the crowd.

I didn't join in.

Fine by me.

I was having second thoughts about the whole thing.

Then I remembered the girls. The reason I was there. I said I'd endure almost anything to help girls being trafficked.

Thirty percent.

That number was stuck in my head. I still couldn't believe it. The government report said thirty percent of underage girls were being sex trafficked.

I was anxious to get on the ground. To start investigating. I wanted to go on this mission to see if the thirty percent number was true.

I had no idea where to begin. Other than go to Yura Lake and shake the trees and see what I saw.

Back in Washington, I'd looked at the satellite photos of the area. The town was right on the lake. More of a village. Maybe a hundred houses. Several dozen businesses. A school. K through 12 in one building.

One of the first places I intended to go. To talk to the principal. Girls could not go missing out of the school without the principal knowing about it.

Outside of the main village was a subdivision. Something similar to what you might see in Virginia. It did seem out of place. Higher-end homes. Gated. Completely surrounded by a wall. All the homes were equipped with solar panels, and the neighborhood seemed to have its own power grid and water system.

In the northern edge of the town was a dome shaped building. An observatory. The Northern Lights were visible in the area. Particularly from October to April. They were supposed to be the most vibrant in the winter months.

The Observatory was free to enter. Another place I intended to go right away.

By the time we circled around to start another approach, my resolve had returned. I wanted to land. Get going on the mission. See the Northern Lights.

First, we had to survive the landing.

The second approach was the same as the first. The pilot accelerated to maintain enough momentum to knife through the high winds. Seemed faster this time. The whole airplane shook from the pressure.

I heard a few more screams.

I said a prayer.

The wheels bounced on the runway. The left wing tilted. I thought I saw a spark when it tipped the ground.

A gust under the right wing would flip us over.

The pilot had no choice but to brake given the precarious position of the aircraft. He couldn't accelerate and lift off again.

The plane bounced again, then steadied.

The runway was 8,605 feet long.

How did I know that? Curly taught me to know everything. To do my homework. Prepare for a mission like my life depended on it. Sometimes it did. I remembered facts. Numbers. Statistics.

Thirty percent.

The girls.

That's why I was there. Now that I was on the ground, they'd be on the forefront of my mind.

The plane came to a halt.

The passengers erupted in applause.

The plane spun around to taxi back to the terminal. The engines sputtered and died.

I could hear the pilot trying to restart them. He was unable to. Probably because of the intense cold on the ground. Maybe the engines were protesting the rough treatment.

"This is your captain again. I'm sorry for the rough landing," he said over the intercom.

Me too.

"Unfortunately, our engines aren't going to restart. I've notified the tower to send a maintenance crew to tow us to the gate. It'll be a few minutes."

At least we were on the ground. What was a few more minutes?

It gave me time to gather my thoughts. Get into mission mode. Once I was in the theater, my mood changed. I felt strong. Resolved. Determined. Stronger than my enemies.

Hopefully, I'd soon have a name or names to go with the villain in my head.

The tow arrived and slowly took us to the terminal. There were no jetways. The steps were lowered. When I exited the plane, the cold wind took my breath away and almost knocked me off my feet.

I couldn't believe it.

I'd never felt cold like that before.

As much as I had prepared mentally and emotionally, nothing could've prepared me for it.

Suck it up, Curly said in my head. *Don't be such a wuss.*

He usually added a colorful word or two to the instructions when he called me a wuss.

I didn't care. I was practically running. I couldn't get inside soon enough.

We were led to baggage claim. I heard English. Also Inuktitut. The local language of the Inuits. The ratio was about fifty/fifty.

The bags came quickly enough. Except mine wasn't there.

I rubbed my face roughly.

I needed my guns and supplies. Night vision goggles. Assault rifle. My trusty Sig. Magazines. Not the kind you read. Magazines filled with bullets. I'd brought more than I probably needed.

Which made no difference if they didn't make it on the flight.

I went to the information desk to lodge a complaint. The lady said she'd track it. It'd have to be brought there on the next flight.

"When will that be?" I asked.

"I have no idea. Probably one to two weeks. This series of storms have settled in for a while."

"Can you bring my bag to me?"

"Where are you staying?"

"Yura Lake."

"Oh. No. I'm sorry. We don't have a way of getting it to you. You're welcome to come back and get it. But I realize that might be impossible. How long are you staying?"

"I don't know."

As long as it takes.

"You can retrieve it when you fly home. We'll store it for you."

I'd have to make do.

There were polar bears on Baffin Island. Lots of them. Surely, I could find high powered rifles. Either steal or buy one.

I thanked the lady. It wasn't her fault and I walked outside to find my ride. He was nowhere to be found. I practically froze to death looking for him.

I went back inside. Asked around. No one knew where he was.

"That's just great," I muttered under my breath.

I remembered what Curly said. "When missions start bad, they usually end bad."

I hoped he was wrong.

4

Iqaluit, Nunavut

The lady at the information desk who handled my lost bag claim was also who I needed to see about transportation to Yura Lake. She was extremely perky considering the nature of her job. Dealing with customers with problems.

I'd anticipated finding a group of people battered and bruised by the weather. In Virginia, the citizenry complained incessantly when the temperature fell below freezing. Or a little ice built up on the road.

These people lived in these conditions nine to ten months out of the year. The locals seemed to have embraced their home and were making the best of it. They weren't bubbling over with personality but weren't depressed either. More resolute and determined. At least that was my impression based on the limited interaction.

It was inspiring. Made me want to suck it up and quit the complaining in my head.

"I need to get to Yura Lake," I said to the lady trying to match her positive tone and the smile on her face.

She shrugged. "That'll be difficult."

"Somebody was supposed to meet me. Atanarjuat. I hope I'm pronouncing his name correctly."

She grimaced this time.

"Ugh. Oh yeah. You did pronounce it right."

"I take it you know him. Can you get in touch with him?"

"My guess is he's at a bar. You wouldn't want him driving you anyway. I could've told you he's not very reliable."

"Hm. Well, I have to get there. Preferably tonight."

It was actually still daytime. The one hour of sunlight was gone and the darkness had my body clock confused.

"I'm sorry. I don't think I can help you. Not today, anyway."

"How far is it to Yura Lake?"

I think I knew. I researched it. I had to cross Frobisher Bay which was frozen over. What I didn't know was if I could get there in a straight shot, the way the crow flies.

"Twelve miles."

That had been my guess. I could run that in good weather. Not in forty below temperature. Or on ice, although I did have the proper shoes for traversing icy terrain. I'd found those before I left Virginia.

"Can I rent a vehicle and drive over?" I asked.

"Do you have experience driving on ice?"

I hesitated. Then leaned to the side and propped my elbow on the counter which came above my waist. To strike an even more casual tone. "How hard could it be?"

"Extremely. You could get lost."

"I simply drive west, right? I'll use the compass on my phone."

She shook her head.

"They aren't always reliable. Given the cold and proximity to the North Pole. The magnetic field and all."

"I'll follow the lights of the village. If it's only twelve miles, I think I'll see the town fairly quickly."

Her head was moving from side to side with more emphasis now.

"It's not just directions. It's not easy driving on ice. A vehicle can flip over if you don't know what you're doing."

"I'll take my chances."

"You also have the elements to consider. What if your engine freezes over? Do you know how to unthaw it?"

"Light a match and toss it in the gas tank?"

Her face contorted into a frown.

"I'm kidding."

She forced a grin.

I knew engines could freeze in the cold. Especially diesel engines. Which I assumed most things were up there. I hadn't thought about them freezing over.

"I'd hate for you to get stuck on the middle of the lake in the dark," she said. "You'll freeze to death."

"Let's not do that."

"Agreed. There is a dogsled."

"Isn't it too cold for the dogs?"

"They can survive up to seventy-five below zero."

"That's amazing."

"They do better than humans in the cold."

"I don't want to put the dogs through that. I'd feel bad for them."

"They love it, actually. Get a good team of dogs and they'll pull you all night."

"I don't need all night. Just twelve miles. How fast can a dog sled go?"

"Twenty miles an hour."

"That'll work."

"It's costly."

"Money is no object."

"Let me make a few phone calls."

I stepped away from the counter even though no one was waiting. The woman dialed a number right away. It gave me a moment to clear my head.

A few steps from the counter were large plate glass windows that looked out into the runway. I touched the window and was surprised by how cold it was. Not able to resist, I leaned in and breathed, fogging it up slightly.

Off in the distance I saw a plane approaching.

"Good luck landing," I muttered to myself. My back still ached from all the jostling.

It did seem like the wind had died down some. The snow on the ground wasn't blowing around with the same intensity. The plane approached and landed safely. A larger private plane. Bigger than the one we had come in on. Not a Gulfstream but something in the seventy-to-hundred-million-dollar range. Not what I expected to see in this part of the world.

The plane taxied out of my view. I'd seen a secured area on the satellite photos with a large hangar. I presumed that's where the plane went. The only place it could have gone.

I looked over and the woman was still on the phone. Having an animated conversation. Our eyes met and she didn't motion me over, so it didn't seem like she was getting anywhere.

A few seconds later, she hung up the phone and said, "I'm waiting for someone to call me back."

"Okay. I'll wait over here."

Instead, I stepped outside. Risking the cold. My curiosity was piqued. On a mission, you did what you had to do. Regardless. I was in full mission mode.

Catching my breath was difficult. The wind *had* died down, but the cold was brutal.

I made my way across the street to get a better view of the hangar. The plane had already parked inside. A bustle of activity surrounded it.

I strained to see what was going on. I wished I had my bags at that moment and could pull out the binoculars.

A huge man exited the plane. I gasped. He had to be seven feet tall. A girl followed him off the plane. I couldn't make out the age from that distance. They walked toward a waiting helicopter. He was holding her arm.

I'd noticed on the satellite photos that the observatory in Yura Lake had a helipad attached to it which seemed odd. I thought it might be for sightseeing tours in the summer, but I didn't find any advertisements for such excursions.

The large man and young woman were no longer in my line of sight. My view was blocked by the helicopter. I could only presume they had boarded. Seconds later, the rotors started spinning and it lifted off. I watched it disappear in the darkness heading out over the bay.

I went back inside and walked over to the counter. "Do you know who owns that helicopter and private plane that just landed?" I asked.

"Mr. Z."

I hadn't heard that name before. It wasn't in the CIA report, and I didn't see any reference to it in my research.

"What does the Z stand for?"

"I don't know."

"Where was the helicopter going?" I asked.

"To Yura Lake."

"I could've caught a ride with them."

"Oh no. That wouldn't be possible. Mr. Z. is a very private person."

"Is he a really tall man?"

"No. Mr. Z. is short. I've only seen him one time. Most people have never seen him."

My heart jumped like it did when a clue surfaced.

"I just saw a tall man. Maybe seven feet tall or so."

"He works for Mr. Z."

"He's huge."

"He's a descendant of the Tuniits."

"I read about them. I thought they were a myth."

She shrugged. "Who knows?"

This man was no myth.

She leaned over the counter and started to whisper. As if what she was going to tell me was top secret.

"According to legend," she said, "Tuniits were the first inhabitants of the Baffin Islands. They came over on the *Bering Land Bridge* from Greenland. Supposedly. Tuniits means giants. They were very tall. Even so, they were passive and shy. Not violent at all."

"Interesting."

"Anyway. The story goes… the Inuits and the Tuniits got along well at first. They shared the land. You know, hunting and fishing and stuff. The Inuits knew how to build kayaks. One of the giants borrowed a kayak without permission and damaged it somehow."

"What happened?"

"The Inuit was so angry he killed the giant in his sleep."

"Wow."

"Stabbed him in the neck. Killed him."

I'd used that same move several times.

"The giants were so afraid, they left. Never to be seen again. I've only seen one around here. Mr. Z.'s bodyguard."

"Why would the giants be afraid? If they're so huge."

"I don't know. Like I said, it's mostly legend. Who knows if it really happened?"

Her phone rang. She answered and turned her back to me. I stayed at the counter with my arms resting on it.

Who was this Mr. Z.? And why did he need a bodyguard?

I'd searched high and low to find out who was the money man behind Yura Lake. I'd only been on the ground for a few minutes, and I thought I had found a clue.

The private jet. The helicopter. The secrecy. It had to be him.

Where did Mr. Z. live?

I didn't see any sprawling mansions in the satellite photos. That's the first thing I looked for. All the houses in the neighborhood were basically the same size.

More importantly, where did he get his money? Was he the sex trafficker? He certainly fit the profile. It took a lot of money to kidnap and house women and young girls. To provide security. Grease the pockets of the local police and politicians so they looked the other way.

For a moment, I admired the brilliance of it. Running an operation out of this area. If there was anywhere on this earth out of the reach of those of us who wanted to bring down these kind of operations, it'd be Nunavut.

My admiration faded quickly. Turned to disgust. Men like that appalled me. They had so much money they could have dozens of girls at their beck and call. Hundreds even. They never had to struggle to put groceries on the table or pay five dollars for bananas.

Why weren't they satisfied? Why did they risk their fortunes to traffic women when it would be cheaper to pay them?

Long ago, I realized it was all about power and control. Goes back to the Garden of Eden and the fall of man. The curse that men would dominate women. That's what turned them on.

Sickening.

The mission was looking up. I already had a thread to pursue. All the minor complications aside, I was pleased and anxious to get across the bay. I was also thankful for my fortune. Had my ride been on time, I wouldn't have seen the plane land, or the helicopter take off. Or the monstrosity of a man. The Tuniit.

He shouldn't be hard to find. I could pick him out of any crowd. I also had a name for his boss.

Mr. Z.

Sounded like a bad guy's name. I took out my phone and called Brad.

"Are we having fun yet?" he answered.

"I can't feel my extremities. Other than that, I'm doing okay."

Actually, I was still burning up from all the layers. Except for the brief time when I exited the plane and went outside to watch the helicopter take off, I'd been sweltering. I wasn't about to let him know that.

"What's up?" he asked.

"I got a name for you."

"Already?"

"I don't mess around."

"That's what I like about you."

"Mr. Z. He's the richest guy in the area."

"That's not a name. It's an initial."

"It's a place to start. Shouldn't be hard. How many people in this area have a last name that starts with the letter Z?

"Z could be a first name initial."

"Either way."

"It's not a lot to go on."

"Do I have to do everything? You're supposed to provide support. So support me."

"I'll miss my racquetball match."

I laughed.

"You've never touched a racquetball racket in your life."

"I'll have you know... You're right. I've never played racquetball. I'm on it."

The line went dead.

Brad hung up before I could tell him my weapons didn't make it. Whatever. Not much he could do about it anyway. Not like he could overnight them to me. The CIA reach was extensive. Brad could usually get me anything I needed within a day. Usually within a few hours.

In this instance, I had no idea when another plane was coming. My bag would arrive before he could get something to me.

The lady behind the counter got my attention, interrupting my thoughts.

"I have a ride for you," she said, beaming with pride that she'd pulled a rabbit out of her hat.

"Great."

A dog sled run would be cold but fun. Something that wasn't on my bucket list but should have been.

"A supply truck is going to Yura Lake," she said, dashing that enthusiasm. "It's a big rig. Leaves within the hour. The driver's name is Leofric Holmee. Don't worry. You'll be fine with him. If he works for Mr. Z., then he knows what he's doing."

Perfect.

An employee of the boss man. I intended to pump him for information.

Curly you were wrong. Missions that start out bad sometimes end good.

The mission isn't over yet, I heard him say emphatically in my head.

5

Leofric Holmee was the first person I'd met in Iqaluit who I didn't like. Instantly. When he saw me, his eyes lit up like a Las Vegas casino slot machine. Filled with lust. He looked me up and down which was laughable. Not a single curve on my body was showing. I was wearing so many layers, I looked like I weighed a hundred pounds more than I did.

My long blonde hair was covered by a snug mountain classic beanie hat. Only a few locks hung out on each side. From my perspective, I wasn't the least bit attractive. I'd been away from home for several days and felt like I needed a hot shower and a bottle of mouthwash.

Didn't matter to Leofric. He seemed like the kind who would hit on anything that moved. Was he also the kind who would have sex with an underage girl being held against her will?

To be determined.

I put on a friendly smile and hid my disgust nicely. Information was gold on a mission. He worked for Mr. Z. which meant he was a potential gold mine. If I had to play up my looks for twelve miles to gather information, then so be it. Wasn't the first time and wouldn't be the last.

I held out my hand when the lady behind the counter introduced us.

"Leo, thank you for giving the lady a ride," she said, not even trying to hide her annoyance at his obvious caddy behavior.

The man tipped his cap at me and clicked his heavy work boots together. He was wearing rugged blue jeans. A long sleeved thick red checkered flannel shirt covered with an unbuttoned jacket. His gloves showed wear. He took one off to shake my hand. His hand was surprisingly smooth. Not what I expected. His face and neck were also deeply tanned. How did that happen in the Arctic Circle? I'd looked up the name of every business in the area. Which didn't take long. I didn't see any tanning booths. He didn't get it from the one hour a day of sunshine.

He also wasn't Inuit. German, I suspected, based on his name. A transplant. Someone who endured the weather for money. Mr. Z. must pay well.

"My name's Jesse," I said. Jesse Winters was my cover name for the mission. Curly said to always keep your cover name as close to your real name as possible. It made it easier to remember. Winters wasn't like Austen, but I wouldn't have trouble remembering it, considering where I was. If I forgot, the cold wind and piles of snow on the ground would remind me.

"Call me Leo," he said, holding on to my hand longer than what would be considered appropriate.

"Thank you for the ride," I said, finally pulling it away when I'd had enough.

"Thank you, pretty lady. This is my lucky day."

Not if you're a sex trafficker. In that case, this was his unlucky day. The ride was going to be extremely unpleasant for him.

"You behave yourself Leo," the lady at the counter said.

"Always," he replied, although I doubted that was true.

Leo gave the woman at the counter a wave, then used the same hand to command me to follow him. I looked back, smiled, and mouthed a thank you in her direction. She had an apologetic look on her face. Not knowing she'd done me a huge favor. I had a ride to

Yura Lake. With a potential target of my investigation. My heart was pumping blood at a fast rate in anticipation. Like it did when I was in full mission mode.

Leo walked quickly. I could've matched his steps but lagged behind a couple of feet so I could size him up. He wasn't tall. Could be considered muscular, but with a shorter build. Not stocky, but he clearly focused more on his upper body in his workout routines.

Mostly, I wanted to see if he was packing heat.

The thought almost caused me to laugh out loud, when the cold hit my face again with a vengeance. It took a second to catch my breath.

Leo didn't have a gun on him. At least not in the noticeable places. If he did, it was well hidden. A concealed gun wasn't easily drawn unless you knew what you were doing.

I felt a twinge of disappointment. I thought maybe I could steal one from him.

Probably just as well. Leo was no threat. The counter lady's concern for my safety was unwarranted. I could twist the man's limbs into a pretzel. He'd be doing me a favor if he tried something. I liked starting a mission by knocking a few heads together. It energized me.

Not the plan.

I could rattle some cages. Come in with a show of force. Send Mr. Z. a message. Make him come after me. But I had my cover to consider. Flying under the radar for a while was a better strategy. Let the sex traffickers think I was a nobody.

In all honesty, I didn't even know if Mr. Z. was the bad guy. He could be a nice church going family man with three kids and a dog. Who made his money legitimately.

My gut told me no, but that wasn't enough to go ballistic on Leo. The truck driver would have to do a lot more than flirt to get a rile out of me. Better to maintain the subterfuge. Not that I'd be undercover for long. I imagined the gossip chain in a small village like Yura Lake was activated the moment a stranger stepped foot on their soil.

Especially a blonde woman from America. Traveling alone.

Fortunately, we didn't dilly dally and walked quickly to Leo's truck. A massive rig. Bigger than I had expected. I'd envisioned an old cargo truck. Beaten down from the weather. This was shiny new. The trailer was as long as two trucks.

My heart skipped a beat when I wondered if the ice would hold such a heavy load. It must or they wouldn't risk it. I assumed the back trailer was filled with valuable cargo.

Girls?

Probably not. Probably food and supplies.

My imagination was running wild. I was seeing everything related to my mission.

The cold was clouding my judgment. I wasn't thinking clearly. Leo didn't seem to like the cold either. He gave me another leering look when he opened the door of the cab and invited me in. Then put his hand on my bottom to push me up even though it was unnecessary. I bit my tongue to keep from saying something. Part of me wanted to execute a rear kick to his chin.

Let him drink his food out of a straw for the next six weeks.

But I needed the ride.

Men were pigs. I already knew that. Not all of them but I'd met too many to count. How a man got a kick out of touching my hind end through three layers of clothes was something I'd never understand.

I really should warn Leo. Too many lustful looks and I'd put his eyeball in the back of his orbital socket.

I told myself to take a deep breath and calm down. My heart was fluttering. The adrenaline rush from the cold wind along with the thrill of the mission had me over excited. I didn't want to do anything rash. I wasn't even to Yura Lake yet.

Truth be told, Leo was an answer to prayer. As long as he got me across the frozen pond safely, then I'd endure a few looks. Actually, I intended to bombard him with so many questions, he wouldn't have time to make a pass at me.

If Mr. Z. was the head of the snake, and Leo knew it, then I'd probably know it in the next few minutes.

Leo started the truck and the powerful engine roared to life. So did the heater inside the cab. I was sweltering again within seconds and started shedding clothes. My hat and gloves were the first to go. Then my jacket.

Leo seemed to be enjoying the unintended strip tease. I stopped with several more layers to go.

For whatever reason, he didn't start driving. My body tensed. I wondered if he was going to try something already.

I looked outside to see why we weren't moving. Not seeing anything, I said, "What are we waiting on?"

"I need to let this baby warm up."

I nodded.

"How much does this thing weigh?" I asked.

"Eighty tons."

More than I expected.

"Will the ice hold this much weight?"

"Yeah. We've only had one truck fall through the ice."

I groaned.

He grinned. "Don't worry. That was in the spring. When the ice was starting to melt. The idiot driver should've never attempted it. We get paid by the load. That's why he took the risk."

I wanted to ask how much they made per load but resisted the urge. I didn't want to seem too anxious for information.

"Runs on diesel, I assume."

He shook his head from side to side. "This baby runs on electricity. I mean, it also takes diesel as a backup."

"I would guess diesel is hard to come by in the wintertime."

"Not really. My boss stores it. We have all we need. We have all the electricity we need as well. Through solar and the electrical grid."

"Who's your boss?" I asked in as casual a voice as I could muster.

Leo changed the subject which seemed odd.

"What brings you to our island of paradise?" he asked.

He put the truck in drive at the same time, looked in every direction, and began moving.

The truck moved surprisingly fast. Not lumbering from the load at all.

If I wasn't impressed by Leo, I was in awe of his truck. The ride was smooth. Automatic transmission. He could tell I was impressed and spent the next three minutes bragging about his rig.

According to Leo, this truck was a part of a fleet of three. Ordered custom for traversing the ice. He had taken great pride in describing it for me like he owned it, even though I was certain Mr. Z. was the one who purchased it. Not him.

Right behind the cab was a mattress. Leo looked at it a couple of times to make sure I noticed.

Fat chance buddy.

There was a better chance of the rig taking wings and flying us to Yura Lake then he had of getting me on that mattress. Either voluntarily or by force.

I did see a gun sitting beside the mattress. Looked away before he noticed that I saw it.

I suddenly remembered to answer his question. "I'm a journalist," I said.

"For a newspaper?"

"A magazine. I'm here to research a story."

"About what?"

Underage girls being forced into sex slavery.

"How fourteen- to eighteen-year-old girls adapt to growing up in this environment? You know. The cold and all."

"Who cares about that?"

As if I could despise him more.

"I think it'll be interesting," I said, not letting my disdain show. "The suicide rate among Inuit girls is thirty-three times higher for girls ages fifteen to twenty-four than non-indigenous people. I'd like to find out why."

That was actually true. I'd done the research. They also had a higher degree of alcohol abuse. Depression.

"I didn't mean anything by it," Leo said apologetically. "It didn't sound like the type of story that would sell magazines. Nobody cares about this part of the world."

I care.

6

Frobisher Bay

"How long have you been working for Mr. Z?" I asked Leo, causing his eyes to widen in disbelief that I knew that information.

"I didn't say I worked for Mr. Z."

"Oh come on. It's obvious. He's the richest man in the area. This rig cost a fortune. No offense, but you didn't buy it. If you did, you'd be paying someone else to drive it."

He nodded, ceding the argument.

"How long?" I asked again.

"I've been driving this truck for three weeks."

My heart dropped to the bottom of my chest.

Not because of the ride which was as smooth as ice cream. I had expected to be bounced around. Even with the rough road, the truck rode like a Cadillac. My concern was related to his experience. Or lack thereof. I wondered if he could get me safely across the frozen ice.

The lady at the airport counter said driving on a frozen bay was tricky. I suspected even more so managing an eighty-ton locomotive.

Leo must've sensed my trepidation.

"Don't worry. I know what I'm doing."

"What were you doing before you came to work here?" I asked, not convinced.

"I was running a dive shop in Costa Calma."

I groaned.

"Costa Calma is an island off the coast of Africa."

"I know where it is. I'm just wondering how you ended up here. Why would you leave a tropical paradise for this?"

I pointed outside. The snow was coming down hard now. We left the airport on what looked to be one of the main roads. I used the term "road" loosely. There might be pavement somewhere under the layers of ice, dirt, sand, rock salt, snow, and gravel, but it wouldn't see the light of day for months.

We also couldn't see the bay because of the snow, but I figured we were close. I considered keeping quiet so Leo could focus on driving, but my curiosity was getting the best of me.

"And how does running a dive shop qualify you to drive a semi? Don't you need a commercial license?"

Leo looked my way and frowned his annoyance and pointed at me.

"For your information, I have a commercial license. I got it in Germany. That's where I was born and raised."

"I figured."

Both hands were back on the wheel which I appreciated. I'd try not to say something to make him take his hands off the wheel again.

He continued. "I went to college at the University of Munich. I got my masters and doctorate from LMU. Ludwig Maximilian University."

"You have a doctorate?"

He took both hands off the wheel and pointed them at himself which made me grimace. Not only were his hands not steering the rig, but his eyes weren't on the road either.

"This is not just a pretty face," he said. One hand was pointing at his chin.

"I didn't mean to offend you."

"Don't judge me until you get to know me. I'm not a dumb truck driver."

He had a point. I'd judged him from the moment I met him. It's what I did for a living. More importantly, I needed to quit interrupting. The story was fascinating.

"What was your field?" I asked when the conversation lagged for too long.

"Science and research. I was a professor."

My jaw would've hit the floor if not attached to my face. Then it occurred to me he could be lying. I was trained to spot liars. Based on tone and facial expressions. The roar of the engine made it hard to decipher the tone and he was staring straight ahead so I couldn't get a read on his eyes and any facial tics.

"How does a university professor end up here?"

I really wanted to know.

"I got tired of the grind. It was boring. I wasn't cut out to be a teacher. Then I had a bad breakup. My ex-wife was a direct descendant of Adolf Hitler. Not literally. But you know what I mean."

"So you threw away all those years of study and money and went to an island to lay on the beach and drink rum."

"There are worse things in life."

I did know that. Alex and I owned an island north of Aruba. I imagined that I'd be dreaming of that place on some of the cold winter nights ahead of me.

"That still doesn't explain how you got from running a dive shop to driving a truck in the Arctic Circle." Clearly, the information was going to have to be pried out of him.

He didn't answer. His jaw clenched. I saw his shoulders tense. His hands gripped the steering wheel like two vise grips. The truck had come to a complete stop.

"What's wrong?" I asked.

"This is the entrance to the bay. We're getting on the ice now."

Visibility was almost non-existent. Without the headlights we wouldn't have been able to see anything. What I could see was a slight decline. A ramp. That presumably led to the ice-covered bay.

I suddenly wished I was on a dog sled. Enduring the cold. I'd prefer that to the warm cab and the thought of driving eighty tons onto a sheet of ice.

"The entry can be a little jarring," he said.

I gripped the handle on my door.

"Not like that," he said. "Unsettling might be a better word."

He inched forward. The brakes groaned. So did I on the inside. I prided myself on being brave. Fearless under pressure. Curly always said the unknown was the worst part of our job. I agreed with him. I'd much rather be facing a man with a machine gun than this icy abyss.

The truck tires made contact with the ice. I felt the difference immediately. Instability. Sort of like walking on ice. It felt like we could slide at any time.

I could see the bay now. More importantly, I could hear it. Popping. Cracking. The ice moaned from the sudden monstrosity sitting on its back. Uninvited.

"That's normal," Leo said.

I chuckled nervously. Nothing normal about driving a truck over a frozen pond. No matter how many times he said it. How normal could it be for him? He'd only been doing it for three weeks.

I let out a breath I didn't realize I'd been holding when the truck found its footing. So to speak. Leo gently accelerated. He seemed to know what he was doing. So far, anyway.

"They say it gets easier, the more times you do it," he said, in what seemed like a relieved voice.

"How many times have you done it?"

"I carry a load three to four times a week. The first time was with a trainer."

The training didn't seem like enough to me.

He must've sensed what I was thinking.

"I've driven a big rig before. It's how I put myself through college."

"In Germany?"

"Yeah."

"I drove a semi from Munich to Northern Italy. In the dead of winter. Through the Alps."

"But you had roads there."

"True. But this isn't much different. Maybe it is. You can't go as fast."

He was only going fifteen miles per hour. I could see the dashboard from my vantage point, lit up in Christmas-light red.

"Why so slow?" I asked.

"Under the ice is water."

I chuckled. Nervously.

"Obviously," he said. "What I mean is... that it's the ocean. There are waves underneath the ice."

I hadn't really thought about it. Ocean water was always circulating. It made sense that it still did even with a layer of ice covering it.

"If I go more than fifteen miles an hour," he explained, "then the waves will intensify and weaken the structure of the ice. It might not get us this time but will the next time we come through. Or the one after that. Or maybe not at all. But we don't want to risk it."

"No we don't."

Leo's confidence soared. He seemed to enjoy being the smartest person in the room. I could see his academic nature coming out. A total surprise. I'd envisioned him being a frat boy womanizer. Not a university professor. He couldn't be more than thirty-five years old. He might still be a player, but I had to admit to myself that I was impressed by his degrees. If they were real.

He continued. "The dangerous part is if we have a mechanical problem and have to stop. Axels could break in the cold. The engine could freeze over."

"What happens if you have a flat tire?"

"I keep going. You don't ever want to stop. For any reason. Unless you have no other option."

"What happens if you stop?" I was almost afraid to hear the answer.

"This rig weighs so much that if it sits on the ice for more than an hour without moving, it'll weaken the ice and fall through."

"Wow! I mean. What do you do if something like that happens? Let it fall through the ice?"

"Mr. Z. has a tow truck on standby. If I run into trouble, I get on the radio and the tow truck is here within a few minutes. They can drive faster since they don't weigh as much. He can hook me up and tow me to safety within a few minutes."

"You just confirmed that you work for Mr. Z."

Leo shrugged his shoulders.

"What's Mr. Z's real name?"

"Nobody knows. I couldn't tell you even if I did. I signed a confidentiality agreement. I don't think I'm even allowed to give you a ride. Don't say anything. I could get in trouble if my boss finds out."

"I won't say anything."

"I appreciate it."

"You still didn't tell me how you got here from Costa Calma."

"I saw an ad on the internet for drivers. The money was too good to pass up. So were the perks."

"Seems like you had it made on the island. No amount of money would make me choose this over a beach."

"Don't get me wrong. I was having a good time in Costa Calma. Lots of alcohol. Lots of women. Girls throw themselves at dive instructors."

I ignored the comment although I was sure it was true.

"There's more to life than partying," I said. "At some point, you have to grow up."

"Exactly. I make three grand every time I cross the bay with a load."

I did the math. That came to almost thirty thousand dollars a month. He'd have to go on a lot of dive expeditions to make that.

"That's good money. It must be lonely though, on the woman front."

Now we were getting to the real questions I wanted to ask.

"Nah. I do okay. That's part of my compensation."

My jaw dropped a second time. I think I knew what he meant.

He looked over at me with a sly grin. The lustful look was back. Then it turned to a partial grimace.

He immediately regretted saying it. "I said too much."

I wanted to ask a follow up question but was stunned. How did I do so without causing him to clam up?

An awkward silence ensued.

Was he talking about the trafficked girls?

My mind made the leap. Mr. Z was a rich and powerful man. He was the only one in the area who could afford to buy girls, house, and feed them. He also wasn't a family man. Not if he paid his male employees with sexual favors.

Leo clearly hadn't intended to reveal that information. A slip of the tongue.

My heart was racing. I almost forgot where I was. Had forgotten about the risk of driving on the ice. Whatever the risk, it was worth it. Leo told me everything I needed to know.

My hunch was right about Mr. Z.

We continued on in silence for a few minutes. Leo obviously afraid to say anything else.

"Please don't tell anybody what I told you," he finally blurted.

"I said I wouldn't."

"You're a journalist. I know your type. I don't want to see my name plastered in a story."

"I don't reveal my sources. Everything you said here was off the record."

"That's good."

In reality, that was the least of Leo's worries. If he was knowingly having sex with trafficked women, he was going down with Mr. Z. and the rest of them. If young girls, then his head would be dislodged from his spinal column. For now, I was giving him the benefit of the doubt.

As deplorable as his behavior was. Having sex with women in exchange for driving a truck, if the women consented, was none of my business.

We both released a sigh when we reached the other side of the bay and pulled safely onto the shores of Yura Lake. It was still snowing hard so I couldn't see much of the village. I gave Leo the address where I was staying, and he knew exactly how to get there.

When he pulled to a stop, I thanked him. Sincerely.

"Can I see you again?" he asked.

"I don't think I'll be here that long. I'll be pretty busy."

"Maybe I'll see you around."

"Maybe."

"Can I at least have a kiss? For giving you a ride."

I laughed.

"Hey! I didn't charge you."

"I'd rather pay you than let you kiss me."

"Ouch. You know how to stab a man in the heart."

"That's not what I meant." I was backtracking because I might need more information from him later. "I don't kiss a guy until the fourth date. Sorry. That's my rule."

"Great. I only have three more to go."

"This was not a date!"

"It was to me."

"Whatever. Thanks again for the ride."

"Don't get out. Let me get the door for you. The step can be tricky."

I had a reason for letting him. He got out and walked around the front of the cab. He opened the door, and the wind slapped me in the face sending chills down my spine. Even though my gloves, hat, and layers were back on.

Leo took my hand and helped me down.

"I'm good from here," I said. The door to my place was supposed to be opened. If not, the owner of the place lived in the house next to it.

"Okay. Nice to meet you," he said. "I hope to see you again."

You will.

As soon as he realized I had his gun.

7

Three days later

It snowed for three straight days. Not a dusting, but piles of snow. Measured in feet. The village of Yura Lake seemed to continue with business as usual according to a radio station in Iqaluit. Schools were open. All businesses were operating. The snowplows kept the roads cleared.

My landlady, Nirliq, was a cantankerous eighty-year-old Inuit woman, who I'd grown to love and admire, even after only three days. She had warned me not to venture out of the house. Not even to walk the thirty feet to her house.

"You could fall on the sidewalk and crack your skull," she said. "You'd be dead in a matter of minutes in this cold."

I appreciated the advice and followed it. I invited her to stay for tea and she accepted. We sat down to talk. I wanted to pick her brain since she'd lived in Yura Lake all her life. Although I learned it wasn't called that until Mr. Z. came to town and built the lake inside the gated community.

Nirliq took one sip of the tea I made, frowned, then stood to her feet. Walked to the front door with a purpose. Opened it and disappeared outside.

"This tea will not do," she said as she was leaving. Almost with disgust.

I wondered if I'd done something to offend her. Nirliq was small, but from my vantage point, she had the constitution of a tree in the Sequoia National Park.

She showed up at my doorstep a few minutes later. Carrying a steaming kettle. Filled with hot tea. She walked over to the stove and set it down and lit a burner to keep it warm. She poured all the tea I made down the drain. Took out two new cups from the cabinet. Mumbling something about not wanting to mix the two. Then poured us both a cup of her tea.

Walked back over to the rocker and sat down. My cue to do the same.

The best tea I'd ever tasted.

I deduced her tea might be spiked with alcohol even though the spirits were illegal in the community of Yura Lake. After several cups, her words slurred slightly. Noticeably, considering her mind was as sharp as a pickax.

The daily visits with Nirliq were the bright spot of my otherwise boring three days. I found it hard to function. But I had no choice and hunkered down in my house and waited out the storm.

Which was driving me crazy. I had so many things to do.

At the top of the list was to surveil the neighborhood where I believed Mr. Z. lived and ran his operations from. Based on satellite photos it looked like a normal gated neighborhood. Except it seemed out of place for the area.

It had a ten-foot-high wall surrounding it on every side. Security cameras were installed every hundred yards. I could understand why a high-end subdivision in Washington, D.C. needed walls, a gate, and around the clock security, but why did a small community in the middle of the frozen tundra need one?

The answer was obvious to me, even though I had no proof.

Not yet anyway. And getting proof would have to wait since I was stuck in that house.

As warm and cozy as it was.

Not a house. It looked like more of a box from the outside. Basically, a one-room apartment. When you entered, the bedroom and only bathroom were on the right, living room on the left, kitchen in the back.

The furnishings were modest. Next to the bed was a nightstand and lamp. The bed was surprisingly comfortable. With soft sheets and plenty of warm covers. A wood stove sat in one far corner, but I hadn't used it. The apartment was well heated with fuel oil. The furnace was sufficient and reliable according to Nirliq.

In front of the stove was a couch and chair.

It had a small kitchen. With everything I could possibly need. Well stocked. Brad paid extra to make sure plenty of food and beverages were on hand.

Surprisingly, the internet service was as good as what I had back home. Plenty of speed and megabytes and I spent most of my time researching Yura Lake and the community. Curly always said to memorize the area if you had the time. Ingresses and egresses.

Laughable.

There was no way out of Yura Lake to the outside world. No roads getting in and none leading out. The only way across the ice was by sled or snow machine. Or catching a ride with Leo. That probably wasn't going to happen. A last resort if it did.

From the internet, I could access CIA resources including the satellite photos. Brad had ordered daily updates, but they weren't current since the snow blocked any surveillance from the sky. From the most recent photos, I could see the community perfectly and studied it until I couldn't look at it anymore.

Only two entrances in and out. Both had guard gates. Which were monitored closely. One was for residents and guests. I was told by Nirliq that no one could enter without a pass. The other gate was for maintenance workers and the supply trucks. I could see the warehouse where the trucks were kept. Three of them like Leo had said.

On the northeast corner was the observatory which could be entered without passing through the gate. Open to everyone.

On my list of places to go. I still hadn't seen the Northern Lights. Too much cloud cover.

Mr. Z's community had three hundred and twenty-one acres. A man-made lake in the center had a concrete walking trail that went all the way around it and a children's playground nearby. No kids on it. Probably only used a few months out of the year.

A large recreational building had a fitness center, swimming pool, two indoor tennis courts, and a spa. At least that's what I deduced from watching people go in and out. I could see the tennis racquets protruding out of bags. The indoor swimming pool was visible through the skylights on the roof of the building.

Nirliq couldn't tell me much about the community since she'd never been inside. Access was limited to those with permission to enter. Even guests were highly scrutinized. She never had a reason to go there.

It seemed like she wasn't that impressed with Mr. Z.

"What's an old lady like me going to do in a place like that?" she quipped.

"It's a place where you could get out of the house and meet other people."

"I don't like people," she said, which caused me to chuckle out loud. I don't think she was kidding.

She did crack a smile. One of the few times.

For whatever reason, Nirliq liked me. Maybe because Brad had paid her a small fortune for the place. To make sure I had everything I needed. Maybe because she welcomed the company as much as I did.

In my three days of internet investigation, I found no evidence of sex trafficking.

I hadn't broached the subject with Nirliq. I had to be careful with her. She was guarded as it was. Information had to be pried out of her.

She warned me to expect that from everyone in Yura Lake. They didn't take kindly to strangers asking questions.

"Most people are going to clam up when they learn you're a journalist."

Maybe that wasn't the best choice of cover. Too late now.

"Don't get me wrong," Nirliq said. "We're a friendly people. We just don't take kindly to unwelcomed intruders. I appreciate the story you want to write. I've seen a lot of young girls commit suicide over the years. Not that I blame them."

An interesting comment. I wanted to ask more probing questions but decided to take it slow.

Nirliq loved telling stories. She was giving me tremendous insight into the community which was unlike any place on earth.

The people of Nunavut were tough. Strong minded.

Yura Lake wasn't perfect. They had their faults and idiosyncrasies. But it was their choice to live this way. They didn't need anyone from the outside judging them.

Nirliq was clear. "We are a misunderstood people."

I was guilty as well. I had prejudged them.

Why would they live there if they didn't have to?

Why would they suffer through the winters when they could live elsewhere?

Fortunately, I kept my mouth shut and didn't let Nirliq know what I was thinking.

"None of their damn business what the rest of the world thinks about us," she said emphatically. "I don't question their choices in life. They shouldn't question ours. It's not like their posh lives are so much better than ours. Look at their divorce rates."

She had a point. Nunavut had the lowest divorce rates in North America. Surprisingly.

"Those people can all go to hell with the rest of us," she said. "I don't mean you," she added, making eye contact with me.

Damn and hell were the only two curse words I heard come out of her mouth. My mom always said that they were in the Bible, so they were okay to use in context. I'm not sure condemning people to hell was what my mom meant as an acceptable use.

So, I had to follow up on the comment. My Christian faith demanded it.

"Aren't you worried about going to hell?" I asked. A segway into talking about heaven and how to get there.

I really had to be careful broaching the topic. Her jaw clenched as soon as I said it. I could see her clamming up completely, even getting angry. Especially if I came across as trying to evangelize her.

"Hell will be a welcomed relief from the cold," she said defiantly.

"Do you believe in God?" I asked.

"No. If he's there, I've never seen him," she said, which made me sad.

I saw God in everything. Even the harsh winter. When the sun came out, I had a feeling the views of the bay and the mountains were going to be breathtaking. I wasn't sure how so many people could look at God's creation and not see the creator.

The local religion was a topic I had researched. The predominant religion of the area was animism. A polytheistic belief system. There were many gods according to the Inuit religion. Even mountains, rivers, and animals could be considered deities. Most Inuits believed that even inanimate objects had a soul.

The discussions were helping Nirliq to open up.

That and the tea.

The topic turned to the Inuit language. She taught me pronunciation.

"Nunavut. Noo nah voot."

I repeated it. She seemed satisfied.

"Inuit. Ee noo eet."

I repeated it until I got it right.

"Iqaluit. Ee kha loo eet."

"Ullakuut. Oo laa koot. It means good morning."

"Qanuippit. Kha noo ee peet. It means 'How are you?'"

Nirliq giggled when I butchered it. So did I. Maybe she spiked my tea as well. I was feeling relaxed too.

"Are there really fifty words in the Inuit language for snow?" I asked. I'd read where that might be true.

She nodded emphatically.

"Qanuk means snowflake. Kaneq means frost. Kanevvluk means fine snow. Qanikcaq means snow on the ground. Muruaneq means soft deep snow. Nutaryuk means fresh snow. Pirta," she pointed out the window, "means blizzard. You get the drift."

Nirliq burst out laughing. "Pun intended. You get my drift. Snowdrift. I made a pun."

The tea was definitely having an effect as she was a little tipsy. Giggling like a college girl at a frat party where the alcohol was flowing. I was sipping mine slowly. Nursing it.

On the third day, Nirliq began telling me wild tales of Inuit culture and lore. I found it hard to separate fact from mythology.

"My name means snow goose," she said.

"I love your name. It's beautiful."

"There's a story behind it. One day my mother was washing our clothes in a large kettle pot in the kitchen. We didn't have running water back then and she had to melt the snow. All she had was a large slab of lye that had to last the winter."

Nirliq let out a sigh.

"Oh the good old days. I don't know how my mother did it."

I didn't respond. I had no context in which to relate. If I could tell her about the precarious situations I faced as a CIA operative, she might understand. But I couldn't blow my cover.

I also didn't want to interrupt the fascinating story.

"A snow goose landed on the windowsill just outside the kitchen. The next day, my mother realized she was pregnant with me. So she named me Nirliq. Snow goose."

"Fascinating."

"My husband called me his goose wife," she said with a hint of bitterness behind the words.

That caused me to chuckle.

Nirliq didn't find it amusing.

"It's not funny," she said. "I didn't like it."

"Why not?" I wiped the smile from my face.

"Years ago, the geese migrated here in the spring and summer. They left in the wintertime. Headed south. Still do."

"I often see geese pass through where I live as well. Some of them probably come from up here."

She nodded. "Back in the day, when the geese stopped, they would take off their clothes and bathe in the bay."

I thought Nirliq had lost it. Either she was suffering from dementia, or she was drunk. I suspected the latter.

Nirliq pointed out the window. The bay was out there somewhere. Brad had told me my apartment had a beautiful view of the bay. I hadn't actually seen it other than driving on it that night with Leo.

"They took off their clothes?" I said.

"Yes." Then she gasped and put her hand to her mouth. "Oh I forgot the most important part of the story. I see why you didn't understand. You must've thought I was crazy. The geese became women. They shed their goose skins and then bathed in the lake. Naked as a walrus."

She whispered when she said the word "naked" like she needed to be discreet.

I bit my tongue to keep from laughing. I loved Nirliq. Already. After only three days. At first, I thought she was kidding. She really believed what she was telling me.

She continued. "The hunters would spy on the geese. You know how men are?"

"Do I ever?"

"This is the best part," Nirliq said. A smirk had formed on her face. "A hunter stole the goose skin from one of the women. He made her his wife. More a sex slave than anything else."

My ears perked up even further. Nirliq had unknowingly ventured into my territory. The purpose of my trip.

"That's where my husband got the term goose wife," she said bitterly. "I hated the term. That's what he thought of me."

"I wouldn't like it either."

"Let me tell you honey. Life is hard for women in Yura Lake. Men have always dominated women up here. And we've let them for far too long. You can put that in your story. Use my name if you want."

It seemed like subjecting women to human trafficking was deeply rooted in Inuit culture. In their mythology. In the hearts of their women who knew the truth.

Had lived it. Endured it. Treatment harsher than the cold.

I may have found an ally in my fight.

8

The next day

A ray of sunshine burst through my window waking me from a deep sleep.

What time is it?

That can't be right.

How long was I asleep?

The clock beside the bed said one o'clock in the afternoon. I was usually an early riser. I couldn't remember the last time I had slept that late. If ever.

My internal clock was really off. I blamed the tea. Nirliq and I stayed up well into the night drinking her special brew and swapping tall tales. I didn't break my CIA cover, but I sensed she knew I was more than a journalist.

I wasn't worried. I was a good judge of character. Someone would have to torture the information out of her. Nirliq despised Mr. Z. The whole compound, as she called it. It divided the community between the haves and the have nots. Those who took his money, benefited greatly. Those who didn't were outcasts.

Nirliq refused to take what she considered bribes. Selling out. She had no doubt Mr. Z. was good for the men. When it all started, she had foreseen that the women would become more oppressed, and she'd been right.

After her abusive husband died, she vowed to never be indebted to a man again. So she told me all she knew about Mr. Z., the compound, and his mode of operation. Which wasn't much.

The main thing I did learn was that Mr. Z. was the one who paid the money for the girls. She'd heard it wasn't fifteen to twenty thousand dollars. It was upwards of fifty thousand dollars and a guaranteed job for the husband working for Mr. Z's company along with a house inside the compound.

What was Mr. Z.'s company? She didn't have a clue. The men were sworn to secrecy, or they'd lose their cushy situation. She didn't ask too many questions. Everyone not in the inner circle was afraid of Mr. Z.

"Their lips are sealed tighter than my underwear," Nirliq said, referring to those living inside the zone.

I burst out laughing.

The conversation had left me with a lot to think about. I was surprised I was able to sleep at all.

The sunshine gave me a jolt of adrenaline. I rushed to the window to let the rays penetrate my face. I saw the bay for the first time. Ice covered, but one of the most spectacular sights I'd ever seen. I'd been all over the world. This was unique. Nothing could compare to this.

A rush of emotions flooded in. I suddenly wasn't tired at all. No headaches. No hangover. The tea must've had some kind of relaxing qualities to it. Something that let your guard down but didn't make you drunk.

I wanted to rush outside and take in more of the sunshine but stopped when I saw the thermometer in the window. One degree above zero. At least we were headed in the right direction.

Nirliq said any day above zero was a good day. She also said when the storms moved through and the sun came out, we'd have about five hours of sunshine every day. Each new day would bring a little bit more sunlight. In April, the sun was out about eight hours a day.

How long has the sun been out today? An hour? Two? Did I wake up when it first came out?

I needed to take advantage of the daylight and get to work.

Regardless, I had to get dressed and start this mission in earnest. Although, it felt like I'd been making progress. I had a target. Targets were good. I'd pursue Mr. Z. until I was proven wrong.

I wouldn't be. He was the man behind the sex trafficking. I was sure of it.

The voice in my head told me to settle down. I had to build my cover. That meant taking things slow. I was in the middle of nowhere, with no viable extraction plan if things went south. That meant surveilling without anyone knowing it. Posing as a journalist. Asking strategic questions.

I needed to get a few breaks. I'd had a few already. Like running into Leo. Securing his weapon. Befriending Nirliq.

A plan formulated in my mind.

Apparently, another benefit of the tea. It cleared your head. I felt like I'd had two B-12 shots. My energy hormones were raging, and I'd only been awake for less than ten minutes.

I'd start at the only diner in town. Make myself seen by the locals at the most public spot. Buy some groceries. Interact with as many people as possible. Then go to the school and meet with the principal.

Make a trip to the observatory. I wanted to see the Northern Lights, but I also wanted to get close to the compound. Walking around it wasn't possible with all the security cameras. That'd seem suspicious. I wanted to draw attention to myself, but not in that way.

Mr. Z. didn't get to where he was in the world by being careless. If he went to this much trouble to secure the compound, he'd be leery of a woman showing up out of the blue claiming to be a journalist. If for no other reason than he wouldn't want to draw attention to his operation.

A journalist was as big a threat as a CIA operative. The right headline in the right medium could expose his corruption and bring the whole thing down.

This was going to be tricky. I had to be smart.

I also didn't know if Mr. Z. responded to threats with violence. I could see where it'd be easy to make people disappear up here. Especially if the police and politicians were in his back pocket.

I had to assume my life was in danger.

It'd help if I knew who Mr. Z. was.

I was suddenly fuming.

Why hadn't Brad called me back with information on Mr. Z.? It'd been four days. He had the entire weight of the United States government behind him, and he couldn't find the identity of one man.

That'd make my job so much easier.

I was tempted to call him, but he would yell at me. Not yell but use his condescending voice which was worse.

He said he'd call when he had the information. Since he hadn't called, I should assume he didn't know anything. To be fair, if the tables were turned, which they often were, he never called me in those situations. He waited to hear from me. An unwritten rule. We had to trust each other.

Constantly bugging the other was only a distraction. Not a major problem on his end. Distractions for him were annoying. For me, a distraction could get me killed. So I tamped down the urge to call him if for no other reason than to maintain the understanding.

My phone and gun were on the nightstand. I went over and picked up the phone. To my shock, I had a missed call.

From Brad.

How did I sleep through it?

He could never know.

I called him back.

"Did you decide to wake up?" he asked, jokingly. At least it seemed like he was kidding.

I hesitated.

The technology was available. Alex had used it many times. He hacked into cell phones and used the cameras and listening devices on the phones to monitor everything a bad guy said and did.

The CIA had that reach. Brad could tap into my phone at any time. Mostly for security reasons. He wasn't supposed to hack into our phones except in an emergency. For obvious reasons.

Brad knew better. If I found out he was spying on me in private moments, I'd break him into several pieces.

I had to assume he was joking. So I went with it. "I've been working."

"Mr. Z. doesn't exist," he said matter-of-factly.

"Well his money does. He's spending it left and right around here like a fortune 500 CEO."

"I'm telling you. I got nothing."

"Dig deeper. You're the Assistant Director to the CIA. You know what the President of Russia had for breakfast this morning."

"A kolbasa."

A sausage sandwich with cheese. My stomach growled. I hadn't eaten anything. I could use something like that right about now.

"And a syrniki," Brad quipped.

"With cottage cheese or cream cheese?"

"Cottage cheese."

"Wrong choice. I prefer cream cheese in my Russian pastry."

Brad was actually kidding, and I knew it, but my point was well taken.

"Nobody runs an operation like this without leaving some kind of digital trail," I said. "You need to find it."

I rarely pushed back like this. If Brad said he found nothing, it wasn't because he didn't try.

"Jamie, I'm telling you the guy is a ghost."

"He has to be incorporated. Businesses leave a trail. He's obviously into real estate development. He built this entire community. It had to take millions of dollars. If not more than a billion. Where is he getting his money?"

"There's no money trail."

"We should be able to track the planes and supply trucks. Where do those come from?"

"I don't know. Whoever he is, he's good."

"That's a clue in and of itself. Why hide your activities if you have nothing to hide?"

"I don't disagree."

Neither of us said anything for a good twenty seconds.

"What about on your end?" Brad finally asked.

"I have confirmation Mr. Z. is the one purchasing the young girls. He offers the parents money and jobs. And a house. Those who don't take it are ostracized. Kept out of the compound."

"What does the compound look like on the ground?"

"I haven't seen it yet. We've been snowed in. I haven't seen the sunshine since I got here. Until about fifteen minutes ago."

"Looks like the storms have cleared for a while. It'll be cold but no snow."

"That's good to know."

"Kaley's on board now."

"She is?"

"Yep. We swore her in yesterday. She's already out on a mission."

Kaley was a nineteen-year-old girl Brad asked me to train. At first, I thought it was a waste of time. After seeing her in action, I changed my mind and recommended that he hire her. I figured it was only a matter of time until she was made an operative. Probably only a matter of time until I worked with her again.

"Good for Kaley," I said. "I always knew she was going to make it."

Brad laughed.

"I distinctly remember you saying, and I quote, 'she doesn't have what it takes.'"

"I don't remember that. You must be mistaken."

"Whatever."

"I'm really happy for her. I like Kaley. You know her and A-Rad are an item."

"I know."

"I tried to discourage it. Operatives shouldn't date."

"The pot said to the kettle."

He was referring to Alex. When we started dating, we were both operatives. Then we got married against Brad and Curly's advice. I wouldn't recommend it for most people. You can't have a normal marriage while working for the Agency where your whole life is spent lying and getting shot at.

"Kaley is frustrated with A-Rad," I said.

"How so?"

"They've been on like six dates, and he still hasn't kissed her."

Brad laughed. "That sounds like A-Rad."

"Kaley doesn't think it's funny. If he doesn't kiss her soon, she's going to take the initiative and kiss him."

"Maybe he's not into her."

"Oh he's into her. Smitten like a kitten."

"Then he needs to get off the pot."

"How many references to pot are you going to make in one conversation?"

"Speaking of pot, have you seen any evidence of drug use up there?"

I remembered the tea. The two empty cups were still on the counter.

"None so far. Did you know that alcohol is illegal in Yura Lake?"

"I think I read that somewhere."

"The Liquor Act. The local communities get to decide. They fall into three categories. Prohibited. Restricted. Unrestricted. It's against the law to bring alcohol into a restricted community. Same with cannabis. Yura Lake is restricted."

"You should fit in since you don't drink."

Why did I feel guilty?

"I don't drink because I don't like the feeling of losing control. I want to always have my wits about me."

Like not sleeping past noon.

"The President of Russia is having a shot of vodka right now," Brad quipped, referring to my previous joke.

I laughed. "You could guess that anytime of the day and be right."

"Yep."

A thought belted me between the eyes sending a jolt through me. I tried to put it into words.

"Mr. Z. pretty much runs things around here," I said.

"That's what you said."

"That means he's rich."

"Yep. What's your point?"

"You said he's got politicians in his back pocket. That some of them are suspected of being involved in the sex trafficking."

"I've read the report. I'm the one who gave it to you."

"How many rich men have you met who don't drink?"

"Not many. But I'm sure there are some."

"That's right. There are some. I know of a few. But I don't know any who would support banning it altogether. Almost every rich man makes money on alcohol. If not in a business, then in wining and dining their guests."

"I agree with you. But I still don't see your point. Some southern states have blue laws. The politicians ban alcohol, even though they drink like sailors."

"Exactly. They cave to the pressure from religious groups."

"I still don't get your point."

"What if it's some kind of religious thing with Mr. Z?"

"Do you think he's running a non-profit?"

"That's what I'm thinking. That's why the politicians were willing to go along with banning alcohol in the community. Religious pressure."

"Interesting. That's why I couldn't find anything. Nonprofits aren't subject to public records. I have to look at a different database for that. You may be on to something."

Rage was building inside of me. A good thing. I need to harness it to bring Mr. Z. down. It helped if I loathed him.

"Drinking is wrong but holding girls as sex slaves is perfectly fine," I said, bitterly.

"I've seen it before. Religious cult leaders are the biggest hypocrites going. It's worth looking into. I'll see if I can find anything."

"I appreciate it."

I hung up the phone slowly. Contemplating that last thought. It hadn't occurred to me until now. The whole town was shrouded in secrecy. I thought it had to do with culture. Now I wasn't so sure.

9

"The men of Yura Lake think Mr. Z. hung the Northern Lights," Nirliq said, as she straightened my parka and sent me out into the cold to start my investigation.

She had loaned me her daughter's coat. I got the impression she hadn't talked to her daughter in years. She didn't offer any information and I didn't ask.

I was thankful for the coat.

What a difference!

The only thing cold on my body was my nose which felt like someone was sticking it with needles. Even with the cold, it felt good to be outside. I walked quickly and with a purpose the quarter of a mile to the diner.

Every building along the way was basically the same. I only saw two businesses. The rest were houses. The structures were modest. Box shaped. One story. Metal roofs. Some were red. Others brown or green. The occasional blue. One had a red front, green siding on the sides, and a brown door.

Curb appeal wasn't something they worried about in Yura Lake. None of the houses had mailboxes or street numbers on their exterior. I wasn't sure how the mail was distributed or if it even was.

Several houses to my right, on the bay side, were on stilts. That might be because of the potential of flooding or simply to have a place to park a vehicle out of the snow. No one had garages. I remembered seeing garages inside the compound. The observatory was visible a short distance away as was the imposing wall.

The power lines were sagging. Probably so they wouldn't snap in the wind or get weighed down by snow. Every fifty yards or so was a telephone pole. Each house had a separate line that ran to it from one of the poles.

No street signs. Not even stop signs. I guessed people knew how to dodge each other and stay out of an accident.

No advertising signs of any kind. I was used to the landscape in Virginia being littered with billboards. Business signs everywhere. Not one in Yura Lake. The only reason I knew it was the diner was because Nirliq described it for me, and it had a red open sign on the door.

The trailer-shaped structure was solid white. Wooden steps led to a doorway. One car was parked in front. A silver SUV. About half a dozen snow machines were parked outside the entrance.

It had a metal chimney which had a steady stream of smoke coming from it.

And security cameras on the outside.

What?

Why did a diner need security cameras?

I walked up the three steps, stopped on the landing, and let out a sigh. Watched my breath form a cloud in front of my face. Then stared at the security camera to make sure Mr. Z. got a good look at me. If he or his men were the ones monitoring it.

Who else could it be?

By the end of the day, I wanted the boss man to know I was there. If he didn't already.

I opened the door and was met by a rush of warm air and the smell of a greasy kitchen. I quickly stepped inside and closed the door to keep out the cold. Took off my hat and gloves and assessed the place. Which didn't take long.

The dining area was even smaller than it looked on the outside. Not a single window in the entire place. Metal lights hung from the ceiling. It had two white tables with four metal chairs that looked uncomfortable and were unused. Two long brown tables were where the men were sitting. On one side of each table was a bench. At both ends were single chairs. On the other side were three chairs.

Five men sat around one table. Three on the other. Some had plates of food in front of them. Some had cups of what I assumed was coffee.

I could smell it and my stomach roared for some.

The only woman I saw was the waitress. Leaning against the counter. With a confused look on her face. They probably didn't get strangers in the diner very often in the middle of January.

Where were the female customers?

The room was suddenly eerily quiet. Grease could pop in the kitchen, and I'd hear it.

"Can I help you?" I asked.

"I'd like some food."

The waitress looked over at the men like she needed their permission to serve me.

"Order up here at the register," she finally said, scoping me out as much as I was her. I was looking for any signs of oppression. Women who were abused had a look. You could see it in their eyes.

This woman seemed tired, but not a victim.

The kitchen was behind her. In plain sight. A man with an apron had his back to me and was cooking something on the stovetop. Something fried.

Every eye in the place watched me walk to the register. A laminated menu was taped to the top of the surprisingly new cash register. She pointed at it.

I looked it over.

I'd read about all the exotic Inuit dishes and was interested in trying some. Because of the lack of agriculture, their diet consisted mostly of higher-fat foods and animal protein. Lower in carbohydrates.

They ate things like seals, walruses, bear meat, whales, and blubber. Animal fat. That's what everything was cooked in. Not oil. Some ate the blubber raw. That wasn't happening with me.

I was anxious to try most things and wasn't bothered by how they were cooked. Although I was reluctant to try the things blubber was added to in an uncooked form. Like cereal.

Akutaq was berries mixed with fat. Bannock was flatbread. Fat could be spread on it like butter. Suaasat was a traditional soup made from seal, whale, caribou, or seabirds. Cooked in blubber as the base.

My first thought when I read about their diet was that heart disease had to be skyrocketing. To my surprise, it was just the opposite. A study I read said cancer and heart disease were the leading causes of death in every province of Canada except one. Nunavut. Which seemed counterintuitive.

The number of deaths in the region from cancer and heart disease were higher among women than men. The opposite was true in the states. If I really was a journalist, that's one of the things I would dig into.

Maybe the diseases were more prevalent in the United States because we mixed our high fat foods with carbohydrates. My mind was getting off track thinking about the food and I tried to bring it back to the task at hand. Getting some food for my starving stomach which hadn't consumed anything but tea in almost twenty-four hours was the priority.

The menu was one page. I expected to see raw fish. Collected straight from the pristine ocean. That I was anxious to try. I didn't want to eat seabirds, which was a delicacy, but I was open to trying whale or seal.

A wave of disappointment came over me. What I saw on the menu was standard fare. Breakfast served all day. Ordered a la carte. Eggs. Bacon or sausage. Toast. Hash browns. No pancakes, but French toast could be made from the bread.

Lunch had two options. Hamburger or cheeseburger. Fries or chips.

Beverage choices were coffee. Soda in cans. Tea. Orange juice. Water.

No prices were on the menu.

Did I want breakfast or lunch? It was going on three o'clock in the afternoon and I hadn't had either.

"What'll you have?" the waitress asked with a forced smile.

"I'll have a cheeseburger and fries," I said. "I'll also take a soda and a cup of coffee."

She didn't write anything down. Didn't need to. The cook had stopped what he was doing and looked our way. Close enough to hear my order. He went right to work.

"Sit anywhere you like," she said.

I smiled and held out my hand. "I'm Jesse. I'm from America."

"I'm Sesi," she said. At first, I thought she said Sissy, but she spelled it for me. I remembered that name. Nirliq said it was one of the fifty words for snow.

"It's a beautiful name," I said. Her lips formed a thin smile. It'd probably been a long time since anyone had paid her a compliment.

Rather than sit down at the metal tables I sat right down on the end of the brown table where the five men were sitting. Facing the door so I could see if anyone entered. Normally, I liked to sit with my back to a wall so no one could sneak up on me. The only two people behind me were the cook and waitress and I could hear them both working.

Several of the men were startled when I sat down at their table.

"Can I sit here?" I asked.

"Looks like you already did," one of them said in a grouchy tone. Could be considered combative.

The others tried to look aloof or coy. None were leering at me. They were various ages. I'd guess between fifty and seventy. Although, Nirliq said everyone looked older than their real age because of the harshness of the climate.

"I'm Jesse," I said.

"What brings you to these parts?" the same person said. Not offering me his name. No "Pleasure to meet you." No "How are you today, Jesse?" His face was colder than the pile of snow outside.

"I'm a journalist. For a magazine. I'm writing a story."

A couple of their ears perked up. Heads titled in confusion or disbelief or both. They made eye contact with each other sending signals, but none looked at me.

"What kind of story?" he asked, roughly.

"About Yura Lake, of course. I want to write about life in the Arctic Circle and during the harsh winter. I want to know what people do to survive. How they pass the time. What they eat. That kind of thing. Next winter, I'm going to Antarctica. To write about the same thing."

After what happened with Leo, I decided not to tell the locals I was writing about the problems facing teenage girls in the region. Nirliq had agreed. None of their business. They wouldn't take too kindly to a stranger prying around about such things. Especially the ones compounding the problem. They'd get defensive and clam up altogether.

Although, these men were as defensive as a hockey goalie as it was.

No one said anything for a good minute.

"Do you mind if I ask you a few questions?" I said.

"Yeah. We do mind."

I tried to remain upbeat and friendly. "Oh come on. Surely you'd like to contribute something to the story."

"Nope. We're good."

"Do you all live in the compound?"

The spokesman's head jerked back. "What compound?"

"You know. The neighborhood. The one that's gated. Where the lower class in the area aren't allowed."

I couldn't help adding some sarcasm to the words.

The man abruptly stood to his feet. The other men followed his lead like soldiers standing for a general. They all put on their coats and left. Without another word. As did the men sitting at the table next to us.

Sesi arrived at the table with my food a few seconds later. Along with a refill on my coffee.

"You sure know how to clear a room," she said.

"I'm not sure what I said to offend them."

"Don't get me wrong. I'm glad they're gone. They're in here every day. Ordering me around like I'm their personal slave."

My heart raced when I heard a woman use that term.

"All I did was ask if they live in the compound," I said.

"What's the compound?"

"That's what they said. I don't know what to call it. The neighborhood behind the gates."

"Oh. That's the Zone."

"The Zone? Where did it get that name?"

"I don't know. I guess Mr. Z. named it."

"Why all the secrecy?"

"I can't say. But I'd suggest you not go around asking those kinds of questions."

"What's wrong with asking?"

"All I'm saying is be careful. Trust me. You don't want to know what goes on behind those walls."

"Actually, I do."

"My advice is to go back where you came from. These are not the kind of people to mess with."

They don't want to mess with me.

"Tell me why."

"I can't."

A tear formed in her eye. She looked back at the cook, who was eyeing us closely.

She stood up straight and composed herself.

"Do you want any ketchup for your fries?"

I'd forgotten about the food.

"No, I'm good."

My turn to whisper. "If you ever want to talk. Off the record. I'm available. I'm living at Nirliq's place. Come and see me. I'll keep everything you say confidential."

"I'm sorry," she said. "I've already said too much."

She hadn't said anything.

I was stunned.

Even more so when the door opened and a man with a hat, badge, and gun walked through the doors.

10

The man with the badge and gun stood inside the doorway for several seconds to make his presence known. He was a tall man. Broad shoulders. Defined jawline that came together in a pointed chin.

On his head was a Texas Rangers style ten-gallon hat. He wore a brown dress shirt and tie. With a badge on the lapel. Matching brown pants. Shiny cowboy boots. A police duty belt was tight around his waist. Which didn't hang over his pants. He looked to be pretty tough. If he was as tough as he clearly thought he was, I might've been concerned.

The duty belt was loaded with tools of the trade. That's what I was most interested in.

Dark wide leather belt with a large buckle in the center. Attached to the belt was a radio. I'd like to get my hands on one of those at some point. A nightstick was loosely hanging held by a loop. A pair of handcuffs were in a pouch. Speed cuffs actually with a plastic grip. The easy kind to get out of.

A small container of chemical spray was inside a pouch. Mace or pepper spray. A basically worthless weapon. Took too long to activate. Also required close contact with the threat. In my case, I could hit him three times before he could take it out of the belt. Same with the nightstick. Extremely awkward to maneuver out of the loop.

A nightstick was only an effective weapon if you had time to draw it. Which I wouldn't give him. Even if he had the nightstick in his hand

and swung it at me, it left him with all kinds of vulnerability. Shots to the ribs. Uppercut. Throat punch. He'd be better off without it.

Not that it mattered much either way. I didn't intend to start anything.

The last thing on the belt was his gun. Like any other. I'd held dozens of them in my hand. This one was in a holster, buttoned in place. The man was a dummy. It took several seconds to undo the strap. More than enough time for me to strike any of the same places.

Why did my mind go there? To a confrontation. He might be there to get something to eat.

I doubted it. The eight men had hightailed it out of the diner in a hurry when I started asking questions about the Zone. They obviously called the Sheriff as soon as they were out the front door. He got to the diner as fast as it took them to cook my cheeseburger and fries.

My stomach was aching for the food. Why couldn't he have come three minutes later? That's about how long it would've taken me to wolf it down.

Wyatt Earp sauntered over to my table and hovered over me.

I didn't acknowledge him. Instead, I took my first bite of food. Started with the French Fries. In case I needed one hand free. The burger would take both hands.

My stomach roared its approval, as did my taste buds. I could see why they liked cooking food in blubber.

Sesi was behind me within seconds. Like she needed to protect me from the man.

"Hello, Mayor," she said, the words dripping with disrespect.

"Go back to work, Sesi," he said roughly. "This don't concern you."

"Mayor and Sheriff," I said, while taking a break in the chewing. "That's quite a resume. Were you the fifth caller to the local radio station?"

Sesi burst out laughing at the joke.

The Mayor/Sheriff didn't seem to get it. His lips twisted to the side in confusion. Then his eyes widened when he realized it was a slight on him.

"That ain't funny," he said.

"It's kind of funny," I retorted. Then took a bite of my burger. The grease poured out the bottom onto my plate. I anticipated it and held it out from me so as not to get any on my clothes. It was all over my hands though.

I moaned my approval.

I took another bite, gripping it with both hands. Probably not the wisest move on my part, but the smell of the fried meat was too tempting to wait for whatever was about to happen.

"Come with me," he said, sharply.

I looked up.

"I'm eating."

"You're done."

"Leave her alone, Buck."

"You stay out of this, Sesi. I told you to go back to work."

She didn't back down. "She ain't done nothin. Let her be."

Before the clock could make its next tick, Buck raised his hand and backhanded Sesi across the side of her face. The smack echoed through the entire diner. She let out a cry of pain.

My whole body tensed. I felt my greasy fist ball. I wanted to crack his skull.

Buck grabbed Sesi's arm and dragged her toward the register and counter. She resisted but was no match for his strength.

It took every ounce of self-control to keep from bolting out of my chair and hitting him.

I couldn't.

At that moment, I felt as vulnerable as I had at any time in my CIA career. I'd been in many dangerous situations. I didn't know what I was facing here, but I was concerned.

Not about Buck. Under normal circumstances, I'd stand up, run after them, and punch him in the kidney. He'd be peeing blood for the next few months. If I didn't hold back on the intensity of the punch, he'd die on the floor. I could take less drastic measures and simply knock him out cold. Choke him out or strike the side of his neck.

Then wipe my greasy hands on his shirt.

But then what?

I had no way of escape. If I was in Russia, or even North Korea or Iran, I had a thousand places I could hide. I could steal a car. Hunker down in the forest. Make them chase me. For that matter, I could simply put on a disguise and go to the airport with a fake passport and get on a plane and get away from danger.

Here, I had no place to go. Where would I hide? Nirliq's house? That's the first place they'd look. I couldn't put her in that kind of danger. I had no idea how many people would come after me and with what kind of weapons.

I had to assume Mr. Z. had a small army at his disposal. At least thirteen girls had disappeared. Maybe more. Those girls didn't have the skills I had, but if I didn't have an escape route, how long could I fight them off?

Hiding outside wasn't an option. In the cold, I'd die within a few minutes or hours, even with Nirliq's coat.

I had a gun. What good would that do me if I couldn't use it to escape?

I had decided to leave it at home and was thankful for the foresight. A nagging voice told me not to carry it with me. Probably Curly's. There was an outside chance Leo had reported it stolen. If a cop stopped me and searched me, he'd find it, and I'd be arrested.

If I was arrested in Canada, the President of the United States would make one phone call to the Prime Minister, and I'd be on a plane back home within hours. Was that the case here? I doubted it.

How would I even notify Brad that I was in danger?

I couldn't. And what would I do with the weapon? Shoot Buck. I never killed an innocent law enforcement man. Never would. I'd give myself up before I'd do that.

I reminded myself that Buck wasn't innocent. He was willing to abuse a woman in public. That made him a low life as far as I was concerned.

But did that mean he deserved the death penalty? Not until I had more information.

Even if I had to fight my way out of this situation, the only ammunition I had was what was in the magazine of the gun. Sixteen bullets. I could take Buck's gun. That'd give me thirty-two. Then what? What was I going to do? Kill every man in Yura Lake who came after me?

Then what about the girls? I couldn't leave them to their plight.

I had to play it cool. I unballed my fist and took in a calming breath. A pain shot through my heart when Sesi cried out in pain.

"You're hurting me," she said.

I turned to look. Buck was in her face. Spewing expletives. If he took it any further, I'd have no choice but to do something.

He threatened her job. He probably did have that kind of power.

I wanted her to back off. Let me deal with it. She had no way of knowing I could handle the threat myself. Curly always said there weren't two men alive who could take me in a fight.

That wasn't my concern. Even without a gun, I could do whatever I wanted to do to Buck. Including killing him.

But I needed to let this play out.

He was back at my table a minute or so later. I still didn't have a good plan.

The only thing I could think of was to scarf down the food. Curly said to eat and sleep when you can. You never know when you might get another chance. I finished all but a few fries.

That was reason enough to kill Buck. I wanted those fries.

"Did you have to hit her?" I said, with my mouth full.

"I told her twice. She should've listened to me."

"Is she your wife?" It seemed like they had more than a law enforcement/citizen relationship. He'd said something about dealing with her when they got home.

"She's my son's wife. And she ain't worth the price of that plate of food."

"Still. Where I come from, a man who hits a woman is weak. He's less of a man."

His whole body stiffened. Like he wanted to hit me. I glared at him, practically daring him to do so.

I wanted him to see what steely resolve looked like.

He didn't take the bait. If he wanted to fight me now, I'd oblige him and deal with the consequences. But based on his reaction, I deduced Mr. Z. had instructed him to question but not harm me. Not until they knew who they were dealing with.

I could get away with being a little sassy, but I didn't want to push it.

"Stand up," Buck said. "I told you twice. I won't tell you a third time."

"Am I under arrest?"

"You will be if you don't cooperate."

"Where are we going?"

"I'm taking you to the station for questioning."

That changed everything. The station was inside the Zone. I'd been wondering how I was going to get inside the compound. Buck was my ticket in.

My heart raced with excitement. Still, I didn't stand up right away. Buck needed to know I was no pushover. If he tried to hit me, I'd break his wrist. Maybe take a shot to his ribs which were wide open for me. I didn't want to do it, but I had my limits.

I picked up the remaining fries and stuffed them in my face. Then took a drink of soda. Took my time chewing.

Buck was getting impatient.

Good.

When I was done chewing, I wiped my face off with a napkin, completely satisfied with my meal, already thinking about the next one. I'd order from the breakfast menu next time.

I hoped there was a next time.

I stood. Slowly put on my parka. Buck didn't say anything.

As I was walking toward the door, he pushed me from behind. I envisioned a swinging elbow to the side of his head. Him collapsing to the floor in a heap. Sesi applauding.

That reminded me.

I looked over at her. She already had ice on her bloody upper lip. Our eyes met. I gave her a reassuring nod. She probably didn't know how to take it. How could she know I was going to rain the full force of my skills on these men at the right moment? They'd get theirs at a time and place of my choosing.

I couldn't help her right now. She was only one woman. And she wasn't in grave danger. Dozens of other girls were in worse shape than her. I couldn't jeopardize the whole operation to help her.

I'd made the right decision.

Maintaining my cover for as long as possible was the only option.

Until I faced a life and death situation.

I had an ominous feeling that it'd come soon enough.

11

Three weeks later

When I regained consciousness, it took several seconds for my head to clear.

Then I remembered.

The giant was lying on my back. Crushing me. Pushing my head in the snow. So I couldn't breathe.

I instinctively coughed. The cough was croupy like I had a cold. Like fluid was still in my lungs. My lungs were burning. My throat hurt. I must've swallowed snow when I tried to breathe in. I could still taste it.

I remembered Lily. She was the last thing I thought about when I was dying. I must not be dead since I was thinking about her now.

The giant didn't kill me. Why not?

How long was I out?

I did a quick assessment of my body. My head didn't hurt. I had no noticeable injuries. My shoulders hurt. And my wrists.

My hands and feet wouldn't move.

Was I drugged?

I shook my head roughly from side to side to clear the fog.

Then I realized my arms and legs couldn't move because they were bound to a chair. My hands were behind my back in an uncomfortable position which was why my shoulders and wrists hurt. My legs were tied to the leg chairs. Tightly.

Ropes circled around my chest and behind the chair. Probably attached to my wrists which was why my movement was so restricted.

Whoever set the bindings knew what he was doing.

Where was I?

This wasn't the cabin. The one I was running toward when I fell in the snowdrift. That's where the giant lived. Inside the Zone. I had tried to lure him back there so I could force him to tell me where Mr. Z. was.

An almost fatal mistake on my part.

It looked like I was in an interrogation room. More of a concrete chamber. Sterile. White walls. Like a prison cell. It had a door with a small window in it and a slot that opened inward. Presumably to deliver food or to secure handcuffs.

Nothing was in the room but me and the chair I was strapped to. I tested the chair and found it flimsy which gave me a glimmer of hope that I could get out of the restraints.

Was this where they kept the other girls? That seemed like a safe assumption. Which sent a rush of adrenaline through me. I'd been searching for them for days with no luck. I had no idea where Mr. Z. was holding them.

Curly said to look at the bright side in every situation.

If I found where Mr. Z. was holding the girls, then I'd made a significant breakthrough in the investigation. If I could call almost dying and being tied to a chair in a prison cell, with no visible means of escape, progress.

The thought almost caused me to laugh.

The room was eerily quiet. It had to be soundproof. I couldn't hear anything coming from outside the room.

I tested the bindings again. No give at all. It'd take me several minutes to figure out how to get out of them.

No reason to wait.

I got started.

I widened my elbows. Flaring them out. With as much force as I could muster. Then relaxed them. I felt a slight give in the tightness around my wrists.

I took in a deep breath and held it. Then released. Repeated several times. This loosened the bindings on my chest.

Next, I flexed every muscle in my body. Making them as taut as possible. I repeated that several times. Each time my muscles relaxed the bindings loosened ever so slightly.

Especially the bindings on my legs. They gave a little bit each time I tightened my calves, then relaxed them.

I tapped my right foot on the concrete floor, over and over again, until the bindings around my calf fell to my ankle. Repeated the process on my other leg until both bindings were loose.

I twisted my wrists back and forth in every direction. The burlap straps bit into them but I ignored the pain and kept doing it. I was glad the straps weren't leather. It wouldn't hurt as much but would be harder to loosen.

Even though the bindings were around my ankles, my legs were still secured to the chair. So, I leaned the chair backwards. The front legs were slightly off the floor. I had to be careful not to tip over. I straightened my right leg out as far as it would go trying desperately to keep the chair upright. I could see myself falling backwards, banging my head on the floor, and being knocked out again.

The binding slid down the leg of the chair and out. One leg was free. I repeated the maneuver until my other leg was as well. I shook them out to relieve the tension from being stuck in that position for so long.

I raised my legs toward my chest in a seated crunch, which gave me an idea. I stood to my feet, Then dropped to the floor. Butt first. The impact caused the chair to break in two.

It hurt. I knew it would. It was the only thing I could think of.

With as much strength as I could muster, I pulled my arms to the right until the back broke in two as well. The chair was in pieces but parts of it were still attached to me and the bindings.

I wiggled my upper body down so the ropes around my chest slipped over my head. The bottom of the chair fell to the floor. The back was dangling behind me.

I got on the floor and maneuvered my body so I could grip one of the chair legs. I used the sharp edge to saw through the rope that held my wrists.

It was painstakingly slow. When I finally succeeded, my wrists were bloodied, and I had expended a lot of energy.

I stood to my feet and walked around. Reassessing my body. Things ached but I was in good shape. Considering.

The fog was completely gone.

I had to act quickly. Someone would be coming soon.

A smile formed on my face. Act how? What could I do?

A lot of things. Curly said to be resourceful. I had ropes and a broken chair. They could be made into weapons. The two legs of the chair were broken but still attached to the seat of the chair. I ripped them off. Roughly. They weren't much for striking, but the sharp points could do a lot of damage as shards.

I could wait for someone to come, then pounce. A quick strike. The element of surprise was one of the biggest advantages one could have in a fight. Along with skill.

Then it hit me.

Right between the eyes.

They were watching me. Any room this elaborate had to have a camera. I searched the room until I saw the red dot.

I let out a groan inside my head.

I'd just shown them I'm more than a journalist. That I had skills beyond a normal person.

I'll show them how much skill I have.

I put one of the makeshift weapons in each hand and waited. I stood back in a corner leaning casually against the wall. I thought about trying to spring a surprise at the door, but if my hunch was correct, they'd see it. Either come in with guns blazing or simply wait me out.

If I backed away, they would be more likely to come sooner rather than later. My curiosity was piqued. I wanted to know who was on the other side of the door.

Could it be Mr. Z. himself?

He was the one holding me. No question about it. The only one who could afford such an elaborate dungeon. My thoughts went to the girls. I wondered how many of them had been in this room. Perhaps tied up.

Bad guys tended to follow the same protocol every time. My heart broke for them. I had to get out of there. To help them.

Mr. Z. would be overconfident. Even with the show I'd just given him.

His big goon had gotten the best of me. They'd figure he could do it again. Even if I had the two flimsy chair legs as weapons.

They'd probably laugh at me. I could see the giant's face. Mocking me.

A horrifying thought burst into my mind.

Did the giant have to resuscitate me? Give me mouth to mouth? The thought sent chills down my spine and nausea percolating in my stomach. If I was out that long, my brain had to be deprived of oxygen for at least two or three minutes.

I coughed hard. Like I could somehow get the awful taste out of my mouth and off my lips. Even if I could, the images were seared in my mind.

"Eww!" I felt my face twist into a grimace.

I'd rather be tortured by nails than have that big galoot put his lips on mine.

The only person who had kissed me in years was Alex. The thought sent a twinge of hurt and guilt through me.

A waste of time and mental energy.

Snap out of it, Jamie.

Curly was screaming at me to focus. I had bigger worries.

I had no idea if I was going to get out of this alive.

I had to. For Alex. For Lily.

The lock on the door jiggled, interrupting my thoughts. A welcomed interruption considering my mind was going to a dark place.

The door swung open.

The giant entered first. He had a quirky smile on his face. I saw his massive lips and wanted to plant the palm of my hand right on his chin and put all his teeth into the back of his skull.

But a man followed him in. Which momentarily stunned me.

"So I finally get to meet the infamous Mr. Z.," I said, when my composure returned.

He was about how I had pictured him in my mind. Short. Good looking. Dressed in a suit and tie. Blond hair. Pushed to the side. Confident.

Neither of them had a gun visible which surprised me. Maybe Mr. Z. thought the giant was invincible.

He wasn't. Not here. Not in this environment. Maybe out in the snow. If they underestimated me, it'd be to their peril.

Mr. Z. clapped his hands together. In mock applause.

"Very impressive, Jesse Winters. If that's really your name. I like how you got out of the ropes."

I rolled my head from side to side. Like a prize fighter in a corner. Loosening the tension in my neck.

I wasn't sure how to play this. He still thought I was Jesse, which meant he didn't know my real identity. He obviously had his doubts.

Which was probably why I was still alive. He was curious.

"A little trick I learned on the internet," I said.

By the look on his face, I could tell he didn't believe me.

"Who are you?" he asked.

"I could ask you the same question."

"Who I am is not important."

"It is to me. You tied me up like a dog. Why are you holding me prisoner? On whose authority?"

"I'm the authority around here. As you are well aware."

"Are you going to kill me?"

He laughed. "I never kill a pretty girl."

"There are dozens of pretty girls missing."

"They aren't missing. I know where they are."

Did he just admit what I already knew? That he was behind the sex trafficking. Why would he admit that? Why was he so confident? Because he'd already assumed I wasn't getting out of there.

"Let me go," I said. "People will be looking for me."

"They won't find you."

This must be a huge facility. That's why the door was open. Even if I got through it, there were layers of security between me and freedom. He probably had armed guards waiting right outside the door.

I should act while I had the chance. Attack the giant. Thrust one of the chair legs into the side of his neck after kicking him in the knee. Then take Mr. Z. hostage. Put the sharp edge of the leg chair against his neck.

He was a mousy man. Should be easy enough to control.

He must've realized what I was thinking, because he said, "Don't even think about trying to escape."

"I wasn't thinking about escaping. I was thinking about killing you."

"Like you killed the Sheriff?" he asked.

It took all of my self-control not to give anything away in my facial expressions.

"Is he dead?" I asked.

"He's missing."

"Hm. I didn't know that."

"You were seen leaving the diner with him. He was taking you to the station for questioning. You were the last person to see him alive."

"If he's dead, the last person to see him alive was the person who killed him."

Mr. Z. rubbed his chin. Thinking.

He and I both knew that was me.

12

Three weeks before

When the Sheriff and I exited the diner, nighttime had fallen on Yura Lake. Not technically night time since it was still afternoon and I'd only been awake about three and a half hours. Nevertheless, we'd run out of sunlight for the day.

My body clock couldn't get used to the changes.

The only vehicle in the diner parking lot was a massive SUV. With large, oversized tires. A set of cross-country skis were strapped to the top.

The Sheriff, aka Mayor, opened the front door for me. A plastic divider separated the front seats from the back. I was glad he was letting me in the passenger seat in case I needed to act. At this point, I didn't know what I was facing.

Was he only trying to question me for information or were they targeting me?

I decided to take a friendly approach until I knew for sure.

"Thanks, Buck. May I call you Buck?" I asked.

I grabbed the handle and pulled myself up. Buck did the same thing Leo did. Put his hand on my butt and pushed me up.

"Call me whatever you want," he grunted.

Jerk wad.

Pervert.

A couple of Curly's four-letter words came to mind. Curly would probably be mad at me for not back kicking the Sheriff into oblivion.

What I did next was impulsive. I hit the lock button on the doors. A stupid thing to do, but worth it when I saw the Sheriff's face when he tried to open the door.

He jerked on the door handle. Violently. Glared at me.

"I'm kidding," I said. I hit the unlock button and he threw the door open. Fuming like a caged bobcat that had been poked through the fence.

"Do you think this is a game?" he asked.

"No sir. But I do find it amusing. I'm no threat to you. Why are you acting like I'm public enemy number one?"

"You broke the law."

"What law? Is it a crime to eat dinner in the afternoon? I'm glad I didn't order breakfast. I could be looking at ten to twenty years in the slammer."

He ignored the comment. My words were dripping with more sarcasm than the grease on my burger.

"Do you have your visa and passport?" he asked.

"I do."

"Show them to me."

I took them out of my coat and handed them to him. He looked them over. Although not carefully. Like it was a formality. He'd already decided what he was going to do. I wished he'd hurry up and fill me in. So I'd know what I was going to do.

He put them in the side pocket of the truck and started the vehicle.

"I'm going to need those back."

He didn't say anything.

Buck put the vehicle in reverse and backed out. The SUV was top-of-the-line. Like Leo's rig. Nothing but the best for Mr. Z.'s men.

Next to the center console on the passenger side was an automatic rifle attached to a holder. I could use that.

From the looks of the dashboard, the vehicle had every added feature available. It was one of those self-driving trucks. Although Buck's hands were firmly in control of the wheel.

To my surprise, he didn't drive toward the Zone. Instead, he went left out of the diner. Headed out of town. Once we reached the outskirts, he made a sharp right. Where there was no road.

It startled me.

"What are you doing?" I asked.

"I'm taking you to Iqaluit."

"Why?"

"To the airport. To put you on the first plane out of here."

Before I could respond, we were on the bay. Speeding across the ice. The fifteen mile an hour speed limit obviously didn't apply to his truck. The tires held the traction. We weren't sliding at all.

A sense of urgency had come over me. Twelve miles across. I had less than ten minutes to decide what to do.

I couldn't kill him. While I suspected he was part of the sex trafficking ring, I had no proof.

Once I got to Iqaluit, how would I get back to Yura Lake? If I somehow managed, how was I going to operate without being detected? I couldn't go to the diner. Or to the school. Sneaking into the Zone didn't seem like a good plan. Security was tighter than Nirliq's underwear. As she had quipped.

Thinking of Nirliq made me sad. I'd miss her if I was forced to leave.

"Why do I have to leave?" I demanded.

My best strategy at this point was to talk my way out of it. To get him to change his mind. Which seemed more set than a pillar of stone.

"Like I said, you broke the law."

"What law?"

"Our immigration laws."

"I'm not immigrating to Yura Lake, you idiot. I'm visiting."

Time for me to get rougher with him. Maybe he'd give me a reason to take him out. Rules of engagement were I could only act in self-defense unless I had definitive proof he was involved in the sex trafficking.

He didn't respond.

"I have a visa. That's all I need."

"Not to come to Yura Lake. We have our own laws. You have to apply for permission to enter the jurisdiction. You didn't do that."

I remembered Nirliq mentioning it. She said her son applied once and was turned down. Even though he was born and raised there. Apparently, once you leave, you can never return.

"What about my things? All my belongings are in my apartment."

"Forget about them. They're the property of Yura Lake now."

"What if I refuse to get on the plane? You can't force me. I have a valid visa for Nunavut. I assumed that applied to Yura Lake as well."

Buck touched on the brake. We began to skid. He expertly steered into it. When he brought the vehicle to a complete stop, he turned off the engine and put it in park.

Then grabbed my hair. Jerked my head backward. Got right in my face.

He had crossed the line to where self-defense was warranted. I still waited. Maybe I could garner some information.

"Let go of me," I said.

I slapped at his arm which held me tight.

He laughed. "What are you going to do? Nobody is here to help you."

"I can take care of myself."

He laughed.

"You should've left well enough alone. Kept your mouth shut and got on that plane. Now you're mine."

"I'm a journalist. People will be looking for me."

"Well, they won't find you."

His intentions were clear. His eyes were filled with lust. He never intended to take me to the airport. He was going to rape me out in the middle of nowhere. Probably kill me and dispose of the body.

He couldn't afford to take me back to the Zone. He didn't know who I was or who would come looking for me. Best to make me disappear.

Buck jerked on my head sending a searing pain through my skull. My fists were balled. I raised the knuckle on the middle finger of my left hand. Short and quick. I struck him right under the armpit which was vulnerable because his arm was extended.

He let out a yell. Clutched his arm. The blow was delivered perfectly. Impact at that spot caused the entire arm to go numb and sent excruciating pain signals to his brain.

He let out a flurry of expletives. "I'm going to kill you," he said.

Now he had confirmed it.

Curly taught me to end fights immediately. With overwhelming deadly force. One blow. Strategically struck. I had several choices. The trachea. I would crush his windpipe and he would not be able to breathe.

Nasty way to die.

I wasn't in that kind of mood.

One blow to the side of the neck would give him a stroke. Knock him unconscious immediately. I didn't want him to get off that easily.

Should I do that thing I never did?

Why not?

He touched my butt before. So, I grabbed his groin and began twisting. Violently. The quickest way to inflict maximum pain and disable a man.

He cried out like a little baby.

It took several seconds for his brain to override the pain. He swung an elbow at my head. I saw it coming and ducked.

I released my grip and brought the same hand back. Then forward. Putting my weight behind it. I lunged across the center console and brought the palm of my hand directly into his sternum.

Dead center of the left ventricle. Perfectly timed and delivered.

Buck grabbed his chest. His eyes widened. He began gasping for air.

"Commotio cordis," I said. "Sounds like a Greek word for toilet."

I tapped him on his chest with my finger.

"It means you're having a heart attack. Eventually, your breathing will stop, and you'll be in V-fib."

He tried to speak but couldn't.

"I could try to resuscitate you. But I don't want to."

His eyes began to roll into the back of his head. His breathing became more shallow.

Now what, Jamie?

I killed the Mayor and the Sheriff of Yura Lake. How did that help my investigation? If anything, it made it more difficult. I was about five miles out on the ice. Almost halfway between Iqaluit and Yura Lake.

What I really should do is drive to Iqaluit, get on the first plane out, and abandon the mission.

Not going to happen. I didn't give up that easily.

Yura Lake was a cesspool of corruption. The Sheriff was trying to get rid of me before I could ask any questions.

Immigration laws my eye. They didn't want anyone coming in there. Snooping around. Girls were missing. The women of Yura Lake were afraid to say anything. They lived in terror. I was their only hope.

I needed a moment to think.

I couldn't drive back to Yura Lake. I could walk back but that wasn't appealing. Now that the sun was down, the temperature was falling.

Eventually, they'd come looking for the Sheriff and find his vehicle. They might think he died of a heart attack. But he likely had a bruise on his chest. I hit him hard. An autopsy would reveal the blow.

I had no place to dispose of the body and vehicle.

Buck's pulse was weak when I checked it. He'd be dead soon.

I turned on the vehicle to warm the inside of the cab. The dashboard lit up like the cockpit of an airplane.

An idea came to me. I fidgeted with the various features of the SUV. One caught my attention. Five hundred and forty-five miles to empty. The vehicle was full of fuel.

In the center of the console was a computer screen. I pulled up the navigation system. I could enter in coordinates and activate the self-driving feature. Set the controls to travel directly south.

Was it far enough?

As the SUV traveled further south, it'd leave Frobisher Bay and into the Atlantic Ocean.

The map confirmed that my idea would work.

Not south, but southeast. As it got closer to the ocean, the ice would thin, and the SUV would fall through or eventually reach the end of the ice and plummet to the bottom of the ocean. Never to be seen again.

I entered the coordinates.

A moment of indecision hit me. I wanted to take the rifle and his gun. But if they were found in my possession, then I would be linked to the Sheriff's disappearance. I already would be. The men in the diner would be able to say they called the Sheriff, and he came to question me. Under pressure, Sesi would say I left with him.

Still, they had nothing on me. As far as I could tell, Buck was the only law enforcement in the entire city. This would turn the tables on Mr. Z. He'd be confused. Not sure what happened to his lackey.

Confusion led to mistakes. It'd give me an advantage. At least buy me enough time to investigate.

Satisfied it was a good plan, I entered the coordinates. I decided to leave the rifle and his gun. I could only shoot one gun at a time. I did take the bullets from his revolver.

When I opened the car door, the cold hit me. I was dreading the walk back. Then I remembered the skis on the roof. I recently won the gold medal at the Winter Olympics. In the biathlon. Which combined cross country skiing with shooting. I could ski across the ice and be back to Yura Lake in no time.

Under the cover of darkness. The skis could be tied to the Sheriff, but those could be disposed of. I could burn them in my stove. Or hide them easily enough. I decided to keep them. They might come in handy.

After getting them off the roof, I checked them out and they were in good working order. His boots were in the back. Too big for me but they'd have to do.

I walked around to the driver's side and opened the door. Double checked the coordinates. Also fastened Buck's seatbelt so he wouldn't fall out.

The vehicle was running and all I had to do was engage the self-driving feature after turning off the headlights and the interior lights.

I gathered a few things. Retrieved my passport and visa. Also his keycard.

Satisfied I had all I needed, I got out of the way as the vehicle sped away. At sixty miles an hour. Based on my calculations, it'd fall into the ocean sometime within three to four hours.

I watched as it drove off.

My only regret was that I didn't have a chance to interrogate Buck. Not that he would've told me anything I didn't already know.

I put on the ski boots, then fitted them into the skis, grasped the poles in my hands, and took off toward Yura Lake. I could see the lights of the Zone in the distance. All I had to do was head toward them.

The darkness engulfed me. After I got into a rhythm, I was no longer cold. The activity warmed my body. Thanks to Nirliq's daughter's parka.

The sky was filled with millions of diamonds. Twinkling stars. I marveled at God's beautiful creation.

A glow emerged on the northern horizon. A small green light. It shot up into the sky like the flame on a stoked fire.

And began dancing.

Pulsating. Waving at me. The most incredible thing I'd ever seen. Multiple green lights filled the sky.

The Northern Lights. I finally got to see them.

13

The next morning

I'd been a CIA operative for years now. Last night, I learned an important lesson. Always have an escape plan. It's not that Curly never taught me that. It's just that I'd never been in a situation where I didn't have an obvious way to flee a dangerous situation.

I had no excuse.

It should've been obvious. Cross country skis. Why didn't I think of it sooner? The average person can travel seven to ten miles per hour on skis. As a professional, I could reach speeds of twelve to fifteen miles per hour.

If I was going all out on a flat surface, I could reach speeds of twenty to thirty miles per hour. That meant I could cross Frobisher Bay in less than an hour. Twenty minutes if I was pushing it.

It's not like I didn't consider skis. But I was too worried about the cold. With Nirliq's parka, I wasn't exactly warm, but I wasn't freezing cold either. At least I could survive as long as it wasn't seventy below zero.

After disposing of the Sheriff, I had skied back to Yura Lake. And had a pleasant time doing it. While watching the spectacular light show, a calm had enveloped me. I felt one with God and was admiring his handiwork.

I was also totally satisfied that I'd successfully eliminated a major threat. The Sheriff was the gatekeeper so to speak. Mr. Z.'s security blanket. With that gone, the boss would be vulnerable.

When I arrived back in Yura Lake, I went straight to my apartment and hid the skis. Ate a power bar and drank an energy drink. Cross country skiers burn an average of eight hundred calories an hour. I burned three times that in the confrontation with the Sheriff. There's no exercise plan as good as killing a man.

All I'd had to eat that day was the burger and fries, so I was starving.

The adrenaline inside was still on fire. The confrontation with the Sheriff had put me in full scorched earth mission mode.

Nirliq came over for tea and asked about my day. I tried to sound relaxed, but she could tell I was on edge.

I told her about the Sheriff confronting me at the diner. I didn't tell her everything. I left out the part about killing him and sending his body and SUV to an icy grave.

I made up some story about him looking at my visa and passport, then letting me go. She didn't believe me, but also didn't question it further.

She did provide insight. According to Nirliq, the Sheriff was the head of the snake from a muscle standpoint. Mr. Z. was in charge, but the Sheriff was the enforcer. He was the law. The judge and jury for that matter.

He didn't have anyone else working for him. Which meant Mr. Z. had a serious problem. He wouldn't know where the Sheriff was and didn't have anyone to maintain control. It'd take him time to regroup. Hopefully, enough time for me to complete my investigation and kill the real head of the snake.

Mr. Z.

The top prize in my quest for justice. The Sheriff was the appetizer. I was just getting started. I'd kill anyone and everyone who got in my way. I didn't see anyone out there who could stop me. The isolation would work to my advantage now. It'd take time for Mr. Z. to bring in reinforcements.

So far, I hadn't seen anything else that was a threat to me. Except maybe the giant. I still didn't know who he was. Nirliq had never seen him but had heard stories she thought were tall tales.

No pun intended.

After Nirliq left and went to bed, a nagging feeling pulled at the pit of my stomach. When I figured out what it was, I realized that I still needed a faster escape route. Someone in an SUV could mow me over if they were chasing me on the ice. The skis weren't fast enough. I needed a vehicle.

No place to hide a stolen truck, so I took the next best thing.

I walked down to the diner, careful not to be seen. Moving through the shadows. From house to house. Once I reached the diner, I used a rock to knock out the light that illuminated the parking lot. It didn't make sense to take out the security camera. That'd alert whoever was monitoring it and make them suspicious.

With no light, the cameras would only see a shadowy figure. In front of the diner were several snowmobiles. They all had their keys in them. Why wouldn't they? Who was going to steal one in this small village where everyone knew each other, and the Sheriff could arrest anyone who tried?

I fired it up and took off down the street. The opposite way from my apartment. The same direction the Sheriff had taken me. Veered off onto the ice of Frobisher Bay at the exact same spot I was at a few hours ago.

Two miles down the shoreline was a cove. I hid the snowmobile there and hiked back to my apartment.

Feeling a lot better about things. I could walk or ski to the cove and be speeding across the bay within a few minutes. A snowmobile was preferable to an SUV. Other than exposure to the elements, it had every advantage. Maneuverability. Traction on the ice. And it could go faster than a truck.

A snowmobile could reach 120 miles per hour on a flat straightaway. That meant I could reach Iqaluit in less than five minutes.

With an escape plan in place, I felt emboldened. It meant I could carry my gun with me everywhere I went. Leo's gun, technically.

I made a mental note to always have an escape plan in place in the future. More importantly, look for one if the plan wasn't obvious. Be resourceful. There was always a way out of danger. Even in the Arctic Circle.

The next morning, I walked right into the diner. The eight men were sitting at their brown tables, joined by a few more. Still no women, other than Sesi whose lip was swollen like a grape and had the same purple coloring from the bruising.

I should've felt anger but was actually thankful that the Sheriff would never hit her again. I smiled at her. She was too terrified to smile back. Her eyes were flitting back and forth. Her face was as tight as a woven basket.

I sat at one of the metal tables. Ignoring the men.

I could hear the jaws dropping. As they stared at me in amazement. Confused. They probably didn't know where the Sheriff was. Or the snowmobile. As far as they knew, I was no longer in Yura Lake. On the first plane out of Iqaluit.

Sesi was beyond panicked. She was paralyzed like a deer in headlights.

I motioned for her.

"I'll have breakfast. Everything on the menu. One of each. And coffee. Keep it coming. I'm going to be here for a while."

I said it loud enough for everyone to hear.

She poured me a cup right away. The coffee was as good as the food. It'd give a racehorse a jolt of energy.

"What are you doing?" Sesi asked me in a nervous whisper. "You shouldn't be here. Buck will kill you if he finds you here."

"Buck and I have an understanding."

He's dead and I'm not. That's our understanding.

"Seriously, you need to get out of here. Walk out and never come back. These men are dangerous."

I looked up like I was thinking, then said, "Nope. I'm hungry. I'm not worried about these men."

"What did Buck say?"

"He said I could stay."

"That doesn't sound like him."

"Put in my order. Everything'll be alright."

She backed away and walked to the counter. The cook was already looking our way. She gave him my order and he went to work on the griddle.

My mouth was watering. I hoped this meal wasn't going to get interrupted.

As if on cue, one of the men stood to his feet and walked out of the diner. Probably to call Buck.

Good luck with that.

Several of the men glared at me. One of them probably owned the snowmobile. I didn't glare back. Simply ignored them.

The man returned from outside a minute or two later and sat back down. I could hear them murmuring. Something about the Sheriff not answering his phone.

There's no service where he is, I wanted to tell them.

After several minutes, the same man stood to his feet and walked over to where I was sitting. I looked up, even though I was already watching him with my head down. I was on full alert expecting trouble. Ready to dish it out if it came. My gun was on my hip just in case.

"Good morning," I said, in as friendly a tone as I could muster.

He sat down.

"Would you like to join me?" I asked with a hint of sarcasm behind the words.

He leaned closer, putting his elbows on the table. Out of the corner of my eye, I could see Sesi pacing.

"Where's the snowmobile?"

"What snowmobile?"

"Don't play coy with me. We know you took it."

"Why would I take a snowmobile? What possible use would I have for it?"

"My friend wants it back."

He pointed to a guy at the other table. Younger man. His eyes were like black coals of fire. If looks could kill, I'd be dead. Thankfully, they couldn't. But the gun on my hip could kill him easily enough. Although blood on the floor might spoil my appetite.

Probably not. I've eaten in worse conditions.

I leaned back in my chair and put my hands up.

"Why do you think I stole it?"

"You come to town, and it disappears. That's suspicious."

"That sounds like pretty flimsy evidence to me."

His jaw was clenched so tight, his teeth had to hurt.

"If I took it, do you think I would've walked here today? Does that make sense to you?"

"I thought the Sheriff told you to leave town."

"Who told you that?"

"I saw you leave with him. Yesterday afternoon."

I nodded. My food was ready. I could see Sesi collecting it.

"I did leave with him. He was kind enough to give me a ride back to my place."

"You drove off in the opposite direction. I saw you."

"He wanted to show me something. Mr. Sheriff is a nice man. I was impressed by him. He was very helpful. Pleasant and all."

"What did you do to him? He's not answering his phone."

Sesi set the food in front of me. I was impressed that she could carry it all. Eggs. Bacon. Sausage. Hash browns. And French Toast. No syrup. She went back to the counter and brought back a small cup of what looked to be blubber.

What the heck?

I poured the whole thing over my toast. Took my first bite. I moaned my approval. Gave Sesi a thumbs up.

"What did you ask me? I'm sorry. I'm really hungry."

"What did you do to him?"

"To who? Or is it whom? I can't ever keep those straight." I leaned forward. "I'm a journalist. You'd think I'd know the difference."

"What did you do to the Sheriff?"

"To Buck? I don't know what you're talking about."

"Nobody's heard from him since yesterday."

"Emmm."

I'd taken another bite and was chewing. Looking off in the distance like I was thinking.

"Did you check Iqaluit?" I asked.

"That's where he was taking you."

Interesting how they knew all this.

I shook my head.

"No. I showed him my passport and visa and he said I was good. He dropped me off at my apartment. While we were sitting there talking, he got a call. Some kind of problem in Iqaluit. He had to go. That's the last time I saw him."

The man was frustrated.

I was satisfied. The story was a good one. The food was also hitting the spot. I might need a nap after consuming it all. Not happening since the coffee was so strong, I could melt gold in it.

My taste buds were happy.

"We're going to find him," he said roughly.

"I don't think he's lost. He told me he'd be gone for a couple of days."

"I don't believe you."

The man stood up. Knocked the chair to the floor in the process. It let out a loud clanging sound.

"I'll let you know if I see him," I said. "What does the missing snowmobile look like? I'll let you know if I see it, too."

He stomped away, ignoring my comment.

Made a motion with his hand. A signal. All the men in the diner cleared out. All at once. Probably to have some kind of conference. They were rudderless. At a total loss without the Sheriff around to tell them what to do.

Once they were gone, Sesi came and sat down across from me. I was eating slowly now that the men had left. Savoring every bite. Kind of like last night when I didn't rush back to my apartment. The Northern Lights had me mesmerized.

"You shouldn't be here," Sesi said. "It's not safe."

She wasn't going to ruin my mood.

"How's your lip?" I asked.

"I've had worse."

"I'm sorry I didn't stop him."

"What could you do?"

I leaned forward.

"Tell me everything you know. Why is my life in danger?"

"These people are not to be messed with."

"Who are these people?"

"I can't say."

"Can't or won't?"

"What's the difference? I have to live here. You've already seen what Buck will do to me."

"And your husband lets him?"

"My husband's a good man. He's not like his father. He's never laid a hand on me."

"He needs to stand up to his dad."

"I don't see that happening. Nobody stands up to the Sheriff. He's all powerful around here."

I wanted to tell her that she didn't have to worry about Buck anymore, but that'd be an admission of guilt. Not beyond a reasonable doubt, but it wouldn't be hard to tie Buck's disappearance to me.

"I'm not afraid."

"I'm telling you to get out of here."

"Not until I find out what's going on. There's a story here. Why are all the women so afraid?"

"Why aren't you afraid?"

"I can take care of myself."

"There's too many of them."

She had a point. It seemed like all the men were in on it.

"I'll be okay."

I tapped my hip for reassurance.

We talked for nearly a half an hour. I couldn't pry anything out of her. It wasn't unusual for the abused to protect the abusers. Out of fear.

After I paid Sesi, I gave her a big tip and a hug. "If you ever want to talk," I whispered in her ear, "you know where to find me."

"Be careful."

I nodded. Before I could leave, the door opened. The thirteen men walked in. Blocking my exit.

I didn't care if it blew my cover. Time for them to be afraid of me.

14

The thirteen men formed a semi-circle trapping me with my back against the counter. Sesi was beside me and I put myself between her and the men.

"Tell us where the Sheriff is, or you're going to regret it," the spokesman for the group said. He was the same one who had confronted me a few minutes before.

I'd faced many threats. I knew when men were ready to fight. They meant business.

I only considered three options. I tried the first one. Threats.

"I'm only going to give you men one chance to walk away. If you don't, then none of you will be able to walk out of here."

A collective laugh filled the room.

"Do you think you can fight all these men?" the man asked.

"I don't figure I have to fight all of them. I only have to fight five of you."

He laughed again. Then started counting.

"You're not very good at math. I count thirteen of us. Unlucky thirteen for you."

"Let me explain."

"This I got to hear."

"I'm going to attack you first. I will hit you so hard, you'll be in the hospital for six months. That's if the blow doesn't kill you."

He let out a nervous chuckle.

He was confident but had to wonder why I wasn't afraid to face the overwhelming odds. I wasn't a fool. I knew defeating them all would be difficult. But I could seriously injure eight to ten of them. Sometimes that was enough to make the rest run away. If they were all committed to the fight, then someone would get in a blow and disable me.

I decided to vocalize my thoughts. "The way I figure it, only about four of your cohorts have enough guts to stay around when they see you unconscious on the floor. The rest of them will run out of here so fast, it'll make the Northern Lights move in the sky."

"Is that what you think?"

"That's what I know. You see, this ain't my first rodeo. I've killed so many men, I've lost count. Men a lot tougher than you."

"I thought you were a journalist."

"Do you care to find out? Come on, tough guy. Why do you need thirteen men to fight one girl?"

"You're all talk."

"Then why haven't you shut me up... That's right. Because you've got a twinge of doubt in the back of your pea brain. A little voice is telling you, 'What if she's telling the truth?' You better listen to that voice and get out of here while you still can."

Sesi chuckled nervously at the pea brain quip. She was clutching my arm.

"You should just leave," she said, pulling on my arm.

I ignored her.

The man looked me up and down. Trying to size me up. I'd definitely stopped him in his tracks. He came inside ready to bully me. I was making him look bad in front of his friends.

"I'm tougher than I look," I said. "I'm trained to kill a man a hundred different ways with my bare hands."

I saw the indecision in his eyes. Trying to decide if I was bluffing.

"Leave her alone," Sesi said to the man. "All of you. You should all be ashamed of yourselves. Threatening a girl. Don't you have any decency?"

"Shut up, Sesi. Or I'll shut you up."

I had no doubt he'd hit her, the same way Buck did. He wouldn't get the chance. Not as long as I was still standing upright.

"Last chance to walk away," I said. "I suggest you take it."

No one said anything. They didn't move toward me either. Which was a good sign.

"Final warning."

Curly always said to make your strikes quick and overwhelming. These men wouldn't expect me to make the first move. None of them seemed to be backing down. I didn't see much fear on any of their faces. Only confusion.

"All right then," I said. "Let's get this party started."

I took off my parka.

The men still didn't move.

"What are you waiting for? Are you chicken? You come in here threatening me. And you can't back it up?"

Spokesman found a spine.

"We're taking you in," he said, with resolve behind the words. "You can do this the easy way or the hard way. Your choice."

"I already made my choice. You're the one who has to decide if you want to walk the rest of your life with a limp."

"You sure have a mouth on you. I'm looking forward to shutting it."

"Why don't we make this a little fairer?" I asked. "You and me. Let's take it outside. Let's see who's the one who shuts the other up."

Once outside, I could run away. But that'd show weakness. That wasn't one of my three options.

Option two was to pull my gun. I'd do that before I'd try to fight all of them. That'd get their attention. Good thing I had an escape plan. Because I'd need it. If I shot one of them, or even threatened them with a gun, then I'd have to leave Yura Lake. I couldn't stay around. All kinds of bad things could happen.

They could come to my apartment. Surround it. With their own guns. Wait me out. Or worse. Take Nirliq hostage. Or Sesi. I'd have to give myself up and take my chances.

If I had to resort to pulling my gun, I'd have to hightail it out of there to Iqaluit and call Brad. Send in the cavalry. I couldn't fight thirteen men, but Alex, A-Rad, Bond, Colonel, and Kasey could fight a hundred men and I'd like our chances. We'd have more firepower with us than half the small countries in the world.

We'd storm the Zone and find Mr. Z. Break up this whole nefarious operation. Round the whole gang up and take them back to the United States to stand trial. Or maybe they'd reach the same fate as Buck.

I wasn't too proud to call in backup. I'd done it many times. This didn't seem like the time to do it. I didn't know how long that'd take. Alex was in the Cayman Islands tracking the finances of some wanted terrorists. Brad said Kasey was on a mission somewhere. Organizing them would take time. We'd probably have to wait until the first thaw.

Mr. Z. might roll up shop and get out of there. He could disappear. I'd miss my opportunity.

So I turned to option three.

It pained me to do so.

I was almost sick to my stomach. I felt like vomiting up my entire breakfast. Right there on the diner floor. That might be enough to get them to leave me alone.

Leader took a step toward me.

Sesi let out a scream.

"I wouldn't do that if I were you," I said.

Before I was standing casually. I straightened and turned slightly to the left. Weight on my back foot. My right hand still held Sesi back. I needed her out of harm's way.

"I'm done talking," he said.

The spokesman took up a fighting stance. I could tell he would be easy to take. I had half a mind to put him to sleep right then and there. Wouldn't take much. But I needed to give option three a chance to work.

"Buck won't be happy with you," I said. "You don't want to get on his bad side."

"What does he have to do with it?"

"I told you. I was with Buck yesterday."

"We know that. Where is he?"

"I'm not supposed to tell you."

"What are you talking about?"

"Buck isn't here."

"I know that. Where is he?"

"I told you. I'm not supposed to say anything. He told me not to."

"You'd better start talking. And now."

I hesitated. Sometimes I felt like an actress. Playing a role in a movie. If I pulled this off, I'd deserve an Oscar.

"Buck went to Salliq," I blurted.

That was in the Kivalliq Region. I remembered seeing it on the map.

"Why did he go there?"

"It's none of your business. If he wanted you to know, he would've told you. He swore me to secrecy."

"He told you why he was going there?"

"Are you deaf? That's what I just said."

"I don't believe you."

"I don't care if you believe me or not. Buck and I spent the afternoon and most of the evening together."

"What were you doing?"

"A girl doesn't kiss and tell."

Gag me with a pitchfork. I was definitely going to lose my breakfast.

"You and Buck are an item?"

"Yeah. If you can call being together one time an item. What of it? Well... I guess it was more than one time. We were together for several hours."

Someone kill me now. Put me out of misery.

I couldn't believe the words coming out of my mouth.

It seemed to be working. Now he was really confused. All of them were. At least they had all unballed their fists. If they weren't afraid of me, they were certainly afraid of Buck. They didn't want to mess with Buck's girl.

The thought was horrifying. I couldn't let it show on my face.

My story was plausible. They knew Buck was a womanizer. He probably would hit on me. It might be a stretch for them to wrap their heads around the idea that we might be an item.

"Sesi can back me up," I said. "She was here at the diner when he dropped me off last night. Around closing time."

Our eyes met. I pleaded with Sesi to back me up. If she didn't, I'd have to pull the gun.

"That's right," Sesi said. "I was here. Buck dropped her off. They couldn't keep their hands off each other."

"You saw Buck with this woman?"

"Yep. I saw them kissing."

Ugh.

This mission was not going as planned.

Sesi could win an Oscar for best supporting actress. She was selling it.

"Look at this," I said. "Buck gave me his gate card to the Zone. Why would he do that if he didn't want me to have it?"

I waved it in the air.

"You could've taken it off of him when you killed him."

That's exactly what I did.

I hoped it was my ticket inside the Zone. If they believed I was Buck's girlfriend and he really did go to Salliq for ten days, then I could operate inside the Zone in plain sight.

"Don't be ridiculous," I said. "Why would I kill Buck? We're lovers."

Sorry Alex.

"Well he ain't around to say it ain't so."

"Why would I lie? Buck'll be back in a week to ten days. You can ask him yourself."

"You'd better listen to her. You know how Buck is," Sesi said. "If you lay a hand on this girl, he'll tear you apart limb by limb and throw you to the wolves."

Several of them nodded in agreement. I let out a breath I'd been holding. Option three was going to work. As sickening as it was.

One by one they filed out.

When they were gone, Sesi almost burst into tears.

"I was so scared," she said.

"You did good."

"So did you. You didn't seem scared at all."

"I wasn't scared. But I'm glad they believed us."

"Could you really beat up all those men?"

"Maybe not all of them. But I'm good enough to put most of them in the hospital. I wasn't bluffing. I know how to defend myself. You have to as a journalist. Sometimes I go into seedy neighborhoods to get a story."

"I can see that."

"Anyway, they're gone now."

"Are you and Buck really an item?" she asked me.

"Of course not. I wouldn't sleep with him if he was the last man on earth."

"I wouldn't either."

"But I didn't know what else to say. I didn't know what they were going to do to me. Thanks for backing me up."

"Us girls have to stick together."

"Yes we do."

"Is Buck really in Salliq?"

"I don't know where Buck is."

"I figured. He doesn't know anybody over there."

"It buys me some time to get my story."

"I don't think those men will be bothering you. At least for a little while. This will get back to Mr. Z. though."

"That's what I'm hoping for."

15

Word traveled fast in Yura Lake.

I still couldn't get used to the idea that I was Sheriff Buck's girlfriend. If not for the fact that everyone treated me differently, I'd have gotten on the tallest building and shouted it wasn't true.

The cover was actually a stroke of unintended brilliance. I fell into the perfect scenario to conduct my investigation inside the Zone. Buck's gate card got me in. The guard didn't even question my right to have it. He had this silly grin on his face. Like he was trying to picture Buck and me together.

I reminded myself that I'm an actress. Playing a role. I thought about the greater good. Curly taught me to do whatever it took for the sake of the mission. Within reason.

When I got back to Washington and wrote my report, I'd leave this part out. I could hear Bond teasing me unmercifully. Alex would find it amusing. Even Brad would get a kick out of it.

Hopefully, they never found out.

The layout of the Zone was exactly what I'd seen on the satellite photos. The buildings were even more pristine than the photos showed. Modern houses with solar panels on the roofs. Most had garages. Although the only vehicles I saw were snowmobiles and golf carts.

The roads were plowed. The snow wasn't piled on the side of the road. It was hauled on golf carts to a place at the back of the Zone. On the other side of the small lake. Yura Lake.

I didn't see one thing out of place.

The center square had about a dozen businesses. A dentist and eye doctor shared an office. Attached was a small hospital. A hardware store shared a building with a grocery store. One restaurant. I was anxious to try it and compare it to the diner outside the Zone.

It had a clothing store, a crystal shop, which seemed odd, and a hair salon.

I didn't see any pets.

Once inside, I didn't need to show the card to anyone. I was able to walk right into any business. Even the fitness center. As I had suspected, it had a swimming pool, sauna, and spa. An area with free weights and circuit training. Similar to what you'd see in the states, only smaller.

A few more blubber meals and I was going to need that facility.

The school was one building. I loitered outside to gather information. It housed all grades. I learned that kids were required to attend through age sixteen. That's when they graduated.

Most of the women and girls I saw were dressed in Amish style attire. They wore long skirts that went below their knees with black leggings underneath. Their heads were covered with some kind of small net and cap. Women didn't make eye contact with men and spoke only when spoken to.

I hadn't seen any sex trafficked women yet. Only a community of brainwashed mind numbed robots. Under someone's thumb. I suspected I knew whose it was.

That wasn't why I was there. If these women voluntarily chose this life and could leave any time they wanted, then I didn't care. I wouldn't want to live that way, but it was their choice.

A warm front had moved into Yura Lake. If you could call it that. The sun was out and the high that day had reached a balmy seven above zero. Most people weren't wearing their heavy parkas. They were obviously used to the cold. I was still freezing. Even in the sunshine. The parka also concealed my gun which was on my hip.

The women's dress reinforced my thought that this might be some kind of religious commune. With Mr. Z. as the head of the cult. Brad still hadn't called me back with any information. Which told me he was having a hard time finding who was behind it.

While I'd like to have that information, it still felt like I was making progress.

The next logical step was to talk to the principal of the school. Sesi said she might be helpful. Beth Shoemaker was her name, and she was not from Yura Lake. She was a school administrator in Minnesota before she came to run the school.

She also ran the medical clinic. Was some kind of medical doctor. She must be a brilliant woman to have proficiencies in both areas. She'd only been there for this school year, and word was that the men in the Zone weren't happy with her. Sesi wouldn't say why.

Even though Sesi tried to be helpful, she was guarded. She was truly afraid of what might happen if she talked to me. She obviously knew more than she was letting on. I decided not to press it. Even though the Sheriff wasn't coming back and could never hurt her again, Mr. Z. could. There were security cameras in the diner. Maybe even listening devices.

For that matter, the security cameras outside the diner would show that I was lying about Sheriff Buck dropping me off and Sesi seeing us. Only a matter of time until the whole charade came crashing down around me.

Which meant I needed to move quickly while the men of Yura Lake believed my story. At some point, Mr. Z. would mobilize against me. Since I didn't know what resources he had at his disposal, I didn't know what threat I was facing.

My hunch was that Mr. Z.'s primary method of controlling people was money. The Sheriff was the enforcer and kept the people in line.

With him out of the picture, Mr. Z.'s money wasn't much of a threat to me. Until he could martial some kind of response.

Sesi said that Yura Lake had strict gun laws. Only the Sheriff and Mr. Z.'s bodyguard carried a gun in the jurisdiction. Men weren't even allowed to own a gun for hunting. My fear of the locals surrounding my apartment with guns was unfounded.

Leo wasn't actually allowed to carry his. Which was probably why he hadn't reported it stolen.

Since I had his gun, it gave me an advantage.

I kept one eye out for him. He would eventually get around to confronting me when he learned I was inside the Zone.

It didn't seem prudent to go inside the school while it was in session. The principal would be distracted and might not be able to talk to me, even if she were willing. It made sense to wait until school let out.

I called Brad to update him. Mr. Z. might be monitoring cell phone communications, but my phone was a CIA issued satellite phone. Encrypted. We could talk freely. I made sure I was out of earshot of any residents of Yura Lake, and my back was to the security cameras which were everywhere.

He answered on the first ring.

"Do you know how many cult leaders there are in the United States?" he asked as his greeting.

I blurted out a guess. "A hundred."

"The FBI has files for more than ten thousand religious extremist groups."

"Ten thousand!"

"That's why I haven't gotten back to you. It's taking forever to sort through them all."

"Did you look at those whose first or last names start with the letter Z?"

He let out what could only be considered a disapproving grunt.

"Don't tell me how to do my job."

"I didn't mean to—"

"To answer your question, no. There's Zen Buddhism, of course."

"From what I see on the ground, that's not it."

"There's the Zealot's Order."

"What's that?"

"They're in Nebraska and have about thirty members. They don't have any money or followers."

I could feel the disappointment rising inside of me.

"Some of the women here are dressed in Amish attire if that helps."

"I'll check out that possibility."

"I didn't say they were Amish, just that they dressed similarly."

"Worth checking out anyway. The Zoar Order originated in Utah. Dr. Bernard Siegfried founded it."

"It starts with a Z."

"Nope. Siegfried is spelled with an S."

"We don't know for sure that the founder's name starts with Z. It could start with an S."

"It's not him. Siegfried is dead. He founded the church in 1947. In Utah. Right after World War II. He said he was a prophet. That God spoke to him more than a thousand times. He told more than seventy women that God had told them to marry him."

"That's an interesting pick-up line. I hadn't heard that one."

"About forty women fell for it."

"He had forty wives?"

"Yep."

"Alex can't handle the one he has."

"He also said he was immortal," Brad said, ignoring my comment. His tone was intense. He was really into this investigation. "Siegfried said God told him he was never going to die."

"I guess God really didn't tell him that."

"Nope. He said that they were all going to move to Zoar. That's a small town east of the Dead Sea. Lot fled there right before the destruction of Sodom. Siegfried said there was a coming destruction. They'd be safe in Zoar in the end times."

Brad paused but I had no comment. This wasn't our man.

"The marriages didn't work out so well either," Brad said. "About half his wives left him. The rest moved to Nebraska. The church is run by some of his children."

"I can't believe people fall for these things."

All I had to do was look around Yura Lake. I didn't know how these women fell into their plight. Maybe it was voluntary. Maybe they were conned. Mr. Z. had some kind of hold on them. Sesi said most didn't want to leave. I wondered if they could if they wanted. Sesi didn't know of one woman who had actually done so.

I saw men come in and out of the gate, but I hadn't seen any women. According to Sesi, their movements were restricted to inside the Zone.

"I need for you to dig up more information," Brad said.

"I'm working on it. I'm inside the compound right now."

"What do you see?"

"Basically, a commune. No signs of sex trafficking yet."

"I need a name. Or something about the cult that would identify it. Some of their core beliefs and teachings might be helpful."

"The name of the compound is the Zone."

"The Zone. I read something about that. Hang on."

The phone went silent for a couple of minutes. I could hear Brad typing away on his computer keys.

"Here it is. The man's name is Lucas Rikki. He's the leader. He fits the profile. At least from a monetary standpoint. He's estimated to be worth several billion dollars."

My heart skipped a beat.

"He was born in Romo."

"Italy?"

"No. Romo, Denmark. It's an island. He was schooled in Copenhagen. Graduated from Oxford with a Doctorate in Science."

Something was ringing true. Born in a cold weather culture. Highly educated.

"Do you know his height?"

"He's five four."

My heart was racing. "Mr. Z. is short according to a woman I met at the airport."

"Lucas Rikki moved to Idaho. That's where he started preaching his religious propaganda online."

"Idaho is a long way from Nunavut."

"He believes in pantheism. That there are many gods. And there are a select number of prophets sent by the gods to reveal to mankind the secrets of the universe."

"I assume he's one of those prophets."

"Of course. So is Buddha. Mohammad. Joseph Smith. Jesus. He's on the same level as all of them. One level below the gods."

I could feel the righteous indignation rising inside of me. I could feel where this was leading. Mr. Z. might not be Lucas Rikki, but I hated men like this. Who misled people to become rich and powerful. Most used the religion to manipulate women sexually.

"According to his teachings, women were created by the gods to serve men."

"Sounds like my guy."

"That's pretty standard with most religious leaders. The prophets can take many wives."

"Classic sexual manipulation. A form of sex trafficking."

It infuriated me. Men in power used religion to force women into submitting to them. Sexually and otherwise.

"According to the FBI file, he was accused of marrying girls as young as fourteen."

"Was he arrested?"

"Yes. Then released on bail."

"What happened to him?"

"He disappeared."

"Moved to Yura Lake?"

"Maybe."

"It's certainly a good place to hide."

But where? I hadn't seen a house that a religious cult leader, worth billions, would own. He wouldn't live among the peons.

"What was it about the Zone that triggered something in your memory and caused you to think of this guy?" I asked.

"Rikki teaches that human beings can become immortal. That people have the ability within them to obtain extraterrestrial attributes. Even while in their physical bodies. Life is a process of continual transformation through a series of levels. The ABCs of spirituality, he calls it. The first level is the Awareness Zone. The second is the Believers Zone. The third is the Chosen Zone. Those are the ones who will become like god and live for an eternity."

"And he sets the rules as to who gets chosen."

"Yep. He's wildly popular. With millions of online followers. People pay a fortune to go through the levels. To reach Chosen status, they must give the church fifty percent of their possessions and half of what they make each year. Then they can live eternally."

Something told me we had found our guy.

16

The principal of the school, Beth Shoemaker, couldn't see me until tomorrow. She had a baby to deliver. I was impressed by her immediately. Pleasant and friendly but harried. Like she had the weight of the world on her shoulders. She seemed as out of place in Yura Lake as a bowl of blubber in a downtown Manhattan restaurant.

Pursuing the source of her uncomfortableness was something I wanted to do as soon as possible. If anyone knew what was happening with young girls, it was her. Since she couldn't meet, I had the rest of the afternoon for more exploring.

My first stop was the observatory.

I walked there slowly. Taking everything in. Watching the people. Looking for anything that seemed odd. Actually, everything seemed odd. The buildings. The roads. The zombie-like look on the face of every woman.

It's like I'd stepped into another world. A sci-fi movie. Hopefully not a horror movie.

The layout of the Zone had me bewildered. Especially around the observatory. The dome shaped building could be accessed from the Zone and also from the village which had a separate entrance. It was open seven days a week, twenty-four hours a day.

On the Zone side of the observatory was the police station. That's where I was standing. Right outside of it. I'd check it out after the observatory. Extending from the police station was a ten-foot-high wall that went approximately thirty yards toward the south. Forty yards west and then another thirty yards on the other side attaching to a building adjacent to the police station.

The walls had security cameras at each corner. No external entrance. How did you access it? From the observatory? I doubted it. Probably the police station.

From the satellite photos, the helipad was inside the open square. The helicopter sat on a big Z in the middle of a circle. I was curious to know if the helicopter was there. Helicopters didn't have locking mechanisms or keys. I could start it up and take it for a spin.

In my CIA training over the years, I had to learn to fly one. I wasn't as proficient as Alex. Certainly not as skilled as the professional pilots on our team. Bond. Colonel. A-Rad. Kaley now. But I could get it in the air. Part of me wondered what Nunavut looked like from the sky. Probably spectacular.

I had another motive. Anything to get a rile out of Mr. Z. It would fry his behind if I took his helicopter for a joyride.

Where was he? He had to be watching my every move. Either helpless to stop me or unable to mobilize against me this fast.

Checking out the area from the air might be a good idea. Mr. Z. didn't live in the Zone. Perhaps he had another compound nearby. If so, I'd change the target of my investigation. Commandeering the helicopter might give me an advantage. The high ground.

As interested as I was in a helicopter ride, the prudent thing to do was go to the observatory first. Ingresses and egresses were always a priority for a CIA operative. Since it could be accessed from the village, I wanted to see that entrance and exit as well.

For purposes of escape, but also to know from where possible threats might come. Curly would be disappointed in me if I allowed someone to sneak up on me because I was unprepared.

A twinge of sadness pierced my heart. Curly's voice was so prominent in my head, it's like he was still alive. That's the only way I could imagine him. Part of what drove me so hard was that I didn't want to let him down. If I had several hours with a therapist, she'd probably say it was because I grew up without a father. Curly filled the void my father never filled.

Through no fault of his own. My father was an astronaut. He'd been sent on a one-way mission to the end of the universe in search of intelligent life. I hoped he found it. Looking around Yura Lake made me wonder how much intelligent life we really had on this planet.

Now that my father was permanently out of the picture and Curly was dead, the void was back. Keeping Curly alive was my way of compensating for the loss. Maybe denial. Refusing to believe they were both gone.

I needed to get those thoughts out of my head. They were bringing me down. Draining me of energy. A sign the stress was getting to me.

The CIA required us to meet with a therapist once a year. Facing the dangers, especially killing large numbers of people, could take an emotional toll. Brad was constantly worried about me flaming out. Either ending up dead or making a catastrophic mistake that caused an international incident.

While I'd done that a few times, I'd still managed to survive. So far, I'd passed the lie detector and therapist's yearly tests. I'd always told the therapist what she wanted to hear. Never wanting to give Brad an excuse to pull me out of the field. Someday, I intended to leave, but on my own terms.

After exploring the outside of the observatory and the wall, I went inside to take a look. A simple layout, two rooms with a dividing wall and a locked door separating them. No worries. The locked door opened right away. Sheriff Buck's key card was an all-access pass. At least so far, it had gotten me anywhere I wanted to go.

The two rooms divided the haves and the have nots. One room was for the villagers, the other for the residents of the Zone. The two groups weren't allowed to interact with each other according to Nirliq. Outside of the Zone, men were allowed to interact with the villagers, but women weren't.

I already knew that based on my experience with the men at the diner.

In each of the two rooms were comfortable leather reclining chairs. Set up theater style. The roof was partially open facing the north with a glass ceiling allowing for ideal viewing but also providing protection from the elements and keeping the room's temperature controlled.

It was still light out, so the Northern Lights hadn't appeared yet and wouldn't until darkness descended on us again.

I knew a lot about the lights. I'd studied them.

The Greeks named them Aurora Borealis. Aurora meant sunrise and boreas meant winds. They believed Aurora was the sister of the sun and moon gods. At nighttime, she raced across the sky in a chariot, proclaiming the dawn of a new day was coming.

One ancient civilization, the Algonquins, believed a local hero, Nanabozho, traveled to the north after he finished creating the world. He built a huge fire so big that its lights were reflected in the sky.

One of the more interesting things I read came from Finland. They believed that a Firefox ran so fast through the sky that he left streaks. Revontulet was his name which literally means Firefox.

One absurd explanation said the lights were caused by the spray of whales in the area. The spume lit up when the water reflected the moonlight.

Nirliq gave me the Inuit perspective.

"My Ddwa told me the Northern Lights were the spirits of our dead relatives," she had said, during one of our late-night conversations. When she was feeling relaxed from the tea.

Ddwa was the Inuit word for Father.

I'd read that in my research. I also knew where she was going with the lore but kept silent wanting to hear it from her.

"I was petrified of the lights," she said.

"Really?"

"Oh yeah. My Ddwa told me if I went outside at night, the Northern Lights would cut my head off. I never went out alone."

I could hear the intensity and fear in her voice.

"He told me the reason the lights move is because the spirits are playing soccer with the dead kid's heads."

Even though I'd read it, it took on new meaning hearing it from her. I'd traveled the world. I'd read about myths and legends in various cultures. Sometimes I forgot that people actually believed these things.

"Aqsalijaat," she said. "That's the name for them. Soccer trails."

"I can see why you were scared."

Nirliq waved her hand dismissively.

"Dqatulakan," she muttered under her breath.

"What does that mean?"

"Stupid. I was stupid for believing it."

"You were a kid. Most kids believe what their parents tell them."

"My Ddwa was mean. I blame my mother for not telling me the truth. I never did that to my kids. I don't know what the lights are, but they aren't the spirits of my dead relatives. I don't know. Maybe they are. What do I care? No way to know."

I wanted to tell her they were caused by solar winds. When the wind from the sun hit the earth's atmosphere, the magnetic field pulled them northward. When the particles in the air, the protons and electrons, mixed with the solar winds, they released energy. That's what caused the Northern Lights. Not dead people.

Nirliq might not understand it. She said she never went to a formal school. Her mother taught her a few things. She was sharp as a moose's antler, but she never actually learned to read or write.

Brad said she didn't require a contract to rent the place. Now I knew why. She wouldn't have been able to read it anyway. Fine with Brad. The CIA avoided putting things in writing anytime it was possible.

Thinking of Nirliq made me smile. She was going to be amazed when I told her about my adventures inside the Zone.

As I was about to leave the observatory and go to the police station, the door opened. I instinctively reached for my gun. Kept it on my hip when I didn't immediately sense a threat.

A man and a woman walked in. The woman was dressed in the same attire I'd seen earlier. Long skirt. Her hair up. She didn't look my way.

The man looked me over. Cautiously.

I nodded.

"Unnukkut," I said oo-nuh-coot. It meant good evening. Or maybe good night. I couldn't remember.

Now I was embarrassed. It wasn't night yet. I'd also probably butchered the word.

If I did, he didn't say anything. In fact, he didn't speak at all. The woman sat down in one of the chairs. The man walked over to the wall and pushed a button.

He went and sat back down next to the woman. They reclined their chairs backwards and stared into the sky. Even though it was still daylight outside.

A voice began to fill the room.

A pleasant sounding voice. Friendly. Soothing. Peaceful. Monotone.

Mr. Z.?

My spirit said yes. I needed to hear more before my mind made that leap.

"My dear ones," the man said, "what you see here today are known as the Northern Lights. A spectacular array of colors and movement. Men marvel at their beauty. Because they don't understand them. Over the next few minutes, I'm going to explain them to you."

He spoke with a Dutch accent. Brad said the man from Idaho was Dutch.

My heart picked up its pace.

The man's tone changed. He lowered his voice. Exaggerated his syllables. Like he was pontificating. An over pronunciation of every word. Like a professor or preacher. Condescending was the best way to describe it.

He continued. I was gripped to every word looking for clues.

"Trying to explain the lights is like trying to describe the entire encyclopedia in a few short sentences. Can't really be done. For you to understand what I'm about to tell you, you will have to suspend all of your beliefs. You will have to allow me to transport you out of your bodies and into another world. My world."

What a load of bull.

"You must let me remove you from earth. You must suspend all thoughts. And feelings. They will only keep you from experiencing complete oneness with the universe. Listen carefully to my words."

How are they supposed to listen to you explain everything and not think?

A hypnotist. That's what he sounded like.

"They are lights," he said.

Duh.

"But they are not what you think. The lights are the spirits of the chosen ones. Those who are now eternal."

As if on cue, the sun began to fade. Darkness invaded Nunavut. It wasn't like most places where you had prolonged sunsets. Here, one minute it was light, the next minute it was dark.

I wanted to sit in one of the chairs and observe the stars. Sit there until the lights appeared. But the whole thing was creeping me out. His voice. It sounded pleasant but demonic. Difficult to explain.

If I sat down, I felt like I'd somehow be sucked in. My mind would be brainwashed. Maybe I'd be hypnotized. I didn't think that was possible, but I wasn't going to take that chance.

The whole thought was stupid, but my guard was up. This had to be Mr. Z.

I wanted to pull my gun. Stand in the corner and wait for a threat to appear.

"Close your eyes."

I thought the whole purpose of an observatory was to observe.

The couple did as they were told. I kept staring into space. One eye on the door and another on the view. The stars had made their entrance.

"Do you see how happy they are?" he said gleefully. "They are playing. Dancing in the wind. I have been there with them. My body is often transported into the heavenlies, and I too have danced and played with them."

I almost laughed out loud.

"It's the spiritual zone. Not all who hear my words will go there."

Here comes the sales pitch.

"Only the chosen will earn eternal life."

Eternal life is a free gift from God to those who believe in Christ.

My mind was having a raging debate with the man.

"You must be worthy to enter the zone. You must earn salvation."

You can't earn it!

I wanted to shout the words at the top of my lungs. Salvation comes by grace, through faith. Not through our own works.

For the next ten minutes, the man bloviated a bunch of nonsense.

"Fifty million years ago, an evil being named Zenu, captured the souls of millions of people and exiled them to earth. I was sent to earth to free the elect. The chosen."

"If you are chosen, you must sign a one-million-year contract. Pledging all of your earthly possessions to the Zone."

"If you keep the contract, you will live for an eternity. If you don't, you will be handed over to Zenu for eternal torment."

Give me a break! I couldn't believe that people actually fell for this nonsense.

"If you are chosen, you will be given a new brain. Every year, information will be downloaded into your mind revealing the secrets of the universe."

"You must never speak a word of what you have seen or heard to an unbeliever, or your body will be turned over to Zenu."

"You will be protected from all the aliens who roam the earth seeking to destroy you."

As if it couldn't get any weirder.

"You are to worship me. I am the one who can save you from eternal damnation."

I'd heard enough. I started to leave and go check out the police station. I felt so sorry for the couple if they believed that pile of manure.

"There's hope for you," the voice said. "If you are in the Awareness Zone, then you can believe. Once you believe, you must wait to be chosen. You must show yourself worthy."

Brad talked about the zones. Awareness. Believers. And the Chosen Zone. It couldn't be a coincidence. That proved it. Lucas Rikki was our man. The fugitive. The man wanted for molesting young girls in Idaho.

How do I find him?

17

Three weeks later

A stalemate had ensued. Mr. Z. didn't know what to say and neither did I.

We stood in the makeshift prison cell, staring at each other. I was off in the corner. He was at the doorway. I held two chair legs in my hands. The ones I had made into weapons. The giant stood next to his boss and was itching to get at me. I could tell.

I was anxious to fight him as well. He'd gotten the best of me once. I blamed that on the snowdrifts. He wouldn't beat me again.

I hadn't acted because I didn't know what my next move should be. Mr. Z. probably didn't act because he wanted answers. I could imagine a thousand questions raging through his mind.

Who is this woman? What happened to the Sheriff? How did she know how to get out of the bindings? Is my life in danger? Does she know who I am?

Either that, or he didn't know what to do either.

He had already confronted me about the missing Sheriff and my response only added to the mystery.

"You were seen leaving the diner with him," he said. "He was taking you to Iqaluit and putting you on a plane. You were the last person to see him alive."

"If he's dead, the last person to see him alive was the person who killed him," I retorted with a bit of an attitude.

He looked at me skeptically. Not realizing I had admitted to killing the Sheriff in a roundabout way.

I could throw out my story about the Sheriff going to Salliq, but I got the impression Mr. Z. had already heard it and rejected it. The men of the Zone might have been fooled, but Mr. Z. would know it wasn't true. The Sheriff worked for him. He wouldn't take off to Salliq without getting permission first. Even if he did, he would answer his cell phone when the boss called. Or he'd at least return Mr. Z.'s call and let him know what was going on.

Since Mr. Z. didn't know what happened to the Sheriff that gave me an advantage. He probably wanted to keep me alive until he knew. The giant could've killed me while I was out cold. I could see why the giant might not take that step on his own and bring me back to this location, but Mr. Z. decided to bind me rather than kill me.

Because he wanted to know what happened to the Sheriff.

Considering he hadn't spoken to him, he had to assume the Sheriff was dead. What he couldn't figure out was how I did it. An armed man. Twice my size. Trained. Skilled. Mean as a junkyard dog. A man who had struck fear in the entire population of Yura Lake for years. All by himself.

One man was able to keep everyone in line. Cover up the missing girl cases. When I went inside the police station, I didn't find anything related to the girls. No case files. No missing persons posters. No notes of any kind.

Even though the girls were reported missing by their families, the Sheriff made no effort to find them. I could only assume because he knew what had happened to them.

I had my own questions. Mr. Z. admitted the girls were still alive. Where were they? Where was I? More than likely at the same location as the girls.

The Sheriff was my leverage to gain information. That's the chess game we were playing. I was about to put the king in check. Checkmate when I killed him. Which wouldn't be that long from now.

I thought I'd repeat myself.

"The last person to see the Sheriff alive was the person who killed him."

"That was you."

"Then you should assume that I'm the one who killed him."

"I thought you said he was alive. That he went to Salliq for ten days. That you were lovers."

"You've been listening to my conversations."

"I know everything that happens in Yura Lake."

"Not everything. You don't know what happened to the Sheriff. Maybe he did go to Salliq. Maybe we were lovers. Maybe I killed him. You don't know and it's eating you up inside."

If I struck a nerve, his face didn't show it. "Why don't you tell me?"

I decided to throw him a curveball. Tell him the last thing he expected to hear.

"I killed him."

His eyes widened.

"The Sheriff is dead," I said.

He shook his head from side to side like he was trying to relieve some tension. "You killed the Sheriff?"

"It wasn't really that hard to do."

"You stole his gate card and keys."

"I wouldn't say I stole them. Is it stealing if he's dead? I don't know. That's a gray area."

My words dripped with more sarcasm than a melting ice cream cone.

"Where is his vehicle and where is his body?" Mr. Z. said roughly.

"I thought you knew everything that happens in Yura Lake. I thought you were god. Isn't that what you tell all your followers?"

His eyes widened a second time. He caught himself. Clearly realizing his face was revealing the truth.

Another long pause ensued.

The Sheriff's keycard had gotten me into the police station. Inside, I found a huge stash of weapons. Including a shoulder fire missile launcher and half a dozen missiles. Why did Mr. Z. need such a powerful weapon?

I desperately wanted to ask him, but the silence was giving me time to think.

Mr. Z. was trafficking women, but not arms. I was sure of both. It didn't make sense for him to be dealing weapons. Those kinds of weapons were generally purchased in the Middle east, Russia, or South America.

Why transport them to the Arctic Circle, then transport them back out? Too expensive. The market was flooded with cheap weapons.

Mr. Z. didn't like me poking around the police station. The next day, I went back to the station and the weapons were gone. Taken overnight.

I thought I knew what had happened to them. I wouldn't give Mr. Z. the satisfaction of asking. Digging for answers showed weakness. It was irrelevant. The only thing that mattered was what weapons were in the room with us at that moment.

That and where were the girls?

I wouldn't even give Mr. Z. the satisfaction of asking that question. I didn't want him to have anything he could hold over me. Asking meant I didn't know the answer. I didn't want him to know how much I knew. That gave me leverage. He'd keep me alive until he knew if his whole operation was compromised.

"I've been watching you," he finally blurted out, when the silence became too awkward for both of us.

I was getting impatient. I wanted to kill both of them on the spot. But I didn't know where we were. Or where the girls were. I didn't know if they would all die a slow and painful death if I killed Mr. Z.

without knowing how to find them. He might be the one providing them with food and water.

"Don't give yourself too much credit," I said. "I wanted you to see me. I want you to be afraid of me."

"Are you FBI?"

"Maybe."

"CIA?"

"That's also a possibility."

"DEA? We don't do drugs here."

"I bet it's keeping you up at night wondering."

"Not really. I sleep well."

Time to drop a grenade in the middle of things.

"You don't know who I am, but I know who you are."

He grinned, but behind the fake smile was a nervous tic. I was trained to spot it. It's the first weakness I'd seen. Up to that point, I only saw confusion.

I decided to mock him. That'd be his kryptonite. Powerful men were all the same. They had egos the size of Texas. They were used to bullying people. Demanding respect. Especially a religious leader like Rikki who pretended to be a god so people would worship him.

This was the quickest way to get him flustered.

"Did your mother drop you on your head when you were a baby?" I quipped.

His jaw tightened. His entire body tensed.

"I even know your name. Lucas Rikki."

His face gave it away. I had my confirmation. Not that I needed it. I already knew who he was.

"Can I call you Luke? Or do you prefer Rick?"

His eyes burned with anger. Steam was coming out of his ears, so to speak. His fists were balled.

The giant was like a tiger ready to pounce. I kept my eye on him. He took an even more aggressive stance as tension filled the room like smoke from a fireplace with the flume shut. I needed a plan in case the giant pulled a weapon or charged me.

"I know everything about you, Luke," I said. Raising the tension even more. "You're from Romo, Denmark. You graduated from the University of Copenhagen. You have a doctorate in science."

His weight began to shift back and forth. His mind was obviously trying to process this information. How did I know this? He must've had a million new questions. If I knew, then who else did?

A Curly tactic. Throw your enemy off his game. The element of surprise was one of our biggest weapons. Confusion led to mistakes. So did emotions. They caused people to act irrationally. Impulsively. Out of anger.

I acted out of anger, but it was controlled. Targeted. Harnessed into overwhelming force.

Mocking him was clearly working.

"Is that where you came up with all that B.S. about the Northern Lights? And aliens? Zenu? Extraterrestrial beings?"

My words were coming fast now.

"The Awareness Zone. The Believers Zone. The Chosen Zone. The Deity Zone. You think you're a deity. That's laughable. Look at you. You're barely five feet tall. All the mythological gods are big, mighty, powerful. You're a weaselly little man."

I was ready to bring the verbal knockout blow.

"I know now why you stay in hiding. Your followers would take one look at you and laugh. You're nothing but a small man who uses lies to trick your believers into following you. You're a fool. Delusional. You're crazy. You're insane. You probably even believe your lies. You've told them for so long."

I saw him take a breath.

The giant still hadn't spoken. He also hadn't moved any closer. Like he was on a leash. He wouldn't act until Rikki gave him permission. Another one of Rikki's mind numbed robots.

"You think you know me, but you don't," Rikki said angrily. "I don't expect you to understand the things of the Zone."

"I do know you. You molested girls in Idaho."

I saw fear flash across his face.

"There's a warrant out for your arrest. You're a fugitive. I'm taking you back to Idaho to stand trial."

His eyes flitted back and forth. Not sure what to say or do. I could see the panic written all over his face.

The gig was up. His mind was already spinning like a top. He had to escape. I'm sure he had contingency plans. Maybe not. He probably didn't think anyone would ever find him here.

Time to ratchet up the pressure even more.

"That reminds me. You have the right to remain silent. Anything you say can and will be used against you. You have the right... Oh, I forgot. We aren't in the United States. Those rules don't apply. I don't have to read you your rights. I can just kill you."

I didn't have arrest authority anyway. I did have the legal and moral authority to kill him.

The giant took a step forward. Toward me.

My body tensed. The makeshift weapons were still in my hands. "I wouldn't do that if I were you," I warned.

Rikki held him back.

"Put down those weapons. I'm a nonviolent person."

"I'm an extremely violent person."

"I assume so. But you can't kill me. I'm immortal."

"We'll see when I slash your throat."

"That's not going to happen."

"Who's going to stop me?"

"You will cooperate."

"Why would I do that?"

"Because I have Lily."

It felt like I'd run into a brick wall traveling a hundred miles an hour.

How was that possible?

18

Three weeks earlier

The principal's office at the school was like everything else I'd seen in Yura Lake. Pristine. Not extravagant, but modern and functional. Beth Shoemaker matched the décor and was modest but smartly dressed. Her long-sleeved blouse came up to her neck and she wore a full-length solid black skirt.

Her hair wasn't in a net though, telling me she wasn't part of the cult. The brown locks were layered and rested on her shoulders flipping up slightly at the ends. She had that typical midwestern girl look with the matching Minnesotan drawl.

Her greeting was warm but guarded.

"What can I do for you, Ms. Winters?" she asked.

"Please call me Jesse."

"You may call me Beth."

"I will. Thanks for meeting with me."

She was behind the desk, and I sat in a chair in front. Neither of us were relaxed even if we pretended to be.

"I understand you're writing a story on Inuit girls ages fourteen to eighteen," she said. "Trying to figure out why so many of them commit suicide."

That surprised me. I'd only told one person that story.

"Where did you hear that?"

"From my boyfriend."

"You're dating Leo?"

Her cheeks reddened.

"He told me the two of you met and he gave you a ride."

Did he tell you he touched my bottom? Did he tell you he was flirting with me? That he wanted to kiss me? That he curried sexual favors from women as part of his compensation, provided for by Mr. Z.?

I kept those thoughts to myself.

She added, "We've been out a few times. The dating pool in Yura Lake is not exactly overrun with eligible bachelors."

"I suppose not."

If Leo were the last man alive, I think I'd still pass.

Should I warn her?

Then a horrid thought entered my head. Surely, Leo wasn't referring to Beth as one of the women who were part of his compensation. She didn't seem like the type who'd stoop that low. Of course, she didn't seem like the type to date a guy like Leo, even if he was the pick of the litter in this small town.

It almost made me laugh. From what I'd seen from the other men in Yura Lake, Leo probably was at the top of the dating chain. As unbelievable as that sounded in my head. I could see why a naïve schoolmarm might be sucked in by his good looks and charm.

Beth must've sensed what I was thinking because she said, "Leo's not so bad. He can be a bit of a flirt."

"That's an understatement."

"He's harmless though. He's all talk. I mean, he probably did sleep with his share of girls when he was a divemaster, but he didn't know me then. We all have a past. Am I right?"

To be honest, I couldn't care less about her relationship with Leo. I had to know if the Midwest gullibility was real or an act. So, I decided to throw a smoke bomb into the middle of the conversation.

I leaned forward in the chair.

"I'm not actually a journalist. I'm investigating sex trafficking. I have reason to believe Mr. Z. is trafficking Inuit girls here in Yura Lake."

Her eyes widened to twice their size. She began whispering. "Something fishy is going on. I felt it as soon as I got here."

"Tell me what you know. What seems fishy?"

Beth stood and walked from behind her desk and closed the door. I assumed the room was bugged. I didn't see a camera, but these days, cameras could be the size of a pencil eraser. That's the reason I blurted out my real reason for being there. If Mr. Z. was listening, I wanted him to be shaking in his boots.

He'd gone to great lengths to hide there. Anonymity made him feel safe. I'd blown it wide open. He had to know he couldn't continue operating business as usual. Even if he figured out a way to take me out of the picture, if I was part of a larger investigation, reinforcements wouldn't be far behind.

I wanted Mr. Z. to be nervous. To make a mistake. I also wanted to see her reaction. To see if she was in on it. Clearly, she wasn't.

"We can talk freely now," she said, after she sat back down.

"What if the room is bugged?"

"Leo checked. It's not."

"Oh. Okay."

I wasn't sure how Leo would know, but it didn't matter to me one way or the other. If it wasn't, then I could continue my cover. If it was, then I wanted Mr. Z. to hear everything I had to say.

My only concern at that point was Beth. That she might say something that could get her killed.

She still whispered even with the door closed.

"I have six girls in my school who are pregnant. Some as young as fourteen."

"Who are the fathers?"

"The girls won't say."

"I understand that fourteen is the legal age to marry, with the parent's permission. It isn't against the law. At least not around here."

Beth nodded. "Leo told me the parents sell their daughters to Mr. Z. Can you imagine that? Selling your own daughter."

"What did you think you were getting into when you agreed to come here?"

"Not this. Mr. Z. told me there was a real need for a teacher and a doctor. I was uniquely qualified since I have both skills. I was a school administrator in Minnesota, but I'm also an OB/GYN."

"How did you learn about the opportunity?"

"I saw it online. At first, I was skeptical. It seemed too good to be true."

"If it sounds too good to be true, then it usually is." The words came out with a look of disgust on my face. I wasn't sure if it was meant for her yet.

"I didn't come here for the money," she said defensively. "Yeah. Mr. Z. pays me a lot of money and he paid off my student loans. But I was making good money in Minnesota. I came here because he told me the girls needed help. They had trouble learning without a qualified teacher. They also lacked proper medical care. I'm a Christian by faith. I considered it a mission opportunity."

She paused and I didn't respond. She seemed sincere. My heart was softening towards her.

"I'm still glad I came," she said, choking back tears. "It breaks my heart to see what's happening to them."

Now I liked her.

"What do you think is happening to the girls?"

"I don't know. I think they're extremely unhappy. I mean, who wouldn't be? The weather's bad enough. But they're also forced into these marriages. I don't think they can get out of them. It's like they're living in the Dark Ages. Figuratively and literally considering we rarely get sunshine. I'm still not used to that."

"Have they told you they're unhappy?"

"You can see it in their faces."

"Have they said why? Do they talk to you about it?

She shook her head. Then dabbled at her eyes. Took a deep breath before continuing.

"They're afraid. The girls in the Zone religion won't say a word. They come to school and do their work and then leave. They're polite and respond when I talk to them, but I can tell they're sworn to secrecy. They won't even tell me where they live, much less who they're married to."

"According to their religion, their souls will be condemned to eternal damnation if they speak one word about their religion to anyone."

"Well, that's just ridiculous! I didn't know that. I've been here all these months and I know nothing about their religion. Other than it's extremely odd. I talk to them about Christ, but they ignore me."

"Religion is Mr. Z.'s way to control the girls."

"Is that considered sex trafficking?"

"I think so. Especially if the girls want to leave but can't."

"I know of one girl who wants to leave."

"What's her name?"

"Her name is Tapeesa."

"That's a pretty name. Unusual."

"It means Arctic flower. She's gorgeous. I call her Tapestry because she's as pretty as an ornament. She didn't know what a tapestry was. These girls are really sheltered and know little about the outside world."

"I can imagine."

"It's worse than you can imagine. They are completely sheltered. I'm their only contact with the outside world. All the curriculum is determined for me. I'm limited as to what I can teach them."

She grinned slyly.

"I kinda break the rules. Teach them things not in the curriculum. So far, Mr. Z. hasn't said anything."

"Have you ever met Mr. Z.?"

"No. I only talked to him on the phone. One time, when he interviewed me for the job. The rest of the time, I talk to one of his employees. His bodyguard. This huge man. Gunvald. He must be seven feet tall. He comes every afternoon to collect the girls."

The giant. I had a feeling I'd eventually be fighting him.

"Back to Tapeesa. How do you know she wants to leave?" I asked.

"Actually, she doesn't want to leave. She can't. She wants me to smuggle her baby out of here."

"She has a baby?"

"She's pregnant. Due in about three weeks. She asked if I could pretend her baby died in childbirth and then hide her."

"What did you say?"

"That I didn't think I could. What would I do with the baby? How could I get her out of Yura Lake without anyone knowing? I'm not even sure I can leave."

"Do you feel trapped here?"

She leaned forward. "I don't know. I've heard rumors about people disappearing."

"Who did you hear that from?"

"From Leo."

"I don't know if you can trust Leo."

"I know I can. He told me if I ever wanted to leave, he'd get me out of here."

"What if he's one of the sex traffickers?"

She shook her head from side to side with emphasis.

"No way. I know Leo."

"Love can cloud your judgment."

"I didn't say we were in love. We've only been out a few times and he's always been the perfect gentleman."

"Leo?"

"He's never tried anything. Other than a goodnight kiss. I'd call it more like a goodnight peck. He doesn't even kiss me directly on the lips."

"That doesn't sound like the Leo I know."

"I'm a bit of a prude myself. Leo makes me look like an Amish girl."

Interesting analogy considering what I thought of the girls in the Zone who looked Amish.

Now I was confused.

Maybe I had misjudged Leo. He hadn't confronted me about the gun. He acted like a cad around me but a perfect gentleman around Beth. Something didn't seem right about the picture.

Regardless, we were getting off topic. Their love life might be interesting, but irrelevant to my investigation.

"Can I talk to Tapeesa?" I asked.

"I can ask her. But don't get your hopes up. She probably won't talk to you. It took a couple of months before she opened up to me."

"Is she here now? At school?"

"Yes. She's in the classroom studying."

"Will she at least meet with me? Even if I do all the talking? I can tell a lot from her reactions."

"She'll do whatever I tell her to do."

"Great. Bring her in."

"I'll be right back."

Beth stood and walked out the door quickly. Closing it behind her. My mind was like a three-ring circus. All kinds of things were going on at once.

How could I get Tapeesa to talk?

The baby was the obvious road into her deepest secrets. I could get that baby out of there. I could get her out as well. All I had to do was get the snowmobile and take them to Iqaluit. If she wouldn't talk now, maybe she would when she was safely out of Yura Lake.

Less than two minutes later, the door opened and in walked Tapeesa. With Beth right behind her. She closed the door.

Beth was right. The girl was stunningly beautiful.

I stood to my feet and reached out my hand.

She looked over at Beth.

"It's okay. You can trust her."

Tapeesa took my hand. Her grip was timid and weak. I maintained my hold on her. I led her to sit down. Then leaned in close. Her hands rested on her lap, and I put mine on them.

My heart was breaking. I could see the pain in her eyes. They were sunken and dark. Hopeless. I didn't get the feeling she was sex trafficked or passed around to multiple men. But I did sense she had been abused. Forced into her situation. Her shoulders were slumped. Her head was down. She tried not to make eye contact with me.

I lifted my left hand and gently touched her cheek. She flinched.

"Tapeesa, I'm here to help you and your baby," I said. "I can get you out of Yura Lake."

For the first time, she looked up at me. I saw a glimmer of hope. Her eyes widened slightly. Tears formed in the corner of her eyes.

She still didn't speak.

"But you have to help me," I said. "Who's the father of your baby?"

My hands were back on top of hers. She pulled them away. The hope was gone. Replaced by terror.

"It's okay. You can tell me. I won't let anyone hurt you, ever again."

Her face drooped and shoulders slumped again.

"Here's what we're going to do," I said. "Ms. Shoemaker is going to put you in the hospital. She'll say that you're having trouble with the pregnancy. That you need to be hospitalized. That way you don't have to go home tonight."

"I can do that," Beth said.

"Then I'm going to take you and the baby to Iqaluit. I'll put you on the first plane out of here. I have people in America who will take you in and help you."

I worked with a Christian group called *Save The Girls*. They had locations all over the world. Not in Nunavut, but I could get Tapeesa to one of their locations. They'd take her in until she could have her baby and get back on her feet.

The slight glimmer of hope was back. Our eyes met. My face wasn't twelve inches from hers. Tears streamed down her face.

"I can't leave," she said. Her voice cracked.

"Yes, you can. I'll help you."

"He'll find me."

"Who's he?"

Her eyes flitted back and forth. She wrung her hands. Rocked back and forth slightly in the chair. Nervously.

"Tell me who *he* is."

"Mr. Z.," she said, barely above a whisper.

"I can protect you from Mr. Z. I promise."

"He won't let me leave."

"He can't stop you."

"You don't know him. He said he'd kill me and my family if I ever tried to leave him."

"I won't let him."

She hesitated. Looked at Beth. Then at me. Back at Beth.

I had a hunch.

"Is Mr. Z. the father of your baby?"

"Yes."

I was going to kill that man.

19

Once Tapeesa started sharing her gut-wrenching story, the words began to flow like water from a levee breach. It'd been bottled up for three long years. Her youth was stolen from her. I blamed her parents.

"My dad was offered a large sum of money for me," she said. "More than most, I guess. They said I was prettier than the other girls."

If the man was standing in the room at that moment, I'd have a hard time not hitting him so hard he'd see stars. I couldn't believe anyone would do this to their daughter. I couldn't imagine doing such a thing to my daughter for all the money in China.

"Where are your parents now?" I asked.

I might want to pay them a visit if they were still in Yura Lake.

"I don't know. Once they got their money, they moved away. To Canada, I think."

I felt a twinge of disappointment. Probably better. I didn't need any distractions. Revenge wasn't a reason to stray from the mission.

For whatever reason, I didn't hear any bitterness behind Tapeesa's words. What she said next explained why.

"They told me it was an honor. You know. To be the wife of a god. I was doing a great service to the world. Only a select number of girls were chosen to serve Mr. Z. in that way."

Only one girl would have the privilege of killing him. *Me.*

"How old were you when all this happened?" Beth asked. I could tell from the look on her face that she was appalled. This must've been eye opening for her. To realize these kinds of injustices were in the world.

I'd seen worse things. That didn't make it any easier to hear.

Tapeesa took in a breath and said, "Thirteen. We weren't married until I was fourteen. I didn't get pregnant until I was fifteen."

"She's due in three weeks," Beth said for my benefit. Not remembering she had already given me that information.

"I was told a pregnancy was the greatest honor," Tapeesa said. "To give Mr. Z. a daughter."

"She's having a girl," Beth said. Looking my way again. That was new information.

Beth had her hand on Tapeesa's shoulder. Doing her best to reassure her.

"I've said too much."

"It's okay, honey," Beth said. "We're not going to tell anyone. Your secrets are safe with us."

Tapeesa shuddered. "He'll know. He's a god. He knows everything."

The rage stoked inside of me. I despised men like Mr. Z. My whole adult life had been devoted to killing these men. I had to be careful that the anger didn't come through in my voice. To the point I made Tapeesa scared of me.

"Mr. Z. is lying," I said, tempering the words. "He's not a god. He's a normal man. He doesn't know everything. He just wants you to think he does."

Tapeesa became animated. Her head bobbed up and down like a bobblehead doll.

"No. No. He does really know everything." Her voice had reverted back to that of a little girl.

Girls subjected to sex trafficking stopped maturing emotionally. They became stuck at whatever age they were when the trauma started. It sometimes took years of therapy to help them heal and start developing normal emotions again.

Tapeesa was insistent. "Sometimes Mr. Z. would tell me things that only I knew. You know. Things I said. Things I did. He'd like... I share a bedroom with another one of his wives. If we talk about something, he knows it. He can tell me what we said, what I was wearing, and when we said it. He's all knowing."

He's a master manipulator. A con man. A magician's trick.

She continued. "I got in trouble many times for saying too much. Mr. Z. said my mouth was going to cause me to burn for an eternity. You know he has the power to banish me to eternal damnation?"

I said, "Oh dear child, Mr. Z. is not a god. He has cameras and listening devices in your room. That's how he knows what you're saying."

Her eyes widened. "Oh."

"He sees what you're doing. He listens to your conversations. Then tries to make you think he's a god. That's all it is. He's tricking you."

Probably getting his kicks from it as well. Watching the girls in their private moments.

"You said he has other wives?" I said. More of a statement than a question. I had already assumed he did.

"Yes. We take turns. Mr. Z. gives us a schedule of when it's our time to please him. That's what he calls it. Since I'm pregnant I haven't had to for eight months. To be honest, it's been a relief."

I could imagine, although, I didn't need all the sordid details.

Beth said, "How many wives does Mr. Z. have?" thankfully changing the subject. If she hadn't asked, I would have.

"Twenty-two including me."

"How many children does he have?" I asked.

"I don't know. All the children are taken from us at birth. They don't live with us."

"They're taken from you?" I asked. I hadn't expected that response.

"Yes."

"Where are they taken?"

"We don't know."

"I can answer that," Beth said. "They're given to men who live in the Zone. Members of the religion."

"How do you know?" I asked.

"One man brought a baby in for childcare. I recognized her. I delivered her. The baby has a birthmark. And I know for a fact his wife wasn't pregnant. Leo told me what was happening."

I shook my head from side to side in disbelief. "That's sick. I wonder if they're raising them as their children or to become their wives when they turn fourteen. I suspect it's the latter."

"Leo said the girls are being groomed," Beth said. "To become wives. Not for the men who raised them, but for other men in the Zone. All boy babies are raised to be just like the men who raised them."

Tapeesa was crying again.

"That's why you have to help me," she pleaded. "I can't let my baby go through what I went through. It's too late for me but not for my baby girl."

"It's not too late for you," I said, resolutely. "Mr. Z. will never touch you again. You have my word."

"I don't see how that's possible. If I don't come home after school, he'll come looking for me."

"Like I said, Beth will tell him you're in the hospital. With complications from your pregnancy. I'll figure out how to get you out of the Zone and over to Iqaluit. Then out of Nunavut altogether. Probably tonight."

"You can do that?"

"I can and I will."

I wasn't going to tell her I was going to kill Mr. Z. He was the father of her baby after all.

I'd kill him if I could find him. He might already be gone. If he had somehow slipped through my fingers, I'd track him to the ends of the earth. I'd find him, before he could ever find her.

Tapeesa reached her hands to her head and began unclipping her hairnet. Roughly. Angrily. Ripping it apart. When she was done, she threw it against the wall. Her beautiful jet-black hair fell. Flowing past her shoulders. She shook it out.

I saw a new resolve in her.

She shrugged her shoulders. "I'm supposed to have my head covered at all times when I'm not at home. Mr. Z. said I'd suffer eternal damnation if I didn't obey his every command."

The first hint of bitterness was behind the words.

"He said that to control you," I said. "It's not true."

"Oh well. My soul is condemned anyway for talking to you. We're forbidden to ever discuss anything with anyone who is not chosen. So, what difference does it make now? Maybe there's still hope for my baby."

She rubbed her stomach which was huge. It looked to me like she could deliver the baby at any time.

"Your soul is not condemned," Beth said. "Don't believe what Mr. Z. told you. None of it is true. Remember what I told you about Jesus. He's the way, the truth, and the life. He's the way to salvation. Not Mr. Z. He's only a man."

"Mr. Z. told us about Jesus. He said he was a prophet. One level below him."

I wanted to refute it. There'd be time for that later. I needed actionable intelligence.

"Tapeesa, listen to me carefully. I need information. You mentioned your bedroom. That you share it with another wife. Do you live in the same house with Mr. Z.?"

"Yes."

"Where?"

"Here in Yura Lake."

That didn't make sense. I hadn't seen any structure that would house twenty-two wives. Two to a room meant it had to have at least eleven bedrooms and half that many bathrooms.

"Where in Yura Lake, honey?" Beth asked. "I think that's what she's asking."

"Yes. Tell me exactly where you live."

"At the observatory."

"I've been in the observatory. No one lives there."

"We live underneath it."

"You live under the observatory."

"Yes."

"Underground?"

"Yes."

I hadn't considered that possibility.

It suddenly made sense. My mind reverted back to when I was in the observatory. I was trying to remember the configuration. I didn't see any access point. No doors that would lead to an elevator.

Were they hidden?

The only thing I saw was a door off the helipad. I tried it, but it was locked. None of the Sheriff's keys worked on it. I had intended to go back there and pick it at some point. Maybe that was the entrance to either the stairs or an elevator.

Rather than trying to figure it out, I just needed to ask her.

"How do you get there? To where you live?"

"There's a door that leads off the observatory."

"Be more specific."

"We go through the police station and outside. Where the helicopter is. There's a door there. It takes us to an elevator. We take it down and that's our home."

"How big is it?" Beth asked.

"I don't know. Pretty big. Our house is huge. We each share a bedroom and a bathroom."

"Think. I need you to tell me everything you've seen down there."

Tapeesa stared off in the distance. Thinking.

"Start from the beginning. Tell me what you see when you get off the elevator."

"We exit into a big area. It has three different hallways."

"Any armed guards in that foyer?"

"Yes. One. Well, I mean, there are four of them. Only one sits there at a time."

"Okay. You're doing good. There are three hallways. Where do they lead?"

"I've never been down the other two. I go to the right."

"That's where you live?"

"Right."

"Any idea where the other halls go?"

"I think one leads to Mr. Z.'s residence. I've seen him walk down that hall."

"Have you ever been there? To his residence."

"Yes. Many times. Well, only in his bedroom. There's a doorway that leads to his bedroom from where we live."

"Any idea where the third hallway leads?"

I saw her hesitate.

My heart was pounding. Like it did when I came upon a break in the investigation. I was already picturing everything in my mind. How I was going to take out the guard. How I was going to find Mr. Z.

I had a feeling I knew who lived in the third section. I needed confirmation.

"Do you know if anyone lives in the third section?" I asked again. Stronger this time. "Who lives down the third hallway?"

"More women live there. But they aren't his wives. I think they're his mistresses."

"How do you know?"

Tapeesa hesitated.

"This is very important. Tell me what you know."

"One day, I was taken to Mr. Z.'s bedroom and left there. You know. It was my time. Mr. Z. was in the bathroom."

I reminded myself to ask her everything she remembered about the suite. I didn't ask now because I didn't want to interrupt her.

"While I was waiting, a woman came out of another bathroom. There are two of them in his suite. One for us and one for him."

"Go on."

"She was frantic when she saw me. She said she was being held against her will. That she was from Peru. She was drugged in a bar and when she came to, she was on a plane. She ended up here. She pleaded for me to help her."

"Did she say if there were more women?"

"Yes. Twenty or so."

The sex trafficking angle was blown wide open. Mr. Z. kidnapped women from around the world, brought them to Nunavut. Hid them underground, so no one would ever find them. Pure evil.

"What did she say next?" I asked.

"Mr. Z. came out of the bathroom. He was furious. He slapped the girl across the mouth. She was bleeding. I thought he was going to hit me."

Tapeesa's hands were shaking.

"He told me to never tell anyone what I saw that day. If I did, my soul would burn for an eternity. I never told anyone. Until now. I was afraid."

"You are very brave," Beth said, stroking Tapeesa's hair.

"Tell me everything else you can remember about Mr. Z.'s bedroom suite," I said.

It didn't take long. She was only allowed in the bedroom and her bathroom. The suite was luxurious. A massive bed against the far wall, with plush linens, and a gold bedspread. Gold everywhere. Chandelier. Thick carpeting. Mirrors on every wall and on the ceiling.

I was mostly concerned about the layout. Trying to picture it.

A plan was forming in my mind.

I'd take the elevator down. When the door opened, I'd shoot the guard. Rather than going to the right where the wives were, or the left hallway where the trafficked girls were being held, I'd go right for Mr. Z. and kill him first. If he was still around. Take out any other threats. Then figure out how to get the girls out of there.

First, I had to get inside.

"Beth, you said that the giant comes every day at the end of the school day to collect the girls."

"That's right. Gunvald is his name."

Tapeesa's eyes were suddenly filled with fear. She was obviously terrified of the monstrosity.

"When he comes, tell him that Tapeesa is in the hospital," I said. "That her water broke, and that she could have her baby at any time."

"I can do that. Where will you be?"

"I'll be hiding. I want to follow Gunvald and find that entrance to the elevator."

20

Why did it have to be so darn cold?

The temperature was ten below zero. Thirty below windchill.

So much for best laid plans.

A cold front had descended on Yura Lake like the black plague. White plague in this instance, although it wasn't snowing. A small consolation.

In Virginia, we called it an Arctic Blast. More like an eruption. A nuclear freeze.

Actually, I was in the Arctic. This was ground zero. Where the cold gathered, built up its anger, and plunged south. Faster than the geese could get away.

No amount of training would've prepared me for these conditions.

Beth warned me to be careful. In this weather, hypothermia could overtake me within ten minutes. Even while wearing the proper clothing.

Curly said to never be careful. Careful gets you killed. I think I'll side with Beth on this one.

Although, careful was staying inside. Not an option. While I'd prefer to fight the giant inside rather than outside in the cold, I had to avoid a confrontation at all costs.

I couldn't do that if I stayed inside.

Gunvald was coming shortly to pick up the girls from school.

Tapeesa was safe in the hospital. Ironically enough, having minor contractions. Beth didn't think the baby was coming yet. Braxton Hicks contractions was what she called them.

I left her my cell phone number so we could communicate if anything changed.

I couldn't hide inside the school. No logistical way to follow Gunvald out of the school, through the streets, into the police station, and then out into the helipad. Not without being seen.

What if Gunvald searched the school? What if the school was bugged and Mr. Z. heard every word we discussed? Knew my plan?

Inside the police station was ideal. I could watch Gunvald on the security cameras. Except for one problem. He had to walk right past the desk where the security screens were located to get from the helipad to the school.

Not that outside was that much better. All the security cameras in every part of the Zone meant my movements could be tracked. Mr. Z. could feed the giant the information in real time.

So I had to improvise.

I changed out of Nirliq's parka and left the school in a disguise. Trying to find a location where I was sheltered from the cold, out of view of the security cameras, but in the view of the school and police station.

Impossible.

After half-heartedly trying, I gave up, went to the police station, warmed up, then turned off the security system.

Up to that point, I had wanted Mr. Z. to see me. To watch my movements. To realize how big a threat I was to him. It was obviously working since he hadn't done anything to try and stop me. For all practical purposes, I had free run of the place. Could come and go at my own discretion.

Now, I didn't want him to see me. I was in full spy mode.

Alex was the foremost computer hacker in the world. The best of the best. One of the few good guys in the arena. He taught me how to shut down an entire security system. Temporarily or permanently.

In this instance, I opted to take it down for a few hours. If Mr. Z. had a technologically savvy person on staff, he could fix it, but it'd take some time. I could turn it on anytime I wanted. That gave me time to search for a good hiding place.

I found one.

The helipad.

The sun had set. Even better. The helipad was well lit, but the corners were dark and provided perfect cover.

That's where I was. Standing in the far-right corner, shaking. Blowing in my hands to warm my face.

How long had it been? According to my watch, I'd been outside for three minutes. It felt like three hours.

I could feel the cold in my bones. Beth went over the symptoms of hypothermia with me. If I had two or more of those symptoms, I needed to get inside immediately. Hypothermia was deadly in these situations.

First symptom she mentioned was shivering. Check. I had that one. That didn't mean I had hypothermia. I shivered in Virginia when it went below fifty degrees above zero.

Exhaustion.

That wasn't a problem. Adrenaline was pumping through me like water through a firehose. I was fully alert. Aware of my precarious position. If the cold didn't kill me, the giant might try.

What if he saw me?

If he did, I had a plan. Pull the gun out of my pocket and shoot him. Assuming I could steady my hand long enough to aim and fire. If my finger was able to pull the trigger. If the gun worked properly in the frigid cold.

All I could do was hope. No way to test it.

I moved around to keep the body heat going. One of Beth's suggestions, although I already knew that. Common sense told me to keep moving.

Confusion was another symptom.

I was thinking clearly.

Maybe I wasn't. If I was thinking clearly, I wouldn't be standing outside in thirty below zero weather.

Fumbling hands was another symptom of hypothermia. My hands were shaking. I kept wringing them. My gloves were warm, but my hands still felt cold. I couldn't hold them still.

Did that count as a symptom? Normally, my hands were as steady as a water tower.

Memory loss.

Why am I here? I don't remember.

I was joking with myself. I knew why I was there.

Tapeesa.

The promise I made to her.

I was taking her out of Yura Lake tonight and over to Iqaluit.

Brad would think I was crazy. Curly definitely would. Alex would understand and would do the same thing.

Normally in a mission, the greater numbers dictated decisions. At least forty women were in that bunker being held as sex slaves. A few were there voluntarily thinking they were doing a service to their religion, but most were there against their wills.

In most cases, saving the forty took priority over the one. That's what Brad would say. The prudent thing to do was to rescue the girls in the bunker. Then help Tapeesa.

But the forty weren't going anywhere. They'd still be there tomorrow. My promise to Tapeesa took priority. She gave me the information I needed. At great risk to herself. She told me about the underground bunker. Confirmed the sex trafficking.

I owed her.

I told her I'd get her out of Yura Lake tonight and that's what I intended to do.

My heart broke for the girl. She'd endured so much. Not of her own choosing. Her Judas parents sold her for thirty pieces of silver. Actually, more like thousands of dollars. Her morally bankrupt father and mother didn't deserve to have children.

I'd feel better once Tapeesa and her daughter were safe and on a plane out of Iqaluit. What if, God forbid, something happened to me in that bunker, and I didn't get out alive?

At least I had the power to save one girl. Two including her baby girl.

I justified it to Brad in my head. Not that I had talked to him. Hadn't had time. When the mission was over, I'd have to include all this in a report. Justify every action. I could spin it however I wanted, but this was a vital part of the story and had to be included in the report.

Rationalization was something I was good at.

The proverbial act first, ask for forgiveness later. Brad was used to it. While he didn't always agree with my decisions in the field, he couldn't argue with the results.

I would argue that I didn't want to rescue the forty girls yet, until I filled him in. In case something went wrong. Brad needed to know what I knew. I hadn't had a chance to confirm with him that Lucas Rikki was Mr. Z. and that he was trafficking women. That they were being held underground.

If I disappeared without talking to him, they'd probably come looking for me, but Mr. Z. would disappear as well. It might take them years to find him again.

Tonight, I would save Tapeesa and call him. Give him vital intelligence information. That way if anything happened to me, he'd send in reinforcements and eventually take down Mr. Z.

Curly was also in my head making his own arguments. What satisfied him was that I needed to gather intelligence.

I don't develop plans on my own. I heard Curly telling me what to do. Guiding me through each step. That was true even before he died. He told me in training that he'd always be in my head. He was right.

The arguments made sense. Even if I were able to find the elevator and the way into the underground, I needed a plan. Curly demanded it.

"You don't know what's down there," he had said. "The ingresses and egresses. Don't go into a confined space without an exit plan."

"There's only one entrance and exit. The elevator."

"You don't know that. I doubt Mr. Z. built that place without having another escape route."

"That's true."

"Of course, it's true. That's why I said it."

I didn't respond.

"You don't know how many guards there are."

"Tapeesa said four. Only one at a time."

"That's all she saw. How many guards would it take to keep forty women in line?"

"Not many, once they're brainwashed. Or drugged. Or so beaten down with fear, they'd never dare to resist."

"Still, there might be more than one. And you don't know the layout."

"Three hallways. Mostly bedrooms."

"That's not much to go on."

"More than I've had in a lot of other situations."

"Even if all goes well, how are you going to get the girls out of Yura Lake?"

"That's a problem."

"A problem you need to solve before charging down there with guns drawn."

"I agree and I need to talk to Brad. Get a plane to Iqaluit."

"The weather might be a problem. Who knows how long it'll take to get a plane in?"

"That will be a problem."

"Lots of problems in this mission."

I was moving around again. Trying to keep warm. The conversation continued to rage in my head.

"When has there never been problems?" I said to Curly.

"There's the giant. He's the biggest problem."

The pun made me laugh.

"Don't you think I'm aware of the giant?"

"He could crush you like a bag of pretzels if you get too close to him."

"Then I won't get close to him."

"You may not have a choice."

"You said there weren't two men alive who could beat me in a fight."

"I'd consider him the equivalent of two men. Maybe four or five if he has skills."

"I don't intend to get close to him. A bullet in the heart or between the eyes will kill him as quickly as it'll kill a jackrabbit."

"No doubt about that."

"I'm going to wait until tomorrow to get the forty girls out."

"I agree."

It was settled.

So I decided to hide and stick to the plan. Find out how to get in the underground, go to the hospital and get Tapeesa, take her to Iqaluit, call Brad and fill him in, then spend the night formulating how I was going to get underground and rescue the girls.

That meant making sure the giant didn't see me now and that we didn't have a confrontation. Not today.

What was I thinking about before I got off on that tangent with Curly?

That's right. I was going through the symptoms of hypothermia.

Confusion. *Did talking to a dead guy in my head count as confusion?*

I needed to get my mind on something else. The giant.

Hurry up, you big galoot. What's taking you so long?

Once he exited the door, and passed through the police station, I could go inside for a few minutes. Turn on the security cameras and watch him walk to the school and pick up the girls. Hide outside in the helipad again when he came back through.

"Hur... ry... up Gun... Gunner.... Gunvald."

My speech was slurred. Only because my jaw was frozen shut. Slurred speech was one of the symptoms of hypothermia.

How many symptoms did I have? At least two.

Sleepiness was one. I did suddenly feel tired.

Shallow breathing. *My breathing is labored.* Every time I took a breath, I got brain freeze. Like I was eating ice cream too fast. So I tried spacing out my breaths.

Weak pulse. I felt my neck. I couldn't feel anything.

That's because you have gloves on, dummy.

I suddenly felt dizzy.

I looked at my watch. My vision was blurred. I couldn't read the time. That wasn't one of the symptoms. Or was it?

I was going in and out of consciousness. Things were black, then bright. It felt like I was going to fall down. For a moment, I saw stars. Or were they the stars in the sky?

"Get inside, immediately when you feel the onset of symptoms," Beth said. "You aren't any good to any of us if you're dead."

I suddenly felt all the symptoms at once.

Could I make it inside?

My legs felt frozen to the ground. I told them to move but they didn't respond. I was surprised they still held me upright.

A panic came over me. My situation wasn't good. I couldn't stay outside. If I went inside, there was no place to hide. I'd have to kill the giant.

What if the giant came before I could warm myself? I wasn't in any condition to fight him. At least I was thinking clearly enough to know that.

A noise.

What was that?

The door opened.

A figure appeared.

I blinked my eyes so I could see him clearly. Held my breath. Tried to hold still. *If he sees me, I'm dead. If he hears me, I'm dead.*

I might die anyway.

You can't die. You have to live.

Remember your promise to Tapeesa.

The figure moved into the light. I could see him clearly.

It wasn't Gunvald. It was Leo.

21

Three weeks later

I've never wanted a man dead more than I did right now.

Mr. Z. said he had Lily. His satisfied look told me it was true.

"Put down your weapons," he said. "Fighting is useless."

"Not going to happen."

"You will cooperate."

"I'm going to cooperate by killing you."

"You're a mere human. You have no power to kill me. I can't die."

"Let's test your theory and see if it's true. I'm guessing not."

I was in an attack position now. Gunvald sensed it. He was standing beside Mr. Z. Prepared to defend and launch his own assault. Clearly, I would have to kill Gunvald first. He wouldn't be easy to kill.

The other problem was it might give Mr. Z. an opportunity to escape.

I might never find him.

The low life piece of human depravity continued to bloviate. Totally unconcerned that he was about to die. "I can never die because I'm immortal. I'm a god."

"You're a madman."

"I have twelve million followers. The chosen. They have forsaken all to follow me. How many people follow you?"

"I don't lie to them. Steal their money. Spout off a bunch of non-sense about Zenu and the afterlife."

"You can't possibly understand the secrets of the universe that have been given to me."

"You're a scam artist. You make billions off the backs of gullible people who want to believe you. You've told your lies for so long you probably even believe them."

Mr. Z. became pensive. His tone retrospective. "I will become a martyr someday. It's my destiny. When I do, my followers will grow by the millions."

I realized something at that moment. I couldn't take him back to the States for trial. He was right. The spectacle would only draw attention to him. If I killed him, he would be a martyr. So I had to make him disappear. Never to be heard from again. Let his followers wonder why he had abandoned them.

"I'm looking forward to helping you fulfill your destiny," I said.

He shook his head. "Today is not my time to leave my human body. I've seen that day. It's not here. Not now. Certainly not by the likes of you."

"We'll see about that."

Then he said something that infuriated me.

"It's too bad about the girl, Tapeesa. I liked her. I'm sad she had to die."

The rage was stoked inside of me like gasoline on a fire.

I raised the makeshift weapons in my hand and prepared to attack.

I'd broken off the two chair legs. The edges were sharp. One for each of them. Strategically placed in the side of their necks. Or slashed across their throats. Or thrust into their stomachs and twisted.

Mr. Z didn't seem at all concerned. Overconfidence worked to my advantage.

"I'm only going to tell you this one last time," he said, strongly. "Put down your weapons."

I dropped them.

But only as a distraction.

I had other weapons. My knees, elbows, fists, heels, and the palms of my hands. Dropping the weapons gave me the element of surprise. The metal clanged on the floor sending an echo through the prison cell.

The giant and Mr. Z. both looked down. I'd thrown them on the floor to my right. They looked that way. Watched them bounce.

Like a cat, I pounced.

Toward the giant first.

I leapt in the air and executed a flying front kick. Perfectly striking him in the chest with force. Before he could back up or raise his arms to defend it.

Any normal man would've fallen to the ground. I'm the one who fell backwards. Like kicking a wall. Gunvald staggered a step but quickly regained his balance.

He was over me before I could get back on my feet.

He grabbed me by the collar of my shirt. I tried a downward blow on his arms to force him to release me. His grip became stronger. I tried an upward maneuver. He grunted. His only acknowledgement of the strikes.

He hurled me against the wall like I was a rag doll. Knocking the breath out of me.

For a moment, I saw stars when my head bounced against the wall.

Gunvald lumbered toward me. I was in no position to go on the offensive, so I protected my face with my hands.

He kicked me in the chest. More of a stomp than a martial arts technique. It felt like I had a cracked sternum. Maybe a collapsed lung because my breathing suddenly became labored. I struggled to take in air.

Adrenaline blocked the pain.

Indecision hit me. I'd never been in a fight that lasted this long.

He picked me up again. My legs were flailing as I tried to kick him. He held me out from him.

He pushed my back against the wall. I was helpless to stop him.

Once he had me pinned, one hand moved to my throat. The other was back, like he was going to hit me.

I tucked my chin and raised my shoulders to keep him from crushing my windpipe. I only had eight seconds to get out of it. Maybe less since he was so big and strong.

Which threat was the strongest? The fist aimed at my head or the hand on my throat?

My lungs screamed for me to do something giving me the answer. I tried.

We were alone in the room. Mr. Z. had escaped.

The least of my worries. If I didn't do something quick, I was going to die.

Throwing punches toward his head wouldn't work. His arms were too long.

I remembered my training. The only time I'd ever been in this situation was years ago, when Curly had me by the neck. Curly was not as big but just as strong. He hadn't gone easy on me. Simulating a real-life fight. Putting enough pressure to render me unconscious but holding back enough so that he wouldn't kill me.

I reached up and grabbed Gunvald's fingers. Pulled them backwards. I heard cracking sounds. It worked with Curly, and it worked now. Curly said his fingers were sore for a week. I held back enough so I didn't break them before. Not this time.

Gunvald let out an expletive. I hadn't used the same discretion. I kept bending his fingers backwards. I broke at least two of them.

He cried out in pain.

I struggled to regain my breath. My throat would be sore for days.

Unphased, Gunvald lowered his shoulder and picked me up in the air. Avoiding my attempts to strike him in the face.

His back was exposed. I rabbit punched him in the kidney.

He cried out again. So I hit him a second time.

Instead of maintaining his grip, he lifted me high in the air and threw me across the room. I landed hard.

The only benefit was that it gave me space and time to clear my head.

He came toward me, but I had the presence of mind to get back on my feet and circle away. Using the only advantage I had. Maneuverability.

I feigned another aerial kick. He instinctively lifted his hands. Instead, I bent down, pivoted on one foot, and swept his legs out from under him.

He fell to the ground. His head cracked on the floor.

Rather than fight, I decided to run. If I could close the door behind me, he'd be locked in the makeshift prison cell.

But my legs didn't move.

I tried to run. I couldn't.

It's like they were frozen to the floor.

Had I broken my back? Severed my spine? If I had, I wouldn't be standing.

Gunvald was back on his feet. Laughing at me. Mocking me. In no hurry to finish me off.

He came toward me.

I swung wildly. Missing. I couldn't put any weight behind it.

Why wouldn't my feet move?

He reared back and hit me in the side. Breaking more ribs. Surprisingly, I didn't fall. My legs were still glued to the floor.

He kept pummeling me. Like I was a punching bag. Rocking back, then forward, into the punches. He was deliberate. Carefully aiming his punches. Every one of them doing damage.

I couldn't last much longer.

A gunman appeared at the door. With an automatic weapon. Gunvald moved away from me.

Nothing I could do. My feet still didn't move.

He opened fire.

Curly said the bullet that killed me was the one I didn't see coming. I saw these. Like time stood still. Everything happened in slow motion.

The first bullet hit me in the stomach. I instinctively grabbed my midsection. The second hit me in the thigh. It felt like a hot poker was placed on my leg. I'd never been shot before.

Well once. A bullet grazed me. I had a scar to prove it. On one of my first missions with the CIA.

Curly said I'd eventually be killed in action. I took too many risks.

My feet moved now. Like the bullet to the leg set them free from whatever bound them. I limped back against the wall. Or at least I think I did.

The gunman aimed. A barrage of bullets came at me at once. Too many to count or see.

This was how I was going to die.

Everything went black.

Was I dead?

I couldn't be. Not and still be having thoughts.

"Are you okay?" Alex said.

I was sweating.

Where was I?

I felt a hand on my shoulder. I flinched away from it even though the hand and voice were familiar.

What was Alex doing in Yura Lake?

"They have Lily," I said. "I have to get to her."

"Lily's in her crib."

I suddenly realized I was in a bed. It felt like our bed back home in Virginia.

How was that possible?

I threw off the covers. Lily's crib was next to our bed. I touched her. She was sleeping. I bent down and put my ear to her head to see if she was breathing. She was.

Alex was standing next to me. He put his arm around me and pulled me close. I let my head collapse on his shoulder.

"You must've had a nightmare," he said. His voice was groggy but loving. I didn't think I'd ever hear his voice again.

Every detail was etched in my memory.

"It was horrible. I tracked the giant to his cabin. We fought. I fell. He held me in the snow. I was in a prison cell. All bound. I got out of them. Mr. Z. was there. He said he had Lily. Gunvald tried to kill me. I fought him again. I couldn't stop him. Mr. Z. got away. A gunman came into the room. He shot me several times. I thought I was dead."

I felt my stomach. And my leg. They didn't hurt. I didn't have any wounds.

What's going on? How did I survive?

"You're safe now. You're with me. We're at home. Lily is here."

"Tapeesa is dead."

"I know."

Alex's words were gentle and reassuring. Comforting.

"I tried to run but I couldn't."

"I have that dream sometimes too," he said. "You've got a little case of PTSD. That's to be expected. You went through a lot in Yura Lake."

"It felt so real."

"It was."

22

Three weeks before

Leo was now on the list of people I wanted to kill. Mr. Z. was at the top. Leo and the giant were tied for second.

I'd been hiding in the helipad waiting for the giant to emerge. To my shock, I saw Leo come through the door that led to where the trafficked girls were being held, walk over to the door to the police station, use a keycard to open it, then disappear on the other side.

As much as I wanted to, I was in no condition to confront him. The early onset of hypothermia had set in. My eyes had trouble focusing. My legs were wobbly. If I didn't get inside soon, I'd pass out and die. Even so, I waited an extra minute to give Leo time to clear out of the police station and also to make sure Gunvald, the giant, didn't come through the same door.

At some point soon, I'd have to get inside. I couldn't withstand much more of the cold. If Leo was still in the police station, then I'd just have to deal with the threat. I waited as long as I could, pulled my gun, and approached the door.

Fumbled with my own keycard. To get it to work, I had to take off the glove on my right hand exposing my hand to the elements. Both hands were so cold, I couldn't feel them.

Somehow, I willed my muscle memory to work and got the door open. The warmth hit me like a refreshing sea breeze. I listened before entering. Not hearing anything, I went inside and shut the door quickly.

Leo wasn't there. Thankfully.

Still shivering, I hurried to turn on the security system. In time to see Leo stroll into the restaurant. Like he didn't have a care in the world.

Another day at the office. Finish work. Then grab a bite to eat. Work being oppressing forty women with fear and depravity.

I wanted to rush over to the restaurant and confront him but resisted the urge. I'd deal with him later. Once I was in better physical condition. The burning rage was warming my insides, but I needed hot coffee to finish the job.

My hands were shaking. My skin felt colder than a penguin's bottom. Not that I'd ever touched a penguin's bottom.

How did they survive weather like this? I could see how polar bears survived. Even walruses and seals. They were filled with blubber. Penguins had very little fur. Were skinny little things. Not an ounce of fat on them.

Yet they seemed as happy as larks. Playing on the ice. In the coldest regions of the world. Another one of God's amazing creatures.

I did an assessment of my body and was satisfied I'd live. Fortunately, my clothes weren't wet, so I figured I'd warm quickly.

I scanned the security system for Gunvald. Looking everywhere I knew to look. No sign of him.

My mind was bouncing back quickly, but my body was having trouble returning to normal. Mostly, the shaking. I still had the gun in my left hand, in case Gunvald showed up. I finally placed it on the edge of the desk for fear of dropping it and having it go off accidentally. My hand was that unsteady.

With my hand now free, I took out my phone and called Beth. If she didn't answer, I'd have to venture out in the cold and walk over to the school. To make sure everything was okay. I could see Gunvald tricking me and taking a different route to the school.

She answered on the first ring causing me to breathe a noticeable sigh of relief.

"Any sign of Gunvald?" I asked.

"No. How about you?"

"Nothing."

I wasn't going to mention seeing Leo. Not yet. Not until I had a chance to confront him. Which would be tonight. If he was ordering food, I had a few minutes to warm myself before going to the restaurant.

"Are the girls still there?" I asked.

"No. They left."

"Where did they go?"

"They're staying with other Zone members."

That was disappointing.

"Do any of them want to leave Yura Lake? Now's the time. I could get them out of here tonight."

"I didn't ask. Although I doubt it. Those three are pretty hard core. The ones Tapeesa was talking about, who think it's an honor to be married to Mr. Z."

"So all three are married to him?"

"According to Tapeesa. The only girls who live underground are his wives."

"And the sex trafficked girls."

"Right. Where do you think Gunvald is?"

"I suspect that Mr. Z. left Yura Lake. Things were getting too hot for him. No pun intended."

She chuckled dutifully. I could hear the nervousness in her tone.

I'd started a pot of coffee. I could smell it brewing. My body was aching for it.

"How are you?" Beth said. "Your voice is shaking. Did you get too cold?"

"I'm alright. I did get too cold, but I'm warming now."

"Get some hot liquids in you."

"I will. How's Tapeesa?"

"I'm not sure. She's here at the hospital. That's where I am. The contractions stopped but her blood pressure is elevated. I think I'm going to spend the night here."

"Probably from the stress. The girl has been through hell on earth."

"Could be. The baby is stressed as well. I'm thinking about inducing labor. Get the baby out sooner rather than later."

"I was going to take Tapeesa to Iqaluit tonight."

"She's in no condition to be moved."

"Is it that bad?"

"Not yet. But I don't want to make things worse. She doesn't need to be out in this cold. Neither do you."

She had a point. I thought about that. The ride on the snowmobile was less than ten minutes but going that fast through the wind might exacerbate the cold and cause my body to cool faster. And how long would I have to be out in the elements to get to the snowmobile and get it started? Then bring it back to the hospital to get Tapeesa?

It wasn't practical.

Once I got to Iqaluit, where would I hide Tapeesa if the planes weren't running? Mr. Z. could also be there. Probably was. If he left Yura Lake in the last week, he would have nowhere to go. Not until the weather lifted.

That got me thinking. I really needed to go to Iqaluit and find him. The thought of hiking to the snowmobile, starting it up, and then riding across the ice, wasn't appealing.

Once I was there, where would I find him?

Probably at the airport. In his plane. That'd be the most secure place. But I didn't know that for sure. He could have a hiding place in Iqaluit. In that case, I didn't even know where to start looking. The cold would make it impossible to search for him.

What was I going to do? Walk around town? Ride the snowmobile up and down the streets questioning people? I'd be the equivalent of a frozen icicle by morning.

A better plan was to focus on figuring out how to get underground and rescue the girls. Which meant confronting Leo. He had a key. I intended to take it from him. Using his own gun.

"Have you talked to Leo?" I asked Beth.

"I talked to him a little while ago."

"Where is he?"

"He had a truck run tonight."

Liar.

I wasn't going to tell her the truth.

"Do you know where he lives?"

"No. He always picks me up at my place."

It explained why he never hit on Beth. He had orders from Mr. Z. to get close to her. Milk her for information. See if she was loyal. With strict instructions not to touch her. Mr. Z. would supply him with womanly companionship when he needed it.

These people were sick.

"I told him about the girls," she said almost apologetically. "You know. About the underground facility. The sex trafficking. Everything Tapeesa told us. I hope that's okay."

It wasn't.

That took away some of my advantage. Leo now knew I knew. That I was setting a trap for the giant.

It made sense now. That's why Gunvald didn't show up. He was forewarned. Leo came to the police station to confront me. He didn't find me because I was hiding in the helipad.

I had to assume he was armed. Even though I stole his gun, Mr. Z. could easily give him another one.

"I don't think that was a good idea to say anything to Leo," I said. "You have to remember that he works for Mr. Z."

"I'm a good judge of character. I think we can trust him. He seemed genuinely concerned. Appalled even. He asked a bunch of questions."

"He might've been fishing for information. It would explain why Gunvald didn't show. Leo hung up the phone and warned Mr. Z."

"I hadn't thought of that. I'm sorry."

"What's done is done. Do me a favor? Don't talk to Leo anymore. Avoid his calls. Until we know we can really trust him."

"Okay. Sorry."

"You said that already. You take care of Tapeesa. I'll take care of Leo."

"He said he wouldn't be back until tomorrow."

He was sitting in a restaurant. Two hundred yards from the hospital. Knowing Beth never went to the restaurant after school. She didn't like eating alone in public. Something she had shared with me earlier.

"I'll wait until tomorrow then. I'll call you later. Call me if anyone shows up."

"I will."

I hung up and poured myself a large cup of coffee and felt the effects instantly. Within a few minutes, I was already feeling like myself again. Even then, I didn't venture right out into the cold. Giving myself a few more minutes to warm up.

Not too long. I wanted to confront Leo at the restaurant since I knew where he was. Rather than wait.

I could watch him on the security cameras and see where he lived, but then I'd have to surveille the house. Determine the best time to enter. Which meant spending hours in the cold to do the job properly.

No thank you. This mission was filled with complications.

I need to simplify things.

Leo was in the restaurant. I could go there now and confront him. I couldn't kill him yet. Not until I talked to him. Or in self-defense.

All I knew so far was that he had access to the keys. Gunvald or Mr. Z. could've given them to him for whatever reason. He may be nothing more than a trucker.

I had to know before I filled him with lead. First sign of guilt, and he was a dead man.

Once I built up the courage, I turned off the security cameras and exited the police station making the short walk to the restaurant.

My pace was quick. I got there before the cold bothered me. Fortunately, the wind was at my back, which meant my face wasn't getting whipped.

From now on, I was going to wear Nirliq's parka. Even if it did make me easy to spot. I'd rather be warm than in disguise.

The restaurant was warm.

Also, nothing like the diner. It felt like I'd walked into an upscale restaurant in Paris. Marble everywhere. Fancy tables and tablecloths. The lighting was dimmed. It took a second to get my bearings. My right hand was in my pocket with my finger near the trigger of my gun. Ready to pull, aim, and shoot if necessary.

Leo sat alone in the corner. With his back against the wall. I walked over to his seat. The restaurant smelled of fancy beef. Chateaubriand and prime rib. I saw a carving station set up along the back wall.

My stomach growled.

So did my emotions. I was itching to kill someone. I'd been in Iqaluit for nearly a week and had only killed one person, the Sheriff.

The room was half filled. Every eye turned and looked at me. Including Leo's who had a plate of food in front of him. He continued eating, like he wasn't concerned at all that I'd just walked in.

"Have a seat," he said, when I approached.

I did.

He took a bite of food. Then let out a moan.

"I recommend the prime rib," he said.

"I'm not here to eat," I said, although my stomach protested. I hadn't eaten in a while. His plate looked delicious.

"Why are you here?" he asked.

"To kill you."

"With the gun you stole from me?"

"That's right."

"You're not going to kill me."

"You have ten seconds to convince me not to put a bullet in you. I don't think you can. When I kill you, I'll finish that plate of food for you."

"This plate of food is worth fighting over."

"You have six seconds."

"Why would you want to kill me?"

"I saw you come out of the area where Mr. Z. keeps the girls. The ones held against their will."

"Oh. I can explain."

"You have four seconds."

"That's probably not enough time to explain."

"Time's up."

"Order some food, Jamie. Let's talk about it."

Jamie?

Did he make a mistake? My cover name was Jesse. Did he forget?

Or does he know who I really am?

23

Leo just called me Jamie. I had to know why. The words stumbled out of my mouth like a drunken sailor.

"Why did you... call... er... me Jamie?" I asked.

"Because that's your name," he said, calmly.

"You don't have a good memory. My name's Jesse."

He rolled his eyes. "Right. Whatever."

I leaned across the table. Hovering over his food. The aroma struck my nostrils. I wondered if he heard my stomach rumbling.

"I'm serious. Why did you call me Jamie?"

"Do you want me to recite your resume?"

We were well out of earshot of the other patrons. I whispered anyway.

"Who do you think I am?"

"Jamie Austen."

I was floored. Like a pen out of ink. I had no words.

"CIA operative extraordinaire," he said with a friendly grin. I didn't see any guile on his face. "You were the winner of the gold medal at the Winter Olympics in Bavaria. Very impressive. The biathlon, wasn't it? Excellent shooting. For a girl."

I didn't know if I should thank him or slap him across the side of the head.

"I'm kidding," he quickly added. "You could outshoot me every day of the week and twice on Sunday."

"Who are you?" I demanded.

"Leo."

I rolled my eyes.

"I really am Leo."

"Leofric? German? Former divemaster? Ice trucker? I don't believe it."

"You're right. That's my cover. Although Leo is my given name. Wentworth is my last name. You know. Keep your cover name close to your real name. So you can remember it."

Many of the rules of mission protocol were universal. Tried and true. Which was why we were encouraged not to stray from them. Curly said to follow the time-tested traditions until they didn't make sense anymore.

"Formal introductions are in order. Leo Wentworth," he said as he sat down his fork and extended his hand. I didn't shake it. He could be lying. I was trained to spot deception. I didn't see any in his mannerisms or tone.

"Who do you work for?" I asked. The words had authority behind them. He needed to know I wasn't interested in playing games. Or guessing. If he wasn't forthcoming, then he'd be sorry. Of course, I'd hold my cards close to the vest until I knew for sure he could be trusted.

"CSIS."

The Canadian Security and Intelligence Service. The equivalent of the CIA.

"So, you're from Canada? Not Germany?"

"Correct. Why don't you go get some food and I'll fill you in?"

"I'm not hungry."

"I heard your stomach growling."

"Okay. I am hungry. I'll be right back."

It didn't take long to have my own plate of food. The carver gave me extra upon request. Sauteed wild mushrooms in a bordelaise sauce was the primary side along with russet potatoes. I passed on the vegetables. I was in a meat and potatoes kind of mood. It made me feel tougher for whatever reason.

I still didn't know what to think of Leo. Was he lying? He clearly knew who I was. But did he work for CSIS? It made sense. I should've seen the signs. A few alarm bells went off when Beth said Leo checked her office for bugs and didn't find any. He also seemed to have a lot of information about the Zone cult and how girls were sold into marriage.

He also had a gun. Something about that didn't make sense. A good operative wouldn't leave it out in the open like that. Sitting next to the mattress in his truck. It had been easy for me to steal. Curly would've never let me hear the end of it if someone had stolen my gun.

"Scoot over," I said, when I returned to the table with my food. "I always sit with my back against the wall."

With a minor adjustment we could both be facing out. Although, it meant we had to sit close together. The close proximity was so I could put him to sleep if I found out he was lying.

"I'm married," Leo said.

"So am I."

"That's right. How is Alex?"

I about fell over. *How did he know so much about me?*

"You know Alex?"

"I know of him. I watched him play football in college."

"Did you play football at the same college?"

"No. I played in Canada. I went on to play in the CFL. The Canadian Football League. I wasn't nearly as good as Alex though."

Alex was the starting quarterback for the Stanford Cardinals. They lost in the national championship game to Alabama. Not his fault. He would've been MVP of the game had the defense not given up a last second touchdown.

Leo continued. "After Alex married you, I followed his career. Actually, I followed yours more than his. His when they overlapped. He must be one heck of a computer hacker. I heard you caught Pok."

The man did seem connected. The average person wouldn't know that information. Not even Mr. Z., unless he had sources within the CIA.

"Why would you be interested in my career?" I asked.

He chuckled. "You're the best of the best when it comes to sex trafficking. I'm in that division with the CSIS. Your name comes up a lot in our training. As an example of what to do."

"And what not to do."

"Sometimes."

Our sentences were short. With pauses between them. Neither of us were allowing the conversation to keep us from eating. The meat was tender and melted in my mouth. Mr. Z. was certainly an enigma. Cold blooded kidnapper and sex trafficker. Who was responsible for this fine restaurant in the middle of nowhere.

A man who demanded perfection in everything. Even the food. That's what had made him so hard to catch.

Time to change the subject. I was tired of talking about me. I wanted proof that Leo was with the CSIS. If so, I wanted to know everything he knew about Mr. Z's operation. He was an employee and had been working for the man for three weeks. Nothing wrong with us sharing information.

Time to begin probing to see if he'd be forthcoming.

"You're married. That explains why you won't kiss Beth."

"I feel bad about that."

"She's smitten with you."

"Like I said, I feel bad about it. Part of the job."

"You touched my bottom. Do you feel bad about that?"

"No. I was trying to get a rise out of you. I knew you wouldn't like it but would want to maintain your cover. Like I was. I had a job to do."

"Is touching my bottom part of your job?"

"You aren't going to let that go, are you?"

"Not in a million years."

"My cover is that I'm a womanizer. My plan was to get close to the school principal. If anyone had information, it'd be her. Turns out she didn't know much. The investigation wasn't going anywhere until you came along."

"So, you knew who I was as soon as you met me?"

"Yeah. I was asked to give you a ride. I was going to say no until I saw you. I really could get in trouble for bringing you over to Yura Lake. But I recognized you immediately. Who doesn't know the great Jamie Austen?"

I wished he'd stop with the brown nosing.

"I wanted to give you a ride. To find out why you were here. Although, I could figure it out. Same reason I was here."

"I'm glad you gave me a ride. I didn't know how I was going to get to Yura Lake. Probably a dogsled."

"I was happy to do it. The lady at the airport counter said your luggage was lost. I figured you didn't have a weapon, so I left a gun in full view. So you'd have one. I laughed when I saw it was missing. I figured if you needed a gun, you'd take it. And you did."

"I appreciate that."

"Did you kill the Sheriff with it?"

I sat down my fork and raised my right hand. "I used this weapon."

"Of course you did. Jamie Austen can kill a man a hundred different ways with her bare hands. I've always wondered if all the stories about you were true, or just urban legend."

"Probably a little of both. Some truth in all of them."

"I assume the Sheriff is dead."

"The last time I saw him he was."

"He's twice your size. Why not use the gun?"

"We were in the cab of his truck. I didn't want to get blood on me."

Leo was almost finished with his food. I'd made a big dent in mine.

"So you're here investigating Mr. Z?" I asked.

"That's right. I assume you read the report. That thirty percent of Inuit girls are victims of sex trafficking."

I nodded.

"We figured out that Mr. Z. was behind it. I was assigned to come here and infiltrate the organization."

"What else do you know?"

"Less than you. I wasn't getting anywhere until you came along. I had no idea Mr. Z. was holding them underground. Not until Beth told me. Ingenious."

"How did you get a keycard?"

"Gunvald lives in a cabin across the lake. I went there and searched it. I found his passkey. It doesn't get me underground though. It only gets me through the door."

"What's on the other side of the door to the helipad?"

"An elevator. It requires a different keycard to activate."

"We have to get downstairs."

"I know. I'm waiting for you to figure out how to do that."

"I need to see it."

"I'll take you there after we finish eating. I understand the dessert is to die for."

"Don't say that!"

His eyes widened in surprise. I said it loud enough for several people to look our way.

"Don't say what?" he asked.

"To die for. We never say that. Not in our line of work."

He chuckled. "It's just a saying."

"A saying that'll get you killed."

"I'm not superstitious."

"I'm not either. I still don't say it. It's a self-fulfilling prophecy."

"I'll try and remember that."

"What do you intend to tell Beth after the mission is over?"

I suddenly felt bad for her.

"Nothing. I intend to disappear."

"She'll be heartbroken."

"Can't be helped. It'll be worse if I tell her I'm married and have two kids."

"Did you have to lead her on?"

"That's my cover. You of all people should know that. Sometimes we do what we have to do. My cover is a sleazy divemaster from Germany. I didn't pick it. Somebody's idea of a joke back at headquarters."

"You play it well."

"I'll take that as a compliment. It's not easy staying in character. As you know."

"My cover didn't last very long. Journalist writing a story."

"The Sheriff's lover. That was a good one."

"That was pretty good. Gave me access to the police station and the security cameras."

He took his last bite.

"You should be glad I asked questions first before I killed you," I said. "I don't always give someone the opportunity to explain themselves."

"I am."

"Any idea where Gunvald is?"

"I assume he's with Mr. Z."

"Mr. Z. is Lucas Rikki. Fugitive from Idaho."

"We knew that. We also knew he was in Nunavut. We tracked his plane to Iqaluit."

"Where is Mr. Z. now?"

"I think he's in Iqaluit."

"Why do you think that?"

"He left right after the Sheriff went missing."

"The helicopter was already gone."

He shook his head.

"Rikki has two helicopters. One that transports the girls. The other transports him."

"I only saw one."

"The other one is not inside the Zone."

"Where is it?"

"A mile or so north. Rikki has a second entrance to his underground hideout. It comes out at a house right outside the walls."

"I looked at satellite photos. I didn't see anything."

"It's shaped like a house. With a retractable roof. The helicopter lands inside. The roof closes. You would never see it on satellite unless the roof was open."

"That makes sense."

"Why do you think he's still in Iqaluit?"

"Planes have been grounded ever since you arrived. He can't leave. Not until the weather breaks. I figure he's at the airport. Nervous. Wanting to get away as soon as possible."

"That's what I was thinking as well."

"We should work together."

"I usually work alone."

"I can help you."

"I need to confirm you are who you say you are."

"Do whatever you have to do? You can talk to my boss if you want. Or talk to Brad. He'll verify who I am."

I pulled my phone out of my coat and called Brad. Already convinced. If he knew Brad's name, then he was connected. He might be dirty. That thought crossed my mind. But I'd give him the benefit of the doubt if Brad said to.

"Do you know a Leo from CSIS?" I asked.

"Leo Baker."

"No. Leo Wentworth."

"Yeah. I know Leo."

I took a picture of Leo and sent it to Brad.

"Is this him?"

"Yeah that's him. He looks a lot older than the last time I saw him."

"I'll tell him you said that."

"I take it he's up there investigating Mr. Z. as well."

"Don't you ever talk to your counterpart at CSIS?"

"I did. That's why I sent you on the mission. They put it on my radar. But I didn't coordinate with them. You work better alone."

"That's what I just told Leo. Can I trust him?"

"With your life."

"Good to know."

I hung up. Scarfed down the last of my food. We ordered dessert and ate it mostly in silence. I was anxious to get out of there and look at what was behind the door that led to the elevator.

After we finished, I ordered coffee. Still not completely back to normal. I asked a series of personal questions while I drank it.

"How long have you been married?"

"How old are your kids?"

"How long have you been with CSIS?"

The conversation turned to shop talk. We shared a few mission stories.

When it was time to leave, I said, "How do we pay?"

"Food is provided for employees. I'll put it on my tab."

"Thanks."

"I need to finish this mission soon. I think I've gained five pounds."

"You should use the gym."

"I like to run outside."

"Not happening here."

"We shouldn't leave together," he said.

"The security cameras are off."

"You are resourceful."

"I try to be."

As we were walking out the door, Leo asked me, "Do you have any kids?"

"No. Alex and I don't have any children."

24

The elevator to the underground facility could be accessed with a key-card, but also by a keypad. The keycard Leo took from Gunvald's cabin didn't work, but I had an idea. Leo and I were in the police station poring over the security footage from the previous day. Looking for when Gunvald picked up the girls from school and returned them home by way of the elevator.

If Gunvald entered the passcode into the keypad, we might be able to see the numbers. The camera was in the right spot. That didn't mean we'd be able to see it. The giant could be standing in the way and blocking the camera's view. His massive fingers could hide the numbers. Mr. Z. could've changed the code. He could've also deleted the footage.

I was encouraged when I found out he hadn't.

"It looks like the system keeps the footage all the way back to inception," I said to Leo. "There are years of data stored in the system."

"That's evidence," Leo said. "We need to figure out how to preserve it."

I nodded although I wasn't sure how to do it. Alex would know, but he was unavailable. Brad might be able to access it remotely. If he could, that also meant Mr. Z. could as well. I had my doubts the footage would be there much longer.

The previous day's archived footage was easy to find, and rewound it to three o'clock in the afternoon. Figuring Gunvald picked up the girls at the same time each day.

"If this works and we figure out the passcode, what's the plan?" Leo asked.

"What do you mean? The plan is to rescue the girls."

"I know that, but how?"

"I'm going downstairs and get them out of there."

"This is my operation."

"Seriously! You're going to get territorial on me now."

"That's not what I meant. But technically, Nunavut is in Canadian territory. We have jurisdiction. I'm the one who should arrest Mr. Z. and take him back to Canada for trial."

"Mr. Z. will not be alive to stand trial."

"I don't think that's your call. My boss wants him alive."

"Then you need to get to him before me. I suggest you get to it. As soon as I'm done rescuing the girls, I'm going to Iqaluit to look for Mr. Z."

"I thought we were working together on this."

"I told you I work better alone. Now you know why."

"We can discuss Mr. Z. later," Leo said. "First things first. You don't know what's underground. You can't go down that elevator without a plan. Not knowing what you're facing."

"I have a plan."

"That's what I'm asking. What is it?"

"Shoot anyone who is a threat."

"Then what?"

"I don't understand the question."

"What are you going to do with the girls after you rescue them?"

"That'll be a good problem to have."

"I can get a plane to Iqaluit when the weather clears. I've got resources ready to go."

He had a point. I was on my own. I could marshal resources, but I didn't know how long it'd take. I didn't mind working with Leo. As long as he didn't get in my way. I also didn't care if he got credit for the rescue. All I wanted to do was make sure the girls were safe and Mr. Z. got what was coming to him.

If Leo had an escape plane ready to go, then that'd make things easier for me. I had already assumed he'd be able to bring in an army of people to investigate and police the area. That wasn't my job. My job was to rescue the girls and end the threat. Make sure Mr. Z. never oppressed women and young girls again.

"Once I know the girls are safe, you can take charge," I said. "But I'm the best person to lead the rescue."

That seemed to satisfy him. He kept quiet while I searched the security camera system.

"There!" I said pointing at the computer screen. A figure appeared on the screen. The giant. And four girls. Including Tapeesa. Getting into the elevator.

My heart leapt with excitement. I was right. Gunvald did have access to downstairs. I could only hope he used a passcode. Which made sense. Passcodes could be changed. Much easier for Mr. Z. to control access than to pass out keys and keycards.

I kept rewinding. Stopped it when they disappeared, then started it again when the giant first entered the area with the elevator. The system had a slow-motion option.

This was the first time I had really gotten a good look at the giant. He was massive. As big as a polar bear standing on his hind legs.

Gunvald walked to the elevator, lifted the keypad, and touched it. Faster than I could discern the numbers.

I hit rewind. Slowed it even more. Figured out how to zoom in closer.

"That's too close," I said. More to myself than to Leo. I'd zoomed in so far the numbers were blurry.

I was optimistic though.

The giant's fingers blocked the numbers but only moved on the right side of the keypad. While I couldn't see which numbers he hit, that narrowed it down. I ran it backwards and forward, over and over again. No way to see the numbers for certain. I had to tamp down the disappointment.

"It looks like he entered four numbers," I said. "All on the right side."

Leo had his phone out. Looking at it. I had already deduced the giant had entered some combination of nine, six, and three. Leo turned his phone toward me.

Seeing it helped me. Although, there were seemingly an unlimited number of combinations.

"What if it's not numbers but letters?" I asked.

"You mean the code is a word?"

"Yes."

Then it dawned on me.

"I know what it is," I said excitedly.

"What?"

"Zone. 9663."

"That's too easy," Leo said.

"Why wouldn't it be? Mr. Z. wasn't worried about anyone being in our position trying to figure it out."

I shut down the security system and turned off the cameras so Mr. Z. couldn't see us if he was monitoring the area. If that wasn't the code, then I'd open things up again and go back every day until I could see the actual code.

Worst case scenario, I could get Brad to access the system. His people on the ground could zoom in on the footage so close they could count the number of hairs on the back of the giant's hand.

My mind turned to downstairs. Leo had a point. If he was going with me, I needed to make sure he knew what to do. I didn't like going into a potential gunfight with someone I'd never been in the trenches with.

"Here's the plan," I said. "I'm taking the lead on the rescue."

He started to resist. I put my hand in the air to silence him.

"Nonnegotiable. You'll get credit for the rescue. It makes sense to use your resources. But I'm entering the hot zone first."

"I'm okay with that."

"Good. We'll ride down the elevator together. I'll exit first. From what I know, there's only one guard. You exit the elevator when I say clear. If something happens to me and I'm down, you take over. You're still in a position to back me up and shoot the threat and get to the girls."

"I'll back you up. Got it."

"There are three hallways. To the right is where Mr. Z. keeps his wives. You go that direction. I don't expect you to run into any hostiles. If you do, take them out. Secure the area."

"What are you going to do?"

"I'm going to the left. That's where the trafficked girls are being held. I suspect there'll be another armed guard watching them. Maybe several. I'll take them out and secure the area."

"I can help after my area is secure."

"No. I'll meet you in Mr. Z.'s place. You can access it from the wives' suite. That's in the middle hallway. After you make sure the wives are okay, enter the suite and secure it. I'm sure you'll find a treasure trove of evidence in there."

"Sounds like a good plan."

"Okay. Let's talk about Iqaluit. Once we have the girls to deal with, things could get chaotic. Some of them might need medical attention. You'll stay with them."

"I'm going with you to get Mr. Z."

"No. Somebody has to stay behind and protect the girls."

"Why should it be me?"

"You have kids. I don't."

"What does that have to do with it? I know the risks of the job."

"You asked me earlier why Alex and I don't have any kids. We aren't trying. I mean, we aren't trying to prevent it, if you know what I mean. But we always said that if I got pregnant, then I would quit running missions."

"Why?"

"Because we wouldn't want our son or daughter to grow up without at least one parent. I'm the logical person to quit. Alex can do the computer hacking out of harm's way most of the time. I can't."

"I guess that makes sense. Young kids need a mother."

"Anyway. You stay behind. Protect the girls. Search for evidence. There may be more girls in other countries. I wouldn't put it past Mr. Z. When the weather lifts, bring your plane in. I figure you can take the girls over to Iqaluit in the back of one of your empty trucks."

"That's true. Mr. Z. might try to stop me."

"Hopefully, he'll be dead by then."

"He's at the airport. In his hangar."

"That's possible. Although, he would know that's the first place I'll look."

"Where else could he be?"

"A man of his means could have a hideout in Iqaluit. Can he get to Greenland? Isn't the ocean frozen over? He could take a car and drive across the ice."

"He can't drive there," Leo said. "Theoretically, he could walk. But not likely. With global warming, the ice is not as thick on the ocean as it is in the bay. You can't even drive an SUV on it. Too thin in many places. I wouldn't even venture out on a dogsled or snowmobile. Good way to die."

"Okay. Then he's probably in Iqaluit."

"Probably."

"Are you ready?"

Leo nodded.

We both checked our weapons. Made sure we had extra magazines.

We exited the police station, walked through the helipad, and used Leo's keycard to open the door to get to the elevator. I walked to the elevator keypad and lifted the cover. Took off my gloves and prepared to enter the numbers.

"Let's pray this code works," I said.

Leo nodded. I could tell he was nervous. I felt calm inside. Almost certain it would work.

"9663," I said, as I entered the numbers on the keypad.

I heard a ding. The door to the elevator opened.

I let out a slight yelp of delight.

A burst of exhilaration flowed through me. Along with a much-needed dose of adrenaline. The energy I would need to face whatever threat might be on the other side of the elevator door when it opened.

Hopefully, all the guards abandoned their posts when Mr. Z. fled.

Probably not.

For the first time, I felt nervous. Stepping inside the elevator did that to me. Not an ideal scenario. Curly said to avoid it when possible.

Enclosed spaces. Unknown threats.

The whole scene played out in my head. The elevator would descend. Then stop. Within seconds. The door would open automatically.

Not a good situation for us. The guard might open fire and ask questions later.

He also might hesitate. Wait to make sure it's not the giant. I had to hope indecision gave me a split-second advantage.

The guard might be confused. The routine was off. Where was the giant? Where were the girls? Why didn't they come home from school earlier that day?

Or, he might be trigger happy. I couldn't imagine him firing without checking out the occupants first.

No. He'd wait.

Unless he knew we were coming.

The elevator was pristine. Like everything else. Not a speck of dirt anywhere. The back of the elevator was so shiny, I could see myself clearly. That'd help. I could take up a position in the front and see what was in the foyer by the reflection on the back of the elevator.

Then I saw it. The security camera in the corner.

A chill went down my spine.

The camera in the elevator wasn't connected to the system I had accessed. That meant they were being monitored somewhere else.

By Mr. Z.?

Was he watching me now? If so, he could be talking to the guard in real time. Telling him to get ready to blast us.

Part of me said I should abandon the plan. Try to enter through the back entrance. The one outside the Zone.

But a guard could just as easily be waiting there. We were already on the elevator. Soon, we'd be past the point of no return.

I took up a position, on the left side. So I could lead with my right hand. Protected by the panel. I was on the side with the button. I motioned for Leo to get on the other side. He'd be protected by the other panel.

It wasn't as wide. I thought about trading places. I decided against it since either side was vulnerable if the guard took the proper angle.

"Stay clear of the door," I said.

He nodded.

I gave Leo the thumbs up. Fear gripped his face. I doubt he'd been in this situation before.

Nothing I could do about it. I pushed the button, and we started the ride down. It took longer than I expected.

I smiled for the camera. I waved my gun at the camera for effect. In case Mr. Z. was watching.

The elevator stopped. The door opened.

I waited.

A barrage of gunfire erupted from outside the open door.

25

Three weeks later
Arlington, Virginia

After waking up in a cold sweat from the nightmare, I wasn't able to go back to sleep. So, I got up and went into the living room so I wouldn't wake up Lily or keep Alex awake. I tried to sleep on the couch but couldn't. Spent the entire time watching the clock as if I could make the sun come up faster.

Lily woke before Alex. I got her up, changed and fed her. Then I had nearly two precious hours with her.

When Alex did get up, I made him breakfast while he had time with Lily. Neither of us had to be anywhere, so we weren't pressed for time. We both had at least the next three weeks off.

Alex needed a break as much as I did. His mission to the Cayman Islands had been stressful. He wasn't shot at but had to put in long hours staring at a computer screen. Following the money trail of terrorists who were hiding blood money in the Cayman banks. From all indications, his mission had been successful.

After he finished his breakfast, he took Lily in the living room and sat with her on the couch while I did the dishes. She seemed perfectly content in his arms. As did I. Alex had been a great comfort over the last few days after my trying mission to Nunavut.

"Lily is so flippin cute," Alex said, when I finally joined him on the sofa.

"She's adorable," I said.

Lily had dozed off in his arms.

After ten minutes of chitchat, Alex asked out of the blue, "Do you want to talk about last night?"

"The sex?"

"No. Silly. I'm talking about the dream."

We didn't usually discuss such things. Curly said it was better not to.

"Nothing to talk about," I said. "A bad dream. That's all. It wasn't real."

"Dreams can feel real. Remember when I was mad at you for sitting on that guy's lap."

I chuckled. I did remember.

"That was your dream!" I said playfully. "It wasn't real."

"I was still mad at you when I woke up that morning. It took a while to get over it."

"That's hardly fair, since I didn't do anything wrong."

A twinge of guilt shot through me. I hadn't told Alex I pretended to be the Sheriff's lover in Yura Lake. While it wasn't real, it still felt strange playing the role.

As a rule, we didn't talk about each other's missions, so I wasn't obligated to tell him. An excuse I intended to fall back on if he ever heard about it. I had put it in the mission report I gave to Brad. Hopefully, that information was buried forever.

Maybe our wedding vows said I should tell him anyway. Alex would think it was funny and I didn't feel like being kidded about it, so I decided not to say anything.

"That's my point," Alex said. "A dream can feel as real as the real thing. It can stir up the same emotions. It felt like you had cheated on me."

"I would never do that."

More guilt which I tamped down.

"I know you wouldn't," Alex said. "It still felt that way in my dream."

"I know how to tell the difference between what's real and what's not real."

"I know you do. But... it seems like you've had several nightmares since you've been back from Yura Lake."

Alex was walking gingerly around the topic. I could tell he didn't want to make me mad. He was, but I wasn't about to let it show. That would confirm he was right.

"I've had a few nightmares since I've been back."

Honesty seemed like the best approach. Since he knew the truth anyway. I'd awakened him almost every night since I returned from Nunavut. I kept having the same recurring dream. The giant at his cabin. Holding my face in the snow. Waking up in the prison cell. Bound to a chair.

It always ended the same. A man with a machine gun. Killing me.

Last night, Alex said I might be suffering from a slight case of PTSD. He had never said that to me before. In the darkness of the night, I had rejected it. I hoped he didn't bring it up again or I'd really be mad. I didn't need my husband playing psychiatrist with me.

"I had my mission debriefing with Brad yesterday," I said. "It stirred things up again. That's all."

That was true. I'd dreaded that meeting. Going through every painstaking detail with Brad. Being grilled about every decision. I could justify my actions. Even though a lot of people were dead.

Mostly, I had to convince Brad that the whole sordid affair was behind me. He thought I did the right things. When it came to debriefings, everything with Brad was by the book. So I acted emotionless. Casual. Almost nonchalant. If he had noticed the least bit of weakness in me, he'd have ordered a battery of tests. Taken me out of the field for an extended period of time. Ordered counseling sessions.

I still had to go on a mission to kill Mr. Z. As soon as we found him, Brad promised me the first crack at him.

He had asked me about nightmares. I lied. I couldn't let Brad see that what happened in Yura Lake was still affecting me. I didn't want Alex to see it either. Harder to do when I kept waking up in the middle of the night in a fright.

"It seems like this mission was harder on you than most," Alex said.

"It was."

A rare admission. Surprisingly, I didn't feel defensive. Probably because of his guarded tone. He clearly didn't want to get yelled at.

That and he was holding Lily. We really shouldn't be talking about these things in front of her.

"I'll get over it soon," I said. Quickly gathering my composure and hoping that'd be the end of it.

"Tell me about the dream," Alex said.

"I don't see the point. It wasn't real."

"Then tell me about what was real."

Lily let out a coo. But kept her eyes closed. She smacked her lips. In that cute way she always did.

The sound calmed the panic inside of me. I didn't want to relive Yura Lake again. Why wouldn't Alex let it drop? I was home. We were both safe. We needed to enjoy the moment.

How could I avoid talking about it? Alex didn't want to let it drop. Somehow, he must've sensed the need to press the issue. He'd never done this before.

It was all I could do to keep from bursting into tears. The whole thing made me sad. Most people on their day off, planned something fun. We were talking about one of the worst weeks in my life.

I'd give anything if we could just be a normal family. That's what I had been thinking about in the dark recesses of the night. That and other horrible thoughts.

What if it had been me and not Leo who was killed? What about Lily? If I went after Mr. Z. again, who's to say I'd come back? Was that fair to her?

What was playing out in the living room that morning was more confirmation. I loved the look on Alex's face. How adoringly he stared at Lily. How compassionate he was being towards me.

How could I risk losing all this?

Which was why I tamped down the anger I was feeling. Alex loved me. That's why he was asking. Even if it made me angry, I couldn't lash out at him. So I bit my lip and fought back the tears.

Maybe talking to him was a good thing. Better than talking to a staff psychologist. If anyone understood what I was going through, it was Alex. He'd been in as many dangerous situations as I had. He'd awakened in the middle of the night before from a bad dream. I was always there to comfort him through it as well.

I never asked him to talk about it though. We had an unwritten rule. Curly had drilled that into us. Never, ever, under any circumstances, talk about the missions after the debriefing. Put the emotions in the vault and throw away the key.

Otherwise, it'd affect the next mission. It might get us killed.

For a moment, I wondered if there should be a next mission. Not if I couldn't get in the right frame of mind.

There was something I really wanted to discuss with Alex. Now didn't seem like the right time. Something more important. We had to get through this topic first.

"What happened in the elevator?" Alex asked. Softly. Gently. Caringly.

Tears welled up in my eyes again. The pain was still raw.

I had no choice. I had to talk about it.

"Leo and I rode the elevator down to the underground area. I told him I wanted to go alone."

The last words came out bitterly.

"He should've listened to me."

Alex shifted positions on the couch. He realized the solemnity of the moment. He turned so he was facing me. I was sitting with my legs folded. Talking barely above a whisper. My head down. I couldn't look him in the eye, or I'd lose it.

"The gunman was ready for us," I said. "He opened fire immediately. Automatic rifle. He emptied it."

"I know what that's like."

"I don't remember ever being in such an enclosed space and so close to the rapid fire. Point blank range. The sound was deafening. The ringing in my ears didn't stop for several days."

"I can imagine."

"The gunman was stupid. He walked right toward the open door. He should've been coming toward us at an angle."

"Curly said to be thankful we are better trained. Of course, he was mostly patting himself on the back when he said it. But point well taken."

"Curly was right. The bullets blasted the back of the elevator. Missed us completely."

"Any ricochets?"

I shook my head.

"Fortunately, the back of the elevator was made of soft wood. The bullets were absorbed into it. No ricochets at all. Otherwise, I wouldn't be sitting on this couch telling the story."

"I'm glad you are."

"The elevator was rendered inoperable though. Which complicated the extraction of the girls."

"An inconvenience. Considering the alternatives."

"The panel protected me. I was on one knee. The gunman was shooting wildly. Spraying bullets."

I took a deep breath. The pain was overwhelming my soul.

"Leo made a mistake," I said.

My voice cracked.

Alex reached out and touched my hand. I still didn't make eye contact.

"He acted too soon?" Alex said.

"Yeah. It all happened so fast."

"Best thing to do was let the gunman empty his magazine," Alex said.

I nodded.

"It only took ten seconds. Felt like an hour. We were protected by the panels on the side. Leo panicked. That's easy to do. The gunman was getting closer to the door. But he was firing straight ahead. Leo must've thought he needed to protect us. I was safe. Below the fire. I wasn't going to let the gunman get an angle on us. As soon as he got close, I was ready to shoot him."

"That sounds like the right thing to do."

"Leo leaned out from behind the panel to take a shot. He didn't have a chance. His body was riddled with bullets."

"Nothing you could do."

"I did do something. I killed the gunman."

"Good."

"That was the distraction I needed. The gunman turned his rifle toward Leo, I had a clean shot."

"Leo died a hero."

"The whole elevator was smoky. Smelled of burnt ammunition."

"I know that smell."

"No reason to check on Leo. He was dead. Stupid. I told him to stay behind the panel. Out of the doorway. Just in case."

"He knew the risks. We all do."

"Doesn't make it easier. He had a wife and two kids."

"Like I said."

Those words didn't help. Leo knew the risks. So what? His kids would grow up wondering why his father would take such risks.

They wouldn't ever see the faces of the girls we rescued. Twenty of them. Plus the thirteen missing girls. And one of Mr. Z's wives.

Leo didn't die in vain. No consolation to his daughter who wouldn't have her father there to walk her down the aisle.

I never told Beth what happened. As far as she knew, Leo never came back from his truck run. I couldn't blow his cover as a CSIS operative anyway. She certainly didn't need to know that he was married with kids. Better she didn't know what happened to him.

"Were there more gunmen?" Alex asked.

"Three of them. I took them down. They never got off a shot."

"That's my baby."

Alex had my hand and was squeezing it. I wiped the tears out of my eyes with the other hand.

"Tell me about the bomb," he said.

I didn't know if I could.

26

Three weeks earlier
Yura Lake

"Focus on the living," I heard Curly say in my head.

Leo was dead. Nothing I could do to change that fact. Dealing with the ramifications would have to come later. On a mission, we had to focus on priorities. The living. The women who needed rescuing and the other men with machine guns.

If there were more threats, they'd be to the left. Where the trafficked girls were being held. The hallway was long and carpeted. It looked like what you'd see at any five-star resort. At the end was a closed door.

Approaching a closed door was as dangerous as coming out of an elevator. No idea who or what was on the other side. In some ways worse. At least the elevator door opened. I had to breach the door to the girl's suite to get to the other side.

Two security cameras were on the wall. One on each end of the hallway. That gave the guards another advantage. Based on the actions of the first gunmen, I had to assume they could see me. I put a bullet through the lenses of each camera. Then went back to the foyer where the elevator was located.

Retrieved the dead gunman's assault rifle. Careful not to touch the end. It was still hot from the barrage of bullets fired. As I suspected, the rifle was empty, but the gunman had an extra magazine on him. Two of them actually. I replaced the empty one in the rifle, stuck the extra magazine in the pocket of my pants, and went back down the hallway.

I approached the door confidently and intended to let her rip. Empty the entire magazine into the door until it opened. The bullets would pierce the door and kill anyone standing on the other side of it.

Then I thought better of it. I'd be acting as foolishly as the guard who had opened fire on us in the elevator. He killed one of us, but he was dead now. If I indiscriminately began firing, I might waste ammunition. More importantly, I didn't know who was on the other side of the door. The gunmen could be using the girls as human shields.

While it wasn't the smartest thing in the world to do, I approached the door, dropped to the floor, and fired one bullet into the lock. At an angle so the bullet would go into the jamb. It had the desired effect. The door swung open.

I braced for another barrage of gunfire. None came, so I crawled on my belly until I was at the door. Pushed it all the way open, then crawled the rest of the way in. With my handgun drawn. I left the assault rifle on the floor in the hallway behind me.

Easier to control the outcome with small arms. A handgun for me in close quarters was actually preferable to an assault rifle. I could shoot with precision. If there were any girls in the vicinity, I could kill the hostiles without hitting a girl. Assault rifles sprayed bullets. The bullets were also more powerful. They could penetrate several walls. Travel right through a man's skull and come out on the other side and kill a person behind him.

No guards were there. To my surprise.

I let out a breath I'd been holding. On the other side of the door was a large foyer. It had a desk and three chairs and a monitor sitting on the desk. After making sure no threats were nearby, I retrieved the assault weapon, came back inside, and walked behind the desk.

As I suspected, the screen was a security monitor. With various frames of the underground complex. Everything except Mr. Z.'s suite. I assumed he demanded complete privacy even though he didn't provide the same to the girls or even his wives.

I scanned each camera angle. Could see the elevator. The hallways. Inside the wives' suite. Two of the images were dark. I presumed those were from the cameras I shot out.

Where were the guards? I didn't see them.

It felt like they'd been where I was standing, maybe seconds before. Why did they leave their posts?

I felt a rush of panic. Were they headed for the girls? I could see Mr. Z. ordering them to kill the girls in the event of a breach of security.

Better not to jump to conclusions. It also made sense that they might've abandoned their positions when they saw their comrade in arms fall by the elevator.

I maneuvered around the screens. Looked at every room in the girls' suite. No sign of the guards. All I saw were twenty or so women huddled in a room. Obviously scared out of their wits. That made me feel better. At least they were out of harm's way for the moment.

I scanned more camera angles. No guards in the wives' suite.

A loud banging sound startled me. Coming from outside the suite. Down the hallway. It caused me to raise my weapon.

I searched the screens frantically looking for the source.

That's when I spotted the guards. They were in the middle hallway. The one that led to Mr. Z's suite. They must've snuck out the back of the girls' suite. Avoiding me.

They were at the door to Mr. Z's suite, pounding on it. Not knocking, acting like they were trying to break it down.

Without hesitation, I sprang into action and bolted out the door and sprinted down the hallway. Assault weapon over my shoulder and gun in hand. I could hear more pounding, then a crashing sound. Telling me they had broken through the door.

When I got to the middle hallway, the door at the end was open. The gunmen weren't in sight.

They were trying to get away.

That wasn't happening.

I sprinted down the hallway with my gun drawn. Paused long enough to take the necessary precautions before entering the suite. I peered around the door. Leading with my gun. Couldn't see the guards, but I could hear them in another room.

I stepped inside the doorway. The finest suite in the finest hotel in Paris wasn't more lavishly furnished. I didn't take the time to admire it.

This was a battlefield to me.

I took more caution now. Reminding myself that the men had assault rifles. They were shouting at each other in the other room.

I crept quietly toward the noise. Got to the opened door and peered around. The men had their backs to me. They were at another door. It had to be the one that led to the tunnel. Accessed by a keycard or by typing a keycode into the keypad. Same as upstairs.

The men were desperately trying to get the door open.

Not paying attention to me at all.

Curly would be laughing about now. The proper configuration would be for two of the men to be behind the man working on the door, facing out, with their guns drawn. Protecting against threats.

Lucky for me they weren't.

One man was fiddling with the keypad. Shouting expletives when he couldn't get it to open.

I fired two shots.

Tap. Tap.

Both found their mark. Struck the two men in the back of their heads. They fell to the floor. Not ever knowing where the shots came from.

The one working the keypad looked back. His eyes widened. Fear flashed across his face when he saw my gun aimed at his head.

I intended to keep him alive. To question him. He might have valuable information. But he went for his rifle. Sort of. It was slung over his shoulder. He tried to maneuver it to the front of his body.

He didn't get a chance. He was lying on the floor with two bullets between his eyes before his finger could even get to the trigger.

I made sure they were dead, then entered the word zone in the keypad. It didn't open. That made sense to me. This was Mr. Z.'s security blanket. His escape route. He wouldn't trust the code to anyone. Not even the sheriff or the giant. Especially not the guards.

I'd have to figure that out later. It would probably be necessary. I doubted the elevator was operational at that point.

I cleared the suite to make sure there were no more threats. Amazed at how much money had gone into the construction of this underground facility. I found another bank of security computers in a room. It looked like the war room at the White House. Television screens lined the wall. There had to be thirty of them. Each one with a different view of the Zone. Facing the screens was a large control area. With a soundboard and state-of-the-art computers.

Alex would love to be in that room to check things out.

The bank of screens to the right showed the view from every room in the underground. The wives' suite. Where they kept the trafficked girls. Every bedroom. Every bathroom. The hallways. The elevator.

I could envision Mr. Z. watching the girls like a voyeur. Sickening.

I got a glimpse of Leo's body. It caused a pain to shoot through my heart. Also propelled me on. I was close to rescuing the girls. Four gunmen were dead. I wouldn't rest until Mr. Z. was as well.

I focused on the cameras in the wives' suite. About twenty more women were standing in the living room. Looking at a large television screen on the wall. I could tell they were his wives by the way they were dressed. Hairnets. Skirts. Blouses that covered their arms and came up to their necks.

I didn't see any threats on any of the cameras.

After I'd seen enough, I found the door to the wives' suite. Off Mr. Z. 's bedroom. It was basically as Tapeesa had described it. The master bedroom had two separate bathrooms. The entire suite was lavishly arrayed. It had to be nearly ten thousand square feet of space. Mirrors everywhere.

The door to the wives' suite was locked. Rather than kick it down, I knocked and one of the women opened it right away.

Her eyes widened when she saw me and the gun in my hand.

"I'm here to help you," I said.

She didn't answer. I didn't see the least bit of fear on her face or in her eyes. It was almost like she was drugged. She also didn't do anything to try and stop me from entering the suite.

The living and kitchen area were massive. Not as nice as Mr. Z. 's living quarters, but nicer than most.

The ladies barely noticed me. Their eyes were glued to the screen on the wall. Lucas Rikki, aka Mr. Z., their husband, was talking.

They were all mesmerized. Like programmed robots.

"What's going on?" I asked.

No one answered. Only one woman looked my way.

Beth had warned me. She said the wives rarely spoke even in the classroom. When they did talk, they were respectful, but monotone. Emotionless. Never wasted a word. Only occasionally was Beth able to solicit more than a yes or no answer out of them.

Most were intelligent. They did their schoolwork on time and with excellence. Other than their strange social behaviors, they were ideal students in every way.

I walked around the group and stood by the television screen facing them. Took a good look at each one. The frumpy dress aside, they were all thin with beautiful faces. Various ages. I'd guess the oldest was in her forties. The youngest possibly fourteen. Several were pregnant.

They barely noticed me. They were intently listening to Mr. Z.

I turned to look at him as well. Got my first good look at him. I was curious. He wasn't imposing. He was short. Good looking. Immaculately dressed. He was standing in front of an ocean with palm trees behind him. I knew that was a visual trick. He was actually standing in front of a green screen. Probably in Iqaluit.

I was more interested in what he was saying. He was talking in a pleasant voice. The same tone I heard in the observatory.

"Aspire to something bigger than materialism," he said.

That almost made me laugh, having just come from his richly lavished suite. Paid for by the hard-working men and women in his cult. *Disgusting.*

He continued. "The chosen must forsake all others to follow me. You must leave your fathers and mothers and daughters and sisters and brothers and friends. Even if they hate you and revile you. You must separate yourself from all earthly possessions to attain eternal life."

Each word stoked the rage inside of me. Most of the sex traffickers I chased knew they were depraved scumbags. They didn't try to hide it. This man thought he was God's gift to the earth. I'd never seen so much ego in one demented personality.

He continued. I wanted to put a bullet in the middle of the screen but resisted. Mostly because I wanted to hear what he had to say.

"I have seen a coming conflict. It came to my mind when I was caught up in the sky. An apocalypse is coming. It will start in the north. Under the shadow of the great lights. The evil ones will come for you. Carrying guns."

Several of the ladies looked over at me. I still had the assault rifle over my shoulder and the handgun in my hand. My whole body was tense as if I anticipated a threat to walk through the door at any time.

"Don't be afraid of them," Rikki said. "They cannot touch you unless I allow it. You will not know if you are strong until you face it. Until you face death."

The word apocalypse was still bouncing around in my mind. What was he talking about? Why did he keep mentioning death?

"Don't think about life or death," he said. "Think about life and the afterlife. Only the very few are chosen to die for me. They will have a reward in the place I have prepared for them."

His words were ominous even if the tone wasn't..

"I see a coming destruction. A city destroyed by fire and ice. The unbelievers will die. You will never die. You will rise to meet me in the sky. In the great lights."

What?

Was he talking about Yura Lake?

Then I remembered the room in the police station that had been full of explosives.

A panic shot through me.

"Today you will be with me in the Great Lights," he said.

Today!

It suddenly made sense. Mr. Z. had rigged the place with explosives. He intended to blow up the entire Zone. With me in it.

I had to hurry.

27

Mr. Z. wouldn't be the first cult leader to destroy his property and even kill his followers. I hoped I was wrong, but feared I was right. It made sense. I had wondered why he had a stockroom full of explosives in the police station. When I went back the next day, they were gone.

Now I knew why.

Before Mr. Z. fled Yura Lake, I was certain he left behind a bomb. One that would destroy all the evidence of his evilness. And kill me in the process.

The ramifications were running wildly through my mind like an out-of-control herd of buffalo. A million questions flooded my mind at once.

How big was the bomb?

How was I going to get everyone out in time?

How much time did I have?

Could he detonate it by remote control?

How could I evacuate the entire town?

Mr. Z. was still speaking on the television screen. "This will confirm once again that I am all knowing," he said, smugly. "And that I am god. The earth will shake. Not one stone will be left unturned."

The man was insane.

He planted explosives around Yura Lake. He pretended to foretell the event that he had created. A coming apocalypse. He intended to blow up the town, then claim he saw it coming by prophesying it hours before. Once again, trying to fool the people into believing he was a deity. The gullible flock would believe him.

"Everyone listen to me," I shouted trying to get the women's attention. "We have to get out of here. This place is going to blow up."

They ignored me.

"You are all going to die."

I waved the gun at them.

"I'm ordering everyone out."

A few looked my way. Most of their eyes were still transfixed to the screen. What kind of hold did this man have over them?

My heart broke for them. They were so deceived.

"You're all going to die!" I said again, with even more emphasis.

"Do not be afraid," Mr. Z. said. His voice was raised. "You won't die."

It's like he could hear my words.

He continued. "The correlation between life and afterlife is fifty/fifty. Both are real. In a few minutes, you will no longer need your earthly body. I will give you a spiritual body."

A few minutes?

"Later today, you will be reunited with your loved ones who have gone into the spiritual realm before you. You will play with them in the Great Lights. I will be there with you."

As hard as I tried, I couldn't get their attention. Only one girl listened to me. She appeared to be slightly older than Tapeesa. She came up to me.

"Are we really going to die?" she asked.

"Yes. But not because Mr. Z. is some prophet. He placed explosives around the Zone. This place is going to blow up. We've got to get out of here."

"Is Tapeesa safe?"

"Yes. She's in the hospital. Having her baby."

Actually, she wasn't safe. No one was. I had more to worry about than just the people in the underground. The entire Zone could be destroyed. Mr. Z. said no stone would be left unturned.

The explosives in the police station were more than enough to level a small town. Especially with this huge facility underground. Everything would be brought down on top of it.

On top of me.

"Do you think you can talk any sense into them?" I asked, pointing at the other wives. Several had sat down. Mr. Z. was still spouting off his lies. I figured that was a good thing. He wouldn't blow the place up until he was finished bloviating.

"I don't think they'll leave," she said.

"Then get your coat and make your way to the tunnel. I'll meet you there."

"What tunnel?"

"It's in Mr. Z.'s suite. Through that door." I pointed at it. "You'll see it. There are three dead guards at the entrance. Don't look at them."

"Okay."

She left the room. So did I. I went back to the suite that held the trafficked girls. They were no longer gathered together. They were wandering around. Frantic. Trying to find a way of escape.

Some were in the hallway. Some by the elevator. One woman was pushing Leo's body out of the elevator. Desperately pushing the button. It wasn't responding.

"I'm here to help you," I said to her. "The elevator doesn't work. I have another way to get you out of here."

She didn't speak English.

I spoke to her in Spanish, and she understood. That calmed her slightly.

"How many of you are there?" I asked.

"There are twenty-two of us."

"Where are you from?"

"Peru. I was kidnapped and brought here."

I nodded.

"Go tell the other girls to get their coats on," I said. "Now! I'm getting everyone out of here."

She did as I said.

I checked the elevator again. To confirm it really wasn't operational. It made sense not to use it even if it was. The elevator was the worst place to be in an explosion. It also led to the Zone. I didn't think we were safe there either.

The best thing was to get the girls out of the Zone through the tunnel. According to Leo, the tunnel led to a building. Outside the Zone. Where Mr. Z. kept a helipad and had used it to escape without me knowing.

As I exited the elevator, I stopped long enough to reposition Leo's body. I searched to see if I could find anything his wife might want. Or anything that might give away that he was CSIS. I didn't find anything. He wasn't even wearing a wedding ring. Neither was I. We didn't on missions.

I crossed his arms over his chest and touched his cheek. It pained me that I couldn't take his body with me. I wondered if it'd ever be recovered if my worst nightmare was about to come to pass.

Not something I could worry about now.

I refocused and sprinted down the hallway to the girls' suite. Most of them were gathered in the living room.

"My name is Jesse," I said. "I'm here to rescue you. Is this everybody?"

"No. There are two more," somebody said.

"Go get them."

Before she could, two girls appeared in the doorway.

"Everyone follow me," I said. "I'm going to lead you out of here through a tunnel. I have to warn you that it's cold outside. I'll try to get you to a shelter immediately."

A few of them acknowledged my words either by nodding or saying something. No one asked any questions.

"Let's go."

I led them out of the suite and into the hallway. Once we got to the elevator, we turned down the hallway that led to Mr. Z. 's suite.

"You're going to see some dead bodies. Ignore them."

We entered Mr. Z.'s suite. They'd all probably been there many times. At least in his bedroom.

I rushed them through the main living area to the hall that led to the door that led to the tunnel. Or at least I assumed it did.

I stepped over the dead guards and instructed the girls to stand back. I entered the word zone into the keypad one more time. Just in case I had entered it wrong the first time. It didn't work. I wasn't surprised.

"Everybody stand back," I said. "Go outside the door."

They hesitated. I had to yell at them.

When they were clear, I took the assault rifle and emptied the magazine into the keypad and lock.

The girls let out a collective scream. I didn't have time to calm them.

The door still didn't open. It was made of solid steel. I had another magazine. I blasted the door with more bullets. It seemed to give slightly, but I barely made a dent in it.

My heart was racing. All kinds of doomsday scenarios were playing out in my head. If I couldn't get it open, I wasn't sure what I was going to do. We were trapped. I didn't think there were stairs anywhere.

I retrieved more magazines from the dead guards.

Emptied two more into the door. It gave slightly. I went over to the door and began pulling on the steel part that was weakened.

A couple of girls stuck their heads in.

"Help me," I said to them.

Together we began pulling harder.

I felt it give.

We were able to bend it. Not open it, but we created enough space that we could fit through it.

"Everybody line up. We're going out this door, one at a time."

The girls started filing into the room.

"As soon as you are through, run down the tunnel until you get to the end. Don't stop for anything."

I could only hope there were no guards with guns at the end of the tunnel. Nothing I could do about it. I had to stay behind to make sure everyone got out safely.

No girl left behind was a motto I lived by.

I helped each girl through the opening. When the last girl was in the tunnel, I ran back to the living room.

"Last chance," I shouted to the wives "You have to go now."

They looked my way, but that was all.

The television screen was blank. Mr. Z. was done speaking. He was probably watching me now on the security cameras. Laughing at me. I was out of time.

I ran back into the main suite and squeezed through the opening and into the tunnel. The tunnel was well lit. Almost like a subway. It was even heated. Not to room temperature, but not as cold as I expected it to be.

I sprinted as fast as I could toward the figures I could see at the end. The girls were all running toward a light. The proverbial light at the end of the tunnel. Not an oncoming train. Our place of safety.

Then it happened.

The first explosion.

A concussion. The walls of the tunnel shook.

It caused me to lose my balance.

A small tremor almost caused me to fall.

I heard a rumbling sound. The lights flickered. All kinds of steel cracking. Beams groaning under the stress.

Another explosion. Knocked me off my feet.

Once I regained my balance and my bearings, I took off running again.

The lights went off completely.

Another explosion. This one stronger. They must be timed. Set to go off in increments.

The ground was uneven. Debris began to fall from the ceiling.

I heard a roar. A large explosion.

Closer this time.

Everything was suddenly bright in the tunnel. The flash of light was behind me. I didn't dare look back. I knew what it was.

A fireball.

I kept my focus. And ran. As fast as I could. I smelled the bomb making materials. The chemicals.

The last bomb had exploded inside the tunnel.

The floor of the tunnel began to move, like a wave in a pool.

The explosions kept coming. One after another. Getting closer to me each time.

I prayed the tunnel would hold.

The last girl cleared the tunnel ahead of me. A consolation. At least I got them all out safely.

Another blast knocked me to the ground again.

I picked myself up and willed myself forward.

The air was filled with smoke. I could no longer see the light ahead of me. I kept moving forward. Blindly. Having to step over debris.

Coughing. My eyes burned.

The end of the tunnel couldn't be much further. My hands were in front of me. Like I was blind. Trying to feel my way.

One more giant explosion. Only a few feet behind me.

The ceiling behind me collapsed.

It sounded like a mountain coming down.

I felt the rush of cold wind as the ground had collapsed into the tunnel behind me. The good thing was that the ice and snow put out the fire.

But I was now walking uphill. Like the tunnel had sunk. Or maybe the end of it had tipped toward the crater that had formed behind me.

I heard a voice ahead. The familiar voice of Mr. Z.'s wife. Calling for me. I answered her. Reached out my hands hoping to make contact.

She clasped my hands and pulled me. I practically had to climb out of the tunnel to the landing where she was standing.

We were in a stairwell. The landing held, even though the earth behind me was sliding into an abyss.

The bitter cold slapped my face as the building disconnected from the tunnel and we were standing partially outside.

"Let's get out of here," I said.

We ran up several flights of stairs and into a large room. That's where the helicopter pad was located. I looked up at the ceiling and could see the retractable roof.

The room was heated. The building seemed to be unaffected by the explosion.

I bent over coughing. Trying to get the smoke out of my lungs. When I had recovered, I said, "Is everyone okay?"

They seemed to be.

I counted the girls to make sure they were all there. They were from various countries. And various ages.

My heart was filled with joy. That I had rescued this many girls.

Once I allowed myself to believe they were out of danger, my mind turned to Yura Lake.

Beth and Tapeesa. Nirliq. Everyone else in the Zone. Those who were still in danger. Perhaps dead.

"Where are we?" one of the girls asked me.

"You're in Nunavut," I said. "In the Arctic Circle. In a town called Yura Lake."

Was Yura Lake still there?

28

Three weeks later
Arlington, Virginia

Alex had a goofy look on his face. I'd just poured out my heart to him. Sharing the pain I had experienced in Yura Lake. I described for him in detail how I almost didn't survive the bomb blast. I was to the point in the story where I made it to the helipad with the girls. I was about to describe for him the utter devastation I saw when I finally got to Yura Lake.

He interrupted me.

"That sounds harrowing," he said.

I knew what he was doing.

"Harrowing?" I said, more sarcastically than anything else.

"It means distressing."

"I know what it means."

Alex had reverted back to one of the games we played. About a year before, he started injecting long words into our conversations. I think he stayed up at night, looking for them in the dictionary. Waiting for the right time.

He'd done it again.

He was trying to bring some levity to the intense conversation. Something Curly taught us. Actually, it came natural to a CIA operative. Our lives were so stressful in the field, when we were not on a mission, we needed to keep things light and fun as often as possible. Even when we were arguing or in an intense discussion.

We often reverted to humor to keep from going off an emotional cliff.

Things probably did need to be dialed back a little. Emotions were stirred up inside of me. Deep and raw hurts. Reliving it was painful.

I hadn't even gotten to the worst part yet.

"I didn't know you knew what harrowing meant, Alex."

He pointed at his face and gave me his standard comeback. "This is not just another pretty face."

I couldn't help but laugh. The tension in my shoulders and neck lifted slightly. Even if I knew it wouldn't last.

I looked at him affectionately. Alex was magazine model beautiful. Even with the last braggadocious comment, he didn't know how gorgeous he was, which made him even cuter.

My husband was as close to a perfect specimen as you could get. Tall. Perfect features. He worked out like a fiend so his six pack abs would be appropriate for the cover of any fitness magazine.

Even though an athlete, he wasn't a dumb jock. Alex had a brilliant mind. He was the foremost computer hacker in the world. Which didn't fit the persona I was looking at right then and there.

He was holding Lily like he was holding a valuable vase. With such tender care, you wouldn't know he was a competitive lion when it came to almost anything else. I had no doubt he'd protect Lily with the fierceness he had protected me on more than one occasion.

"Harrowing is an adjective," Alex said. "The word harrow originally comes from the Old English."

"You're into etymology now?"

He had a confused look on his face. His lips twisted to the side and his eyes wandered, like he didn't know what the word etymology meant.

When I first met Alex, his vocabulary was limited. Not in the arena of computers. I'd heard many of the terms. Latency. Integrated Development Environment. Boolean. Application Programming Interface. Algorithms. Topology. Phishing. All those words went over my head. Alex knew them like the back of his hand.

Since we'd started the game, his vocabulary had expanded as well.

Alex was a whiz with computers, but not a wordsmith. It amused me that he kept trying to impress me with long words interjected within a sentence. So I played along and kidded him about it.

"Harrowing comes from the word hergian," he said. "As in to harry or despoil."

"You're making that up."

"I am not! Look it up. It was seen in the homilies of Aelfric around one thousand A.D."

"I'll take your word for it."

I couldn't tell if he was lying or had memorized the information. His straight face didn't give it away. I was trained to spot a lie. Alex was trained to hide one. We were at a stalemate.

"It was also an agricultural term," he added.

"Are you done yet?"

"Not yet."

I let out a noticeable sigh.

"I'm trying to educate you."

"Please continue."

He was going to anyway. Might as well humor him. At least, he was distracting me from the story that I'd just as soon not talk about.

"Harrow was an agricultural implement. A heavy wooden rake. Comes from the word, hearwa."

"Now I know you're making it up."

"It's an Old Norse term. Affiliated with harrow. Or harvest."

"How long have you been waiting to tell me all that?"

"One day. I looked it up yesterday. I found it in a thesaurus. I figured we were going to discuss your mission at some point. Harrowing is an antonym of distressing."

"You mean synonym. Antonym has the opposite meaning."

"Whatever."

My heart was warm. I enjoyed the banter. It felt good to be home. Even though my soul was still troubled.

Harrowed.

Distressed.

The word described how I was feeling perfectly.

Reliving Yura Lake was difficult enough. I knew there was more pain inside. The source of my angst was deeper. Unimaginably painful. So much so I had been dreading it. Putting it off.

I needed to talk to Alex about Lily.

I wasn't sure I could do it. I had no confidence I could force the words out of my mouth when the time came.

"Thank you for the English lesson," I said.

Lily seemed to stir a little. She'd probably wake up soon.

"You're welcome. Finish telling me about Yura Lake," Alex said. "I understand the entire village wasn't destroyed."

"No. Thank God. I decided the best thing to do was to leave the girls at the helipad house and go to Yura Lake to see the extent of the damage. See if I could help with the rescue."

"Were you concerned about Mr. Z. coming back to Yura Lake? If he came back, he'd go to the helipad."

"Not really. The temperature outside was still thirty below zero. I didn't think he'd risk flying a helicopter in that weather. Anyway, it's a risk I had to take. The helipad was heated. They were away from the danger in the Zone."

I paused to see if Alex had a response. He didn't so I continued. We both knew better than to question the other's judgment in the field. Alex had come about as far as he dared with that question, and he knew it.

"I asked if any of them knew how to shoot a gun," I said, a little defensively. As if I still needed to justify my actions. "Several did, so I left the assault rifle and told them to stay put. To shoot anyone who walked through that door unless it was me."

"Sounds like the prudent thing to do."

"Not now."

"What?"

"Prudent?"

"I wasn't trying to use a big word. I use prudent all the time in a sentence. If I were trying to use a big word, I would've chosen sagacious or perspicacious. Would you have preferred nimble-witted?"

"May I continue with my story?"

"You're the one who got us off the rails by questioning prudent."

Now I was getting annoyed.

"A prudent thing for you to do would be to quit interrupting me."

"Sorry."

The smirk told me he wasn't sorry.

"I made the two-mile hike to Yura Lake," I said. "Almost froze to death. And yes, half the village was gone. The observatory was no longer standing. Normally, you could see it from miles away. The police station was gone. All that was left was a huge crater. Have you ever seen those big sinkholes in Florida?"

He nodded.

"It's like that. A huge hole had formed in the middle of the town. Everything collapsed on top of Mr. Z.'s underground facility. I figured several hundred people were buried. Nothing I could do about it. Nothing anyone could do. It was too cold to mount a search and rescue. Everyone was standing around in a daze. Some people were actually throwing themselves into the crater."

"Committing suicide?"

"Yeah. To join their fellow cult members. I guess they were upset that they didn't get to die and go play in the Northern Lights."

"I hate that man. You've got to get Mr. Z."

"Yes I do."

I took a deep breath and continued.

"Fortunately, the hospital was outside the blast zone. It was still standing. It shook like everything else and had some minor damage. The lights went out, but the hospital had a backup generator. Beth wasn't hurt. She was doing her best to help the people who came in injured. I spent several hours helping as well."

"That's tough."

"Yeah. Beth was amazing. But she was limited in what she could do. The hospital really didn't have the capacity to help that many people. There's not much she could do for the most seriously injured. A few of them died."

"That's unfortunate."

Alex's phone rang interrupting the story. Causing us both to jump.

"It's Brad," he said, after answering it. "He wants to talk to you."

I reached across the couch and took his phone.

"Hello, Brad."

"Why didn't you answer your phone?" he said roughly. Not bothering to return the friendly greeting. "I've been trying to call you."

"My phone was on silent. I didn't want it to wake Lily."

"You can't use Lily as an excuse," he said roughly. "I need to be able to reach you at any time."

"I thought we were off for a few weeks."

"You are never off. You know that. Twenty-four seven. You need to be available."

I tamped down the anger because he was right. That's what we signed up for. We had to be available at a moment's notice to go anywhere in the world. My phone was on silent, but it should've been near me so I could feel the vibrations.

I didn't think Brad would be calling me in the middle of the night. I should've taken it off of silent when the sun came up.

"What's up?" I asked, changing the subject.

It wasn't worth getting into an argument over. An argument I couldn't win. Brad was the assistant director of the CIA. While we had a good working relationship, and I was invaluable to him, he had fired me before. Would do it again if he thought I was a liability. Not being able to reach us when we weren't on a mission was one of his pet peeves.

Sometimes I thought getting fired would be a blessing.

"We found Rikki," he said.

I sat up. Fully engaged now. My heart started racing. I'd gone from despondent to full mission mode faster than a corvette can go zero to sixty.

"Where is he?"

"In Greenland. We think."

"I knew it!"

"You were right. You said to look for observatories. Especially ones that had been built in the last few years."

"I had a hunch Mr. Z. had more underground facilities. The observatory is a perfect cover."

"He has at least one. It's outside Nuuk. That's the capital of Greenland. Used to be called Godthad. He built an observatory there. Also another community. Smaller than the one in Yura Lake, but it's growing. I've seen the satellite photos. It looks like Yura Lake. I'm ninety five percent sure he's there. That's where he recorded the doomsday message. We think when he left Yura Lake in the helicopter, he flew straight to Greenland."

"That's why we couldn't find him in Iqaluit. Do you want me to go there?"

"No. I only called to let you know I booked you a pedicure for this afternoon."

His words dripped with sarcasm.

"Shut up. When do I leave?"

"Give me until lunch to gather more information. This just came across my desk. I need to build you a cover."

"What's the temperature in Nuuk?" I asked.

"Not as cold as Iqaluit."

"That's nice to know."

"I'll check." I heard him typing on his computer. "The low tonight is minus eight. The high tomorrow will be a balmy eighteen degrees above zero."

"I'll bring my suntan lotion."

Brad hung up.

I sat Alex's phone on the coffee table where it was before Brad called. Lily had drifted back into a deep sleep. I'd need to wake her soon. If she slept too much in the day, she didn't sleep at night.

"That was Brad," I said. Then realized my mistake.

"I know."

"Right. You answered the phone."

I was still stunned. Trying to process all the ramifications. It made my conversation with Alex about Lily that much more important.

"They found Rikki."

"I figured."

"Brad wants me to go there."

"I think you should."

"What about Lily?"

"What about her?"

"I've been thinking about Leo's kids. They are growing up without a father."

"That's the risk of the job."

"I know. But we always said that when we had a child, I would quit."

"Is that what you want to do, quit?"

"No. I want to go to Greenland and kill Rikki. And rescue more girls. I also want Lily to grow up with a mother. There are no guarantees I can do both."

"You could get hit by a bus in downtown Washington, D.C. Life is full of risks."

"Our risks are different. You know that."

"I do. I know how much you love what you do. Think of all the girls who have a better life because of you. You've rescued thousands of girls. You're the best in the world at it. I'd hate to see you quit."

"What if I don't come back from Greenland? You'll have to raise Lily all alone. Then you'll have to quit."

"I can't quit. I love what I do."

"So do I."

"Then what are our options?"

I couldn't contain the tears that had built up in my eyes. They began flowing down my cheeks.

"I think we have to put Lily up for adoption," I blurted.

Alex sat straight up. His eyes widened as large as the saucers in the kitchen cabinet.

"But what about your promise?" he asked.

"I know. I can't believe I'm suggesting it."

"Talk about distressing."

"Harrowing doesn't even begin to describe how I'm feeling."

There are no words.

29

Three weeks earlier

The scene unfolding in Yura Lake could only be described as utter chaos. I was being torn in several different directions.

The rescued girls were still hiding in the helipad. I had to figure out what to do with them. They needed food, water, and better shelter. The hospital was too small to hold them. So was the school. They wouldn't all fit in my small apartment. I had no doubt Nirliq would help, but her resources were limited.

I could load them on a truck and take them to Iqaluit. Although, I dreaded the thought. I had no experience driving on ice. Could I maneuver it? What if I jackknifed the big rig? What if I killed the engine and couldn't get it started? What if the fuel line froze and we were stuck?

I wouldn't be able to go and get help. Leo had warned if a truck was stationary on the ice for longer than an hour, it'd fall through. If that happened, we'd have no choice but to walk to Iqaluit. I could envision trying to lead them across the ice by foot. We'd all freeze to death.

The snowmobile was another option. But I couldn't realistically carry them to Iqaluit one at a time. It'd take many hours to do so. I'd freeze to death after one or two trips.

And wherever I decided to take them, they'd need around the clock protection. I couldn't leave some girls in Iqaluit, while I came back to get more. Not with Mr. Z. possibly in the vicinity.

Even if I could get the girls there by truck, then what? Were we supposed to loiter in the concourse while I waved my gun around like a crazy woman if anyone came near us. Guns weren't allowed in airports. The authorities would be there in a second.

For all I knew, Mr. Z. had them in his back pocket as well.

I also knew me. One look at Mr. Z.'s airplane hangar and I'd be over there in a second. To kill him and the giant.

What if I wasn't successful? The girls would be enslaved again.

What if I was successful? Were the Iqaluit authorities going to sit back and let me murder one of their most prominent citizens? It'd be one thing if I could kill him and had an escape plan. Maybe I could get away if it was just me. With this many girls in my charge, I had nowhere to go.

What a mess!

The best place for the girls was right where they were. Until I could figure it out. But I doubted they'd see it that way. If I didn't get back to the helipad soon, they might panic and do something stupid. Like leave. Wander out in the cold.

It was dark out. They wouldn't know where to go. They might die from hypothermia. How would I round them up again? I had to go back to the helipad soon and explain the situation to them. With food and water. Blankets and pillows. With a viable plan.

Where would I get enough food for that many people? I'd passed the restaurant coming to the hospital. Or at least where it used to be. It was at the bottom of the crater. I could take them to the diner out-side the Zone. But that'd mean getting them from the helipad, hiking two miles through the brutal cold, then getting them out of the zone and over to the restaurant.

It might be closed. Even if it was open, what if the cook refused to feed them? I'd have to force him. At gunpoint, if necessary. What if men were there and tried to stop me? I'd almost welcome that. I needed some bad guys to take out my frustrations on.

I hadn't thought this through when I went down the elevator. In my defense, how could I have possibly known about the bomb?

I felt a huge burden lifted when I saw that the hospital was still standing. I went inside, found Beth, and filled her in on the developments.

She had news as well. Tapeesa had started her labor. Beth was concerned.

"Her blood pressure would not come down," Beth had explained. "So I had to induce labor. All that did was put more stress on her and the baby."

"Can she handle a long labor?" I asked.

"I don't know. If things get worse, I may have to do a C-section."

"Are you set up for that?"

"Yes. I've done them before. It's not ideal, but manageable."

"How can I help?"

"Can you protect us? Tapeesa and me?"

"Don't worry. Mr. Z. is gone. He's not coming back. He knows if he comes back to Yura Lake, I'll kill him."

"I'm talking about protecting us from the men who live here in the Zone."

"What men?"

"Before the explosion, two men came to the hospital."

"Who were they?"

"Members of the Chosen. I recognized them. They live in the Zone."

"What did they want?"

"They demanded Tapeesa's baby. I told them the baby hadn't been born yet."

"Why did they want the baby?"

"They said it belonged to one of them. Mr. Z. promised it to him."

"They aren't getting that baby!"

"That's what I told them. They wouldn't listen to me."

"What happened next?" I asked.

"They demanded to see Tapeesa. I tried to stop them, but how could I?"

"I'm sorry I wasn't here."

"That only made things worse. Tapeesa was shouting at them. Telling them they'd never take her baby. It sent her blood pressure skyrocketing."

"I can imagine."

"The men said they'd be back when the baby was born."

"They might not be back," I said. "Not if they got caught up in the bomb. Let's hope that's the case. If not, I'll be ready for them when they come."

I touched the gun on my hip for my own benefit. It always gave me a boost of empowerment.

"What if you're not here?" Beth asked.

"I can leave you a gun."

"I don't know how to use it."

I let out a huge breath. Then a sigh.

"I'll figure something out. You're safe until the baby is born. They won't be back until then. I'll just have to make sure I'm here."

That seemed to satisfy her. She left to check on Tapeesa and the baby.

I started pacing the hallway. Could I keep that promise? I didn't know. How could I be in two places at once? Protect Beth and Tapeesa and also protect the girls? I could only hope that Mr. Z. thought the girls perished in the blast.

Did the helipad have security cameras? I didn't stop to look.

Of course, it did.

Mr. Z. would be monitoring them. I had to assume he knew the girls survived. That I was alive. He'd be making alternate plans at that very moment.

I'd been two steps behind him this whole mission. Somehow, I had to get ahead of him.

I called Brad.

"There was an explosion," I said, when he answered on the first ring.

"I know."

Brad knew everything. The CIA reach was seemingly endless.

"I'm okay. Thanks for asking."

"I assumed you were okay, since you're calling me."

"You're such a man. I could use a little bit of sympathy here. I'm in a precarious situation."

"If you want sympathy, call your pastor. If you want help, call me."

"That's what I'm doing."

"What do you need me to do?"

"I have more than twenty girls who need to get out of here. They were being held by Mr. Z. in the underground facility. That facility is gone. The bomb destroyed half of Yura Lake. There are hundreds of casualties. A search and rescue team needs to be brought in. Along with a forensic team to gather evidence."

"That I can't do. Not our jurisdiction."

"I know. But you can call CSIS. They can bring in whatever resources are necessary."

"Have Leo call them and coordinate what you need."

"Leo is dead."

The line went silent.

"I'm on it," Brad finally said in the same emotionless voice. "I'll call them and let them know."

"Leo said CSIS has a plane ready to come to Iqaluit and pick up the girls."

"They might, but I don't want to use it. On second thought, maybe I won't call them. Let's get the girls out of there first. I don't want a territorial war."

"That's the problem. I don't know how to get them out."

"You'll need a good size plane."

"We'll cram them into whatever we have. We just have to get them out of here. They're not safe in Yura Lake."

"Hold on a sec."

I couldn't hear anything. Brad had me on hold. When he came back on the line, he said, "Are you there?"

I said yes.

"Not you, Jamie. Can you hear me A-Rad?"

"I can hear you."

"Hello, A-Rad," I said.

"Hi. Jamie. Good to hear your voice."

"Likewise. Where are you?"

"I just left Germany. I'm headed home."

"Good timing. I need you to make a detour," Brad said. "Go to Iqaluit. There are packages there. Pick them up and bring them here."

A-Rad would know packages meant rescued girls since I was on the line.

"I can do that."

"No you can't," I said. "From what I understand, the airport is closed. Because of the weather. Iqaluit is in the Arctic Circle. You can't land until you get a break in the weather."

"I used to fly into the eye of a hurricane. I can land anywhere."

"Have you ever flown in the cold?"

"Do missions to the South Pole count?"

"I didn't know you flew to the South Pole."

"I haven't. But it sounded like a good comeback. Don't worry about it. I fly the northern route all the time. Over Finland. Greenland. We go that way a lot when the volcanoes aren't erupting. Landing in the cold is tricky, but I can handle it."

"I don't want you to take any unnecessary risks."

"I won't. Although, waiting would be better. What's your situation, Jamie?"

"Dire."

"Then I'm coming to get you now."

"How soon can you be here?"

"Five hours and sixteen minutes," he said after a brief pause.

"Perfect. It'll take me that long to get the women to Iqaluit."

"Kaley is changing our flight plan now."

"Kaley's with you?"

"Yep. She says hi."

"Great. I could use her here."

"She's excited."

"Do you feel like shooting someone, A-Rad?"

"Always."

"There's a seven-foot giant here who needs killing. Not even you could miss him."

"Ouch. That hurt."

"That was a compliment."

"It didn't sound like one."

"You have a lot of skills. Shooting isn't your best one."

We kidded him about it all the time. He was twice as good as a good marksman. Our standards were a lot higher than that.

"I've gotten a lot better. Kaley's been teaching me some things."

"I bet she has," Brad said.

It made me smile. I pictured A-Rad's cheeks turning bright red.

"Anything else?" A-Rad asked.

"No. I'm disconnecting you now," Brad said.

"Hang in there, Jamie. I'll get to you as soon as possible."

"Thanks."

Once A-Rad was off the line, Brad said to me "How are you going to get that many girls to Iqaluit? I'm looking at the weather. It says the temperature is thirty below zero."

"I don't know. But I will. I have to. They aren't safe here."

"Better get off the phone and get on it."

"Thanks. I'm glad I called you."

"I'm glad you're safe."

I hung up the phone thinking I didn't feel safe.

The predicament hit me right between the eyes. I'd felt confident while talking to Brad. Not so much now. How could I get the girls to Iqaluit? What were my options?

One of Mr. Z.'s trucks seemed like the best choice. But I didn't know if the trucks were operational. The bomb might've taken down the warehouse.

Then I decided it hadn't. Mr. Z. wouldn't risk it. He'd want to preserve those assets. He might need them later. Those trucks were expensive.

Then I realized how foolish that thought was. The maniac had just destroyed his entire town. The observatory. Twenty or thirty thousand square feet of underground living quarters. He wouldn't care about a few million dollars in trucks.

If the trucks weren't an option and I couldn't take the snowmobile, then I could steal an SUV and drive them across out of the cold. A few at a time. I did the math. Seven or eight trips.

But how would I protect them? I couldn't drive a handful of girls across the bay and drop them off at the airport. All alone. With no protection. None of the girls would be safe. The ones I left in Iqaluit would be vulnerable as well. I wouldn't put it past the men of Yura Lake to blame me for the bomb and organize against us.

The truck was the only option. I had to keep the girls together and stay with them so I could protect them.

I had a question for Beth.

As I was looking for her, I heard screaming coming from one of the rooms. It sounded like a woman in labor.

I knocked on the door, but didn't get a response so I walked in.

Tapeesa was sitting up in the hospital bed. Sweating profusely. Clutching her stomach. Clearly in the throes of labor.

Beth was by her side. With one hand on her shoulder, speaking words of encouragement to her.

Our eyes met. Beth smiled nervously.

"You're doing good," Beth said to Tapeesa. Once the contraction stopped, Beth gave Tapeesa some ice chips. And used a washcloth to pat her forehead. Tapeesa slumped back in the bed. Obviously exhausted.

I walked over so I was on the other side of her.

Tapeesa let out a shriek. Then grabbed my hand.

"They're going to take my baby! Don't let them! Please!"

She was hysterical.

"I'm not going to let them take your baby. I promise."

"How are you going to stop them? That's what they do. I told you Mr. Z. wouldn't stop until he had my baby."

"You let me worry about that. You focus on doing what Dr. Beth tells you to do. That baby will be here before you know it. I promised you I'd get you to Iqaluit and to safety and I meant it."

Not today. In reality, the girls were the priority. I had to consider them first. Tapeesa and the baby were safe at the hospital for now. I wouldn't be able to move her and her baby for a couple of days anyway.

No way to get Tapeesa on the plane with A-Rad. I'd have to make other arrangements.

"Can I talk to you for a second, Dr. Beth?" I said.

"Sure."

I pointed toward the door. She nodded.

Beth patted Tapeesa on the hand and said, "I'll be right back."

Once we were in the hall and out of earshot, I said, "How much longer do you think before she has the baby?"

Beth shrugged. "I don't know. The contractions are strong, but she's not that dilated. I'd say at least three to four more hours."

"How's her blood pressure?"

"It goes up during the contractions. To dangerous levels. But then comes down when the contractions stop. I'd like to give her an epidural so she's not in so much pain, but I don't want to slow down the delivery process."

"I have to take the rescued girls to Iqaluit. We're meeting a plane to get them to safety."

"Are they okay? Do any of them need medical attention?"

"I think they're okay for now. Healthy enough to travel."

"How are you going to get them across the bay?"

"I intend to use one of Mr. Z.'s trucks."

"Are the trucks still there?"

"I don't know."

"I tried to call Leo. I haven't been able to reach him. I left him a message. I warned him not to come back to Yura Lake until we see the extent of the damage."

"Good idea."

"He hasn't called me back. Where is he?"

"I don't know."

"I left him several messages. Why won't he call me back?"

I changed the subject.

"Beth, I have a question. Is it safe for the girls to ride in the back of the truck? You know with the cold."

"Leo said the trucks have heaters in the back. To protect merchandise that can't get cold."

"That's good to know."

I had to hope the trucks survived the blast.

Tapeesa started screaming again, so Beth went back inside the room.

30

Iqaluit International Airport

When I said I worked better alone, that wasn't entirely true. Euphoria came over me when I saw A-Rad masterfully land the plane at the Iqaluit airport, under extremely difficult conditions. It felt good to have other members of my team in the arena.

I was standing in the airport terminal counting down the minutes until he arrived. The girls and I all rushed to the window when the woman behind the counter said the plane was approaching.

Up until then, I was halfway expecting men with machine guns to burst into the airport at any time and attempt to arrest me. My missing bag had arrived, so I had a small arsenal at my disposal. My guns were hidden, but I was violating a number of local laws. The concealed weapon in my coat pocket being one of them.

To be used as a last resort. Only in an extreme situation. If any of Mr. Z.'s goons showed up, I wouldn't hesitate to use deadly force. Even in an airport.

The local police would be problematic. I only killed cops if I knew they were dirty. And as a last resort. Protecting the girls seemed like a good enough reason to me. No way I'd let anyone detain them. They were getting on that plane. Even if it was by the end of my gun.

Thankfully, no threats emerged, and I burst into applause when A-Rad and Kaley landed. The girls didn't understand everything happening but were excited as well. Once they were on that plane, their nightmare would be over. The healing could begin.

It warmed my heart to know I'd been the one to rescue them. With Leo's help. It pained me to think about him and his family. The loss was excruciating if I allowed myself to go there.

I wondered if his wife knew yet.

This mission had had so many tragedies already. My heart even broke for the wives who had lost their lives. For no sensible reason.

I know.

Some of those women chose to marry Mr. Z. Others were sold into the forced marriages but chose to stay anyway. I gave them a chance to leave.

It wasn't entirely their fault. They were brainwashed by a madman.

Early on in my career, I decided not to judge the women. Many chose to get into prostitution. For a variety of reasons. Some financial, others because they didn't think they deserved anything better out of life. I still considered them victims. I wouldn't risk my life for them, but I did have compassion for their situations.

Those forced into slavery were a different story. They were the ones I would help and invest my emotional energy into. I felt an overwhelming passion to take whatever risk necessary for the ones who couldn't help themselves.

Like the women at the airport. Who were trapped underground. Chosen because they were beautiful. Targeted. Intelligent, but at the wrong place at the wrong time.

While we were waiting for A-Rad, I had a chance to hear some of their stories. A few were snatched off the streets. Most were in a bar. Always alone. Their drinks were drugged. The next thing they knew, they woke up on a plane. Brought to Iqaluit. Although they didn't know that was the destination. They only knew it was cold. From there, they were helicoptered to Yura Lake under the watchful eye of the giant.

Some had been underground for more than two years. Under armed guard the entire time. Forced to do unspeakable things.

Apparently, those women were only available to a select group of men. The same ones each time. Occasionally Mr. Z. Other times with men I presumed were high up in the Chosen cult. Other than being forced to have sex with the men, the women were treated well. Never physically abused. They always had good food and water. The fine restaurant I had eaten at prepared them three meals a day.

They had nice clothes. Jewelry. Shoes. Amenities you might find in a five-star hotel. But they didn't have their freedom. The most important thing. The niceties of life can't replace the void present when you lose your freedom.

Thirteen of them were Inuit girls who were kidnapped. The ones reported missing to the authorities. I still don't know Mr. Z.'s motive. Maybe boredom. Maybe just because he could. Those girls were born in Nunavut and their families were looking for them. Most had given up hope.

We were taking them to the United States anyway. Until everything could be sorted out and they could be returned to their families. If that's what they wanted.

The girls kept thanking me. Over and over again. I refused to accept the accolades until they were in the air. Something could still go wrong. The mission wasn't a success until they were safe.

We were close now. I felt more confident as time passed, and nobody showed up to stop us. The lady behind the counter, who had helped me with my bags the week before, was sympathetic. She was instrumental in arranging everything we needed from the airport authorities. Including a meal at a local restaurant which was brought to us.

While the girls were eating, I was reflecting. Allowing myself to consider the events of the last few days. Unlike anything I'd ever experienced before.

The stress felt like a weight on my shoulders. I was second guessing myself. That happened when someone died alongside me. When bombs exploded and I barely survived.

It was during those times that I felt inadequate. Like I should've done things better. Rescued more girls. Thought of the underground facility sooner. Gotten to them before Mr. Z. got away. Before the bomb exploded.

Curly was in my head rebutting those arguments. *You did the best you could.*

An interesting dynamic. When I was feeling good about myself and how well I did on a mission, Curly was telling me everything I did wrong. When I was down on myself, he was telling me everything I did right.

Like I had a devil's advocate on my shoulder.

At the end of the day, his words were like fuel. My resolve was given a shot of adrenaline. Like a car running on empty, that suddenly had a full tank of gas.

I had to keep doing this as long as I was physically able. This was what I was born to do.

A report estimated that two and a half million girls worldwide were being held as sex slaves. I thought it was two to three times that. Maybe twenty times that number.

The girls I'd rescued in Yura Lake were a drop in the proverbial bucket. Sadly, I was doing more than anyone else in the world to combat it. The task seemed overwhelming. It took on so many forms.

Some sex trafficking rings were government sponsored. Many were run by terrorist groups. In this instance, these girls were held by a religious zealot. A man who pretended to be a god so he could marry young girls. How many Mr. Z.'s were out there? Did he have more underground facilities?

I intended to find out.

I was on my phone. Looking for religious zealots like Mr. Z. I came across a man who was recently arrested in the United States for having twenty wives. A cult leader who proclaimed himself to be a prophet. He even married his own daughter who was eleven. He had sixty followers. He passed the young girls around to the other men in the cult. Claimed that God told him to do it and also to watch.

He claimed to have the power to restore the girl's virginities after each time.

Disgusting.

He would stand trial.

A sudden anger came over me. I wondered why the local authorities of Iqaluit hadn't done anything about the depravity happening in Yura Lake. Why did I have to come from miles away to do their jobs for them?

They were part of the problem. Even if only because they looked the other way. Or didn't pursue it hard enough. Mr. Z. brought those kidnapped girls from other countries to the Iqaluit airport. Right under their noses. Or maybe with their knowledge. Either way, they were partly to blame. I almost wished one of them would show up so I could give them a piece of my mind. Or one of my bullets if I found out they were part of the problem.

The anger was good. It kept me focused.

This was a battle of good versus evil. These men were the vilest of the vile. I couldn't rid the world of all of them. But I could kill some of them.

Mr. Z. being number one on my most wanted list.

Watching the girls get excited when A-Rad landed the plane, made it all worth it and pushed the negative thoughts out of my head. At least temporarily.

A-Rad taxied the plane up to a gate near us. Even though the private planes loaded at a different location, the woman behind the counter arranged it so the girls could board from the terminal. A-Rad didn't even have to get out of the plane or shut off the engines. She even arranged to have the plane refueled.

I boarded the plane, made sure the girls were settled, then told A-Rad to get out of there as soon as possible.

Kaley stayed with me. I could use her in Yura Lake. I didn't know what threats I was facing there. Tapeesa and her baby still needed to be rescued. There might be more women we could help as well.

After A-Rad was in the air, Kaley and I got in Mr. Z.'s truck and I started it up. She was clearly impressed by the ride. Especially after she learned I stole it from Mr. Z.

I hadn't told her we had to drive across the ice to get to Yura Lake. She actually knew little about what we were doing.

"I can't believe it's so cold here," she said. It wasn't cold in the cab. I had the heaters on full blast. We'd be roasting soon.

"It's hard to run a mission in this cold," I said. "Surveillance. Reconnaissance. Spy craft. Those things are impossible to do in this type of weather."

"I heard we lost one. Someone from CSIS."

"Yep."

I thought about telling her what happened. To use it as a teaching moment. Then thought better of it. Brad had put me in charge of training Kaley at the Farm. He made me her mentor. At first, I didn't think she had what it took to be a good operative. I'm glad I didn't go by my first instinct. She was doing well, according to Brad. I was looking forward to seeing how much she had progressed.

Kaley now had a mission under her belt. I needed to see her more as a peer than a trainee. I'd continue to teach her if she wanted me to. Otherwise, I'd run the mission and she could learn by my example.

Although, I doubted her skills would be tested much in Yura Lake. I thought the worst of it was over. All we had to do was wait for Tapeesa to have her baby then get her out of there.

The trickiest part of my plan would come once we were back in Iqaluit. I intended to steal Mr. Z.'s plane. Kaley was a proficient pilot. I was counting on her to fly us out of there. Alex would change the tail number on the plane, and it would become the property of AJAX.

The airport authorities were helpful this time, but there were no guarantees they were going to sit back and let me steal a plane. I didn't consider it stealing. Compensation. What Mr. Z. owed me for my trouble. Punitive damages.

"Tell me about what you were doing in Germany," I said to Kaley.

"Need to know basis."

I laughed.

"I guess I deserve that."

In training, I'd drilled in her that we didn't talk about our mission to third parties. That information was limited to need to know. She was entitled to throw that back in my face.

"I'm kidding," Kaley said. "We were running a sex trafficking mission."

"In Germany? Prostitution is legal."

Germany was like Amsterdam. Prostitution was government sanctioned. Girls had to be licensed. The pimps had to form businesses. That didn't mean trafficking didn't exist. It was just harder to find. The sex industry was mostly legal. Most of the girls didn't need rescuing.

"Listen to this," Kaley said. "There are more than four hundred thousand prostitutes in Germany now. Over 1.2 million men a day pay for sex. Prostitution has exploded since they made it legal."

I had seen those stats.

"What was your mission?"

"As you know, there's an underground."

Ironic that she would mention underground sex trafficking. Considering what I had faced in Yura Lake.

Not what she meant. Underground in Germany was sex trafficking in plain sight. In some ways, that made it easier to run operations for the traffickers. Authorities weren't looking for prostitution rings. Other than the occasional sting to make sure the businesses had the proper licenses.

Even the sex traffickers had the licenses.

"How did you play it?" I asked.

Kaley chuckled nervously.

"I dressed up as a prostitute and stood on a corner where several girls were congregated. Muscled in on their territory."

"I bet that didn't go over very well."

"No it didn't. They confronted me. I didn't give in. Their pimp showed up within a couple of minutes. Proprietor is what they call them there. The owner of the business license is a proprietor."

"Yeah right. Sanctioned Pimp."

"Anyway. He tried to run me off. He was one of the ones I suspected of trafficking. It worked. We got him out of the weeds. A-Rad followed him. I got in my car and tracked A-Rad by his phone. The man led us to his hideout."

"That sounds like a good plan."

"To make a long story short, A-Rad and I crashed their party. Killed the bad guys and rescued a bunch of girls. Turns out, they were running a legitimate business, but had a certain clientele who would pay more for girls who were forced into having sex with them. The ones who were there against their wills."

"Unfortunately, those guys exist. They keep us in business."

"We found where they were holding the girls and freed them. Seventeen of them by the time we were done."

"Good job, Kaley. I'm impressed."

I meant it.

Kaley let out a scream.

"What are you doing?" she shouted.

I'd pulled off the road and was about to drive onto the ice. I should've warned Kaley but wanted to see her reaction. Same as mine the first time it had happened to me.

Kaley clutched the handle of her door.

The entry on the ice still shook my nerves. I could feel the ice moving. We could hear the cracking. It took a few seconds for the massive truck to get its footing, so to speak.

"Are you trying to get us killed?" she asked.

"It's perfectly safe."

"This is a big truck. What if we fall through the ice?"

"I've done it a couple of times now. We won't fall through."

Kaley was still clutching the handle.

Seconds before, she was talking about how she had stormed a hideout and killed a bunch of bad guys. How fearless she was. Right now, she was spooked by the thought of driving on ice.

Not that I blamed her. It was amusing, nonetheless.

"Look over there," I said. Pointing to the Northern Lights.

"Wow!"

"I know. I'm amazed every time I see them."

"Those are spectacular."

"Yes. They are."

That got Kaley's mind off the ice.

"Are you hungry?" I asked.

"Famished."

"I know just the thing that'll hit the spot. A blubber cheeseburger and fries."

"Blubber?"

"Yes. There's this great diner over at Yura Lake. They cook everything in blubber."

"Fat?"

"The fat of a seal, walrus, or whale."

"And that's good?"

"Best burger I ever ate."

My phone rang interrupting our conversation.

"Hello, Beth."

"Where are you?" she asked.

"On my way back to Yura Lake. Is something wrong? Has Tapeesa had her baby?"

"Not yet. But any minute now."

Something had her worried. I could hear it in her voice.

"Those two men are back. They are in Tapeesa's room. Waiting for her to have the baby. I don't know how to make them leave."

"I do. We're on our way."

I floored it. Then I remembered what Leo said. Driving faster than fifteen miles per hour caused instability in the waves underneath the ice. It could weaken the ice and cause us to fall through.

I did the math. At this rate it'd take us forty-five minutes to get there. I had no choice. I crept the speed up to thirty miles an hour. I needed to cut that time in half.

"Is there a problem?" Kaley asked.

"A big problem. The blubber sandwich will have to wait."

31

As we approached the hospital, I could hear screaming inside. Not labor pains, but a confrontation. Kaley instinctively pulled her gun. I told her to hide it but keep her finger near the trigger.

To my knowledge, none of the men in the Chosen cult had weapons. From the looks of the men I'd seen, a dozen of them together couldn't best Kaley and me even if they were armed.

Mr. Z. preached pacifism to his followers. Of course, he didn't follow that rule himself. Typical hypocrisy from despotic rulers. Even those who hid behind the veil of religion. Mr. Z. had armed guards around him at all times. Held young girls hostage at the barrel of a gun. Assault weapon no less.

Leaders didn't want their followers to have weapons. Otherwise, they might get overthrown. Americans should remember that. Politicians who want to take the people's weapons have an ulterior motive. It's not public safety. They want to be able to control the population and establish their authoritarian rule. Made much easier when the people are willing but unable to fight back.

A philosophical distraction for another day.

I had more pressing matters.

Once inside the hospital, the screaming was at a fever pitch. I could pick out the various voices. Tapeesa was hysterical. Screaming at the top of her lungs.

"Give me my baby! Don't let them take my baby! She's mine!"

That meant she had delivered the baby girl.

Beth was shouting as well.

"Let go of her! She's in no condition to be taken out of the hospital!"

I assumed she was talking about the baby. The men must be trying to leave with the girl. We had gotten there with no time to spare.

The men weren't shouting but making their case.

"She's rightfully ours. Get your hands off of me or I'll tell Mr. Z."

I burst through the doors. With a plan.

"What's going on here!" I demanded.

"Who are you?" one of the men asked.

He was holding the naked newborn who hadn't even been cleaned off yet. Beth was beside him, with one hand on the man's arm and the other grasping the baby.

The infant was now screaming at the top of her lungs. She looked and sounded healthy.

The only thing louder was Tapeesa. She was sitting up in her bed. Still attached to the monitors. Dripping in sweat. Her hair was matted. She seemed almost too weak to stand. All her energy was behind the words. She was begging now.

"Please don't take my baby! Please!"

I whistled to get everyone's attention. The room wasn't big, and the piercing sound had the desired effect.

Everyone stopped instantly. Looked at me. Then the din started again as they all felt the need to make their case to me. Which was what I wanted. For the men to see me as the authority in the room.

Tapeesa was the most hysterical.

"Jesse, they have my baby. You said you wouldn't let them take her. Make them give her back to me."

"This baby needs medical attention," Beth said.

"The baby is legally mine," the man holding her said.

Beth and the man were almost in a tug of war. Each had their hands on the girl and weren't going to let go.

"Everyone shut up!" I shouted.

The noise died down. Except for the baby crying and Tapeesa sobbing.

I walked over to the man and reached for the baby. He pulled her back. Beth still held a firm grip.

"Let go of the girl," I said to the man. "You too, Dr. Beth. Give the girl to me."

Beth released her grip, but the man didn't.

"Who are you?" the man asked again.

"I know who you are," the other man said. "You're Sheriff Buck's girlfriend."

"That's right," I said. Trying my best to keep a straight face. "I am the Sheriff's girlfriend."

Kaley's eyes widened and her mouth opened so wide, it couldn't go any further. She twisted her head to the side in a confused look. I didn't even bother sending her a signal. She'd know soon enough that it wasn't true. If she hadn't figured it out already.

"I just got off the phone with Buck," I said. "He sent me here to take charge of this situation. He's on his way back to Yura Lake. He'll be here tomorrow morning."

"Good," the man said. "He knows this baby belongs to me."

"This baby is Mr. Z's daughter!" I said roughly. "Everything in the world belongs to Mr. Z. And you won't get her if you continue to act with such impudence."

I thought maybe a big word would give me more credibility. I knew it because Alex had used it recently in one of his word games with me.

"Mr. Z. promised that girl to me," the man said.

"That's right," the other one chimed in. "I'm supposed to raise her until she's fourteen. Then she's going to marry him."

"I know all that," I said. "And I'll make sure that you get her. Just not right now."

"I knew I couldn't trust you!" Tapeesa shouted. She was sitting up again.

She tried to get out of bed but collapsed into Beth's arms. Beth helped her back onto the bed and pulled the covers over her.

Tapeesa pointed her finger at me. If looks could kill, I'd be deader than a doorknob. I felt bad putting her through this. No way I could signal her either. To let her know it was part of my plan. I needed to get the men out of there. I could do it with my gun. But this would be easier. Cleaner.

"You're with them!" Tapeesa shouted.

"Be quiet, Tapeesa," I said.

I hated using that harsh tone. Couldn't be helped.

Beth seemed to know what I was doing. She took Tapeesa's hand to reassure her. Tapeesa's head collapsed into Beth's chest. She was sobbing again.

Beth kept looking at the monitors. Tapeesa was connected to machines that were monitoring her vital signs. I looked over at them and could see a red-light blinking. Putting out an annoying alarm sound. Adding to the din. Tapeesa's blood pressure and pulse were dangerously high.

I needed to diffuse this situation quickly.

The man still maintained his grip on the baby. I glared at him. What I really wanted to do was knee him in the groin. I was in a perfect position to do so. Then he'd release his grip. But I resisted the urge. Maybe I could talk some sense into him. If I played it right.

Kaley stood off to the side. Her whole body was tense, but she didn't say or do anything. She would follow my lead.

The man said, "If you are who you say you are, then you know that this baby belongs to me. She's to be my wife when she turns fourteen."

I had to hide the disgust on my face.

"Of course. That's right. But you can't take her now."

"Why not?"

"Because she's a newborn. She needs to be examined. Given her vaccinations. Dr. Beth needs to check her out thoroughly. Mr. Z. wants to make sure she doesn't need medical attention or have anything wrong with her. Dr. Beth can't do that if you take her from here. It's also thirty below zero outside. The baby needs to be swaddled."

He didn't seem impressed by the argument.

"Who is that woman?" the man asked. Pointing at Kaley.

"She's with me. Mr. Z. sent her."

"You're not from around here. Are you from Greenland?" the man asked.

That was important information. Maybe I was right, and Mr. Z. had another operation in another country.

I answered for her. "Yes. Her name is Katherine. She's going to escort you out of the hospital. You can come back in the morning for the baby. As soon as the Sheriff gets here and says you can."

"We'll wait here."

"No you won't. You're upsetting Tapeesa. Mr. Z. will not be happy about it. She's his wife."

That seemed to satisfy him.

He released his grip on the girl. She was now fully in my arms. I brought her close to my chest. She wasn't screaming anymore, but she was crying. Probably cold. Such a harsh way to be brought into the world. My heart melted for her.

An army of men couldn't pry her out of my arms.

I moved closer to the man so Tapeesa couldn't hear me. Spoke slightly above a whisper.

"It'll be alright. I'll talk to Tapeesa. Then I'll call Mr. Z. and let him know. I'll get everything straightened out. You'll get your baby. Tomorrow morning. Come back then."

"How do I know you're telling the truth?"

"You doubt me?"

"I don't know you."

"I work for Mr. Z.," Kaley said.

"How do I know that?"

We were talking in our regular voices now.

She took out her phone.

"Let me call him right now. He can tell you himself."

"Uh... that won't be necessary."

I was impressed. Good move, Kaley.

"Good. Then it's settled. She'll take you outside," I said, pointing to Kaley. "You'll see that I'm driving one of Mr. Z. 's trucks. Would I be driving *his* truck if I didn't work for him?"

A skeptical look was still on his face. His forehead was furrowed, and his lips twisted to the side. I wanted to take a free hand and smack him into oblivion. I couldn't risk it since I was holding the baby.

It also seemed like my plan was working. I needed to be patient a little while longer.

This was why I didn't want to come in wielding guns. Better for them to give her up voluntarily.

"Everyone get out of here!" Beth said with a sense of urgency in her voice. "Tapeesa is coding."

I looked over and saw Tapeesa slumped back in the bed. Her eyes rolled into the back of her head.

I responded quickly. "Katherine. Take care of these men. Escort them out."

The men hesitated.

"Now!" I said. "I don't want to have to tell Buck and Mr. Z. that you weren't cooperative."

That did the trick. They scurried out. Kaley followed. She looked back and shrugged like she wasn't sure what to do.

I thought I was clear. Take care of the men meant to kill them. I didn't want them coming back tomorrow. Not ever. I wanted them dead. Any man who thought he had the right to rip a baby out of her mother's arms and marry the girl when she was fourteen against her will, that man didn't deserve to breathe.

Kaley shut the door behind them. I was confident she wouldn't let them come back in the room, even if they tried.

Beth's full attention was on Tapeesa. Who seemed to be losing consciousness.

"Is she okay?"

"I don't think so."

"You said she was coding."

I knew what coding was and it didn't seem like that was the case. Her condition did seem serious though.

"I made that up. To try to get rid of the men."

"Good thinking."

"You aren't really going to give them the baby, are you?"

"Of course not. I was trying to get rid of them as well."

"It's a good thing you got here when you did."

"Can I help with Tapeesa?"

"I don't know what to do."

Beth got a stethoscope out and was listening to her chest.

I looked at the monitors again. Tapeesa's blood pressure and pulse rate were no longer high. They were dangerously low.

"What's going on?" I asked after she was finished.

"Her pulse is weak. I think she's had some kind of HF."

"What's that?"

"Heart Failure. A cardiomyopathy. It's the most common complication in pregnancy these days."

"What can you do about it?"

"I don't have what I need. I asked Mr. Z. for the equipment. We don't even have a defibrillator. He said that it wasn't necessary. That he decided if the women lived or died."

As if I could despise him more.

"She's not going to die, is she?"

"I can't do anything for her. Other than try to make her comfortable and pray."

Beth took the baby from my arms. Took her over to the crib and began to clean her up. Get her warmer.

I went to Tapeesa's side. I felt tears welling up in my eyes. I couldn't believe she might die.

"Tapeesa, it's Jesse. I'm sorry, honey. I was trying to get rid of the men. I won't let them take your baby. I promise."

She opened her eyes slightly. Her breathing was shallow. She tried to lift her head but couldn't.

I moved closer to her so I could hear what she had to say.

"Her... name ... is Lily," Tapeesa said, forcing out the words. "Will you promise to take care of her?"

"You are the one who is going to take care of her. She's your daughter. Don't give up. I'm going to get you out of here."

Tapeesa coughed.

"I want you to raise her for me." Her voice cracked as she said it.

"Give her some water," Beth said.

I held Tapeesa's head and let her drink through a straw. That seemed to give her enough strength to speak more clearly.

Tapeesa looked deep into my eyes. "When Lily gets older, tell her that her mother loved her with all my heart."

"You can tell her. You aren't going to die. I'm going to get you out of here."

Beth had the baby clean and swaddled. She put her in Tapeesa's arms.

I saw a smile form on Tapeesa's lips. The baby looked contented. She looked down at her daughter. Lovingly. Lily was staring back at her mother.

A tear escaped from one of Tapeesa's eyes and ran down her cheek. She didn't bother brushing it away.

I choked back my own tears.

Tapeesa brushed the baby's cheek with the back of her hand.

"I love you, Lily," she said. "Jesse is going to be your mother now. You be a good girl for her."

Tapeesa looked at me. I nodded, reassuringly. I didn't know what else to do.

Before I could say anything, Tapeesa's head slumped back. Her arms relaxed. Her body went limp. I took Lily from her.

Tapeesa's eyes were closed. She took one last breath.

Dr. Beth took Tapeesa's hand. Felt for a pulse on her wrist. The monitors were silent. Showed no signs of life at all.

Beth shook her head. Didn't speak or do anything about the tears rushing down her cheeks. They said it all.

My heart broke into a thousand pieces.

32

Three weeks later

"How could we even think about giving Lily up for adoption?" Alex said to me.

"I don't see any other choice," I answered.

Alex grimaced. I'd never seen such a pained look on his face. Not since Curly died anyway.

"I love her already," he said. "I know it's only been a couple of weeks, but I feel like she's part of our family now."

"I love her too. But I have to make a choice. Go after Mr. Z. in Greenland or quit the CIA for good."

"Why does it have to be either or? Maybe there are other options. Let's think this through."

I shook my head.

"I have thought about it. Ever since Tapeesa died. That's all I've thought about."

"You promised you'd raise her."

"Not exactly. I mean. Tapeesa asked me if I would. You know. I didn't actually say—"

I was struggling to find the right words.

"Everything happened so fast. I'd just rescued all the girls. Kaley and I got back to Yura Lake and two men were trying to take her baby. We got rid of them. Then Tapeesa was dying. She wasn't thinking clearly. Neither was I. Tapeesa is the one who mentioned me being Lily's mother. I didn't offer."

"I thought she asked you to take her and to raise her as your daughter."

"She did. But what was I going to say? I couldn't tell her no."

How could I explain it to Alex when I didn't understand it myself? I was ridden with guilt for even speaking the words.

"Tell me exactly what happened," Alex said.

I didn't think I could relive it. The whole thing was a blur. After Tapeesa died, I found out Kaley didn't kill the two men. She sent them away. Mr. Z. sent another message to his followers. To not trust the journalist from the United States. That I wasn't working for him. To do whatever it took to stop me.

We had to get out of there. I wasn't worried for my safety. I was worried about Lily. The men were going to come back for her.

Lily was awake now. We were still sitting on the couch. Alex was holding her. The girl was looking up at him. Making the conversation that much harder.

"What difference does it make what happened?" I said, almost bitterly. "We say things all the time in the heat of the battle. The only thing that matters now is what's best for Lily. You and I are not what's best for her."

Alex twisted his head to the side, clearly not willing to accept that as an answer.

"I think we would be great parents for Lily."

"We don't know anything about taking care of a newborn."

"I think we're doing fine. I don't hear her complaining."

Alex was cooing with her. Playing with her chin. It was so cute. My heart was warm and cold at the same time. If that were possible. My emotions were saying one thing. My mind was looking at things logically. In a stone-cold methodical manner.

Lily made it nearly impossible to think clearly. She would sometimes burst out laughing when I was playing with her. If I tickled her. Her laugh was infectious. Alex and I didn't laugh much. Lily had brought life to our house in a way we had never experienced before.

She'd definitely made a big difference in our lives. Alex and I were antisocial for the most part. We were homebodies. We were gone for such extended periods of time, that when we were home, we rarely went out. We didn't go to movies or out to restaurants. We mostly stayed at home and chilled. Went to church on Sundays.

Other than that, the only time we went out was to exercise. To the gun range to hone our skills.

Lily had completely changed our routine. She was the center of our world now. Which we didn't mind. Even waking up in the middle of the night wasn't an issue. On missions, we were used to grabbing sleep whenever we could.

Having a baby was surprisingly easier than I thought it'd be. The stress of having a baby around was nothing compared to what we faced on the mission field.

That was the problem. The next mission. It'd eventually come. It'd be a lot more complicated as soon as one or both of us had to leave.

"Lily looks like her mother," I blurted out. "She has that beautiful Inuit look."

"That's a good thing. I'm glad she doesn't look like her father."

"That's for sure."

Mr. Z.'s face was seared into my memory. I couldn't wait until the day I put a bullet between his eyes.

"Look at it this way," Alex said with a sly grin on his face. "You get to have a baby and keep your girlish figure."

"I'm not exactly girlish."

I was tall and thin. Freakishly strong. I worked hard at it. Alex had a point. I could have a baby without going through the nine months of pregnancy.

I still felt the need to explain myself and wasn't going to let him get me off the point of the conversation. Which I had been dreading.

"I promised I'd take care of Lily. And protect her. I never said I'd be her mother for her whole life."

"That's not what Tapeesa thought."

What was Alex doing?

Making me feel worse.

Did he really want to keep her? I thought he'd hit the ceiling when he learned I brought a baby home. I was prepared to make the arguments he was making now. Until I realized it wouldn't work. We couldn't keep her.

I raised the intensity behind my words.

"I did what I said I was going to do. I got Lily safely away from Mr. Z. Everything was chaotic. Kaley didn't kill those two men, which meant they were going to come back the next morning. So I had to get everyone out of there. We packed everything and left. Took Beth with us. I barely had time to get my things and say goodbye to Nirliq."

I took in a breath. The words were coming at a rapid pace.

"We took the truck to Iqaluit, stole Mr. Z.'s plane, and flew to Washington, D.C."

"With Lily."

"I certainly wasn't going to leave her behind."

"No. You did the right thing."

"It's not like Kaley or Beth were going to take her. Kaley is nineteen. Madly in love with A-Rad. He still hasn't kissed her, by the way. You need to have a talk with that boy. Beth is single as well. But she's still pining away for Leo. She said she couldn't take on the responsibility of a baby without talking to him."

I wanted to tell Beth the truth about Leo but couldn't. It wasn't my place. Revealing the identity of a CIA operative in the United States was a felony. Punishable by up to ten years in prison. It was a crime in Canada as well. Besides, Beth didn't need to know the whole thing was a ruse. That Leo was married and not romantically interested in her at all. Using her to get information about Mr. Z. for the mission.

I let out a sigh. Another regret. Beth would go the rest of her life wondering why she never heard back from Leo. The CSIS had no doubt disconnected his phone.

Couldn't be helped.

The thoughts solidified an argument in my mind which I could make to Alex.

"I couldn't agree to take Lily without talking to you anyway. It wasn't my decision to make. Even if I inferred to Tapeesa that I would do it, I would've said anything to that poor girl. She was dying before my very eyes."

"I understand how hard that was."

I'm glad he was sympathetic.

"I didn't lie to Tapeesa," I said defensively. "But I didn't have time to think it through."

"You shouldn't feel guilty. It's not your fault. You did the best you could, under the circumstances."

"Thank you for understanding. I already feel bad enough."

Alex chuckled. I wasn't sure why.

"I was a little shocked when I got home and saw a crib in our room," he said. "Diapers. Baby powder. Bottles of formula in the fridge."

I laughed.

"I meant to be home when you got here. Lily and I went to her doctor's appointment."

"We got back early. It didn't matter. I took one look at Lily and fell in love."

"Are you going to love her more than you love me?"

"Impossible. I have enough room in my heart for both of you."

I smiled, even though I didn't feel happy on the inside.

"Does that mean we're going to keep her?" he asked.

"Look. We both knew it would never work," I said soberly.

"We could hire a nanny."

"Sometimes we're gone for months at a time."

"We'll alternate missions. We'll never be gone at the same time."

"Do you think Brad's going to agree to that?"

"We'll quit the CIA. We can run all our missions through AJAX. We'll decide how long we're gone."

I got choked up.

"What if… "

"Don't say it. It's not going to happen."

"I have to say it."

"I know. What if one of us doesn't come home from a mission?"

"It could happen."

"It hasn't happened yet."

"But it could."

"Look how long Curly lived. He died of natural causes. A heart attack. He was working a mission up until the day he died."

"Curly would say we were crazy for even thinking about it. He said to never have kids. It wouldn't work. That's why he never had any."

"He said to never get married either. We didn't listen to him. I'm glad we didn't."

"Me too. I love you."

"Lily can work with AJAX when she gets older."

"She deserves better."

"No one would be a better mother than you."

"Why are you arguing with me about this? You know I'm right."

"I know. I'm trying to convince myself you're wrong."

"It's hard."

"It's excruciating. I can't even imagine giving her up. Never seeing her again."

"It's what's best for Lily. Brad can arrange an adoption. She'll have normal parents."

"Boring parents."

"Parents who don't get shot at."

"Like I said, boring."

"So you agree? That we're doing the right thing?"

"I don't agree. But I guess you're right."

I exhaled. Loudly.

"I'll call Brad before we change our minds."

He answered on the first ring.

"I was just about to call you," he said.

"What about?"

"Get this. Mr. Z. has more than one location."

"I know. You told me. He has a location in Greenland."

"More than that. He has observatories in Norway. Finland. Sweden. Iceland. And Russia."

My heart skipped a beat.

"I bet he has an underground facility at each one of those observatories."

"I don't doubt it. I've been looking into things. There are more missing girls. Hundreds of unsolved cases. You're leaving tomorrow morning," he said. "With Kaley, A-Rad, and Alex."

"Alex is going?"

"Yes. I need all hands on deck. Colonel and Bond are going too. You've stumbled upon one of the biggest sex trafficking rings I've ever seen. I want you to bring this man down. I want Alex to find all his money. Rikki has billions. In my mind, stolen from his followers. I want Alex to empty his bank accounts. I want you to find him and bring him to justice. Dead or alive."

"Alex is sitting right here. I'll tell him."

"What did you want?" Brad said.

"What do you mean?"

"You called me."

"Oh yeah."

I'd gotten so excited about the mission I had forgotten why I called him. It came rushing back at me like an emotional tsunami.

"I need for you to go ahead and arrange Lily's adoption. She's Rikki's daughter. I don't want there to be any way that she can be traced back to him. We can't leave tomorrow unless we have arrangements for someone to take care of Lily."

Brad and I had discussed it in my debriefing meeting. I told him to hold off until I talked to Alex about what we should do.

"I've already made arrangements. In fact, I already started on the paperwork. We have a couple picked out."

I wanted to yell at him for being so presumptuous, but he knew we'd eventually come to this conclusion. Typical Brad. Getting a step ahead of us.

"Then it's settled. We'll bring her by tomorrow. Before we leave."

"I'm on it."

As quickly as Lily came into our life, she was leaving.

I hung up the phone and told Alex everything.

"Looks like we did the right thing," he said.

"Yeah. We could be gone for three or four months tracking down all these locations."

"We wouldn't even recognize Lily when we got home."

"I guess I'll never have children."

I was pouting now. Feeling sorry for myself. My upper lip was bulging out.

"Don't say that. Let's take it a day at a time. Now's not the right time for us to have a baby. That doesn't mean it will always be the case."

"Why is it so hard?"

Lily started to fuss. Like she didn't like the decision either. I took her from Alex and held her close. Rocked her back and forth. Asked her to forgive me.

"You saved her life, Jamie. Think of it this way. There are hundreds if not thousands of girls who are being held as sex slaves by Rikki. Living underground. You'd be a great mother for Lily. But someone else can do that job. No one else can save those girls, but you."

I nodded. Bit my lip. Fighting back the tears. He was right. That didn't make it any easier.

"Some of those girls are pregnant," Alex continued. "No telling how many babies like Lily we are going to rescue over the next few weeks."

"I have to stay focused on that."

"Not tonight."

"No."

"Tonight, we'll focus on Lily. We'll enjoy every second with her. And when we give her up tomorrow, we'll cry. Bittersweet tears."

"Tears of joy, because she's going to a good home," I said. I had to keep telling myself that.

"Joy because you are free to fulfill God's call on your life. To rescue girls."

Alex scooted over so he was next to me on the couch. "I'm proud of you, honey," he said, stroking my head. "It takes a big person to think of the greater good." He wiped the tears off my cheeks. My shirt was wet.

"I'll keep telling myself that."

Tomorrow was going to be one of the hardest days of my life.

33

Six weeks later
Nuuk, Greenland

Coming up with a plan to take out Mr. Z. was taking longer than anyone had anticipated. Having more Type-A personalities involved added to the difficulty in reaching a consensus. Not that I was complaining. It felt good to have everyone together working on the mission. I don't think I could've done it alone.

We were standing around a conference table in my hotel suite, discussing a plan. Alex, Bond, and Colonel weren't shy in expressing their opinions. A-Rad was the only one who kept quiet. He said to tell him where to point his gun and he'd be ready when the time came.

Kaley was as worthless as A-Rad. She was too busy flirting with him to care what we did. They were in the other room giggling like middle school children.

The problems were many. Which was why we hadn't acted.

When I waltzed into Yura Lake with no clue what I was facing, I had to make decisions on the fly. Now we had the luxury of knowing what we were getting into which was what was giving everyone, including me, pause.

My mistakes and successes provided valuable intelligence. We had a lot of things to consider.

The main one being, what if Mr. Z. rigged the compound with explosives?

We could be walking into a trap. We were risk takers, but not fools.

"We don't even know for sure Mr. Z. is here," Colonel said.

Colonel was the oldest on our team. The most experienced. He planned more missions on the ground in Afghanistan than anyone could count. We looked to him in times like this. When we needed to storm a fortress or breach a compound.

"I think he is, mate," Bond said.

Bond was a Brit. A former MI6 operative. He'd been a part of our team for years now. He was fearless and masterful at analyzing intelligence.

"This compound has more security," he said. "That tells me the boss man is here."

We had mountains of satellite photos at various times of day to back up that conclusion.

I added my thoughts. "When Mr. Z. left Yura Lake by helicopter, he didn't land at Iqaluit airport. According to the lady at the airport counter. And I didn't see the helicopter there when A-Rad landed to pick up the girls. That tells me when he left Yura Lake he flew somewhere else. To another compound to hide out. The closest one is Greenland."

"The helicopter had the range to fly all the way to any of the other locations," Colonel said.

"Yes. But radar would've picked it up," Bond retorted. "I talked to my friends at M16. They checked. No helicopter left Nunavut and landed in a European nation. He certainly didn't have the range to fly to Russia."

"He's right," Alex said. "On the date in question, no helicopter entered the airspace of any of the other countries. I followed the air traffic patterns for that day."

"Like I said, that means he's likely here," Colonel said, with a rare grin.

"He's here," I said. "I can feel it."

I had a sixth sense about these things. It's like I had spiritual discernment. I could feel evil in the air.

And what the guys were saying made sense. Over the last six weeks, we'd surveilled every one of Mr. Z. 's compounds. Finland, Norway, Iceland, Sweden, Russia, and Greenland.

We had a lot of circumstantial evidence that Mr. Z. was in Greenland. Which was why we set up our command headquarters there.

Alex was working on hacking into the security system. Once he did that, we could look for the giant on the security cameras. If Mr. Z. were in Greenland, then the giant would be nearby. Or vice versa.

Colonel had insisted we go to each compound in each country and see them in person. That took valuable time, but it had been a smart thing to do. We had satellite photos of each compound but there was nothing like seeing things with our own eyes.

To get a feel for the area. The topography. The ingresses and egresses. The number of guards. To watch the activity. Who came in and out? What was the local police presence like? Could we get in and out of the country with no problems? A major consideration when it came to the Russian compound.

Mr. Z. built his observatories and compounds in places where the Northern Lights could be viewed. Since it was still winter, that meant we had the weather to contend with. Another reason not to act right away. We had more hours of daylight now, and the temperatures weren't as cold.

Even then, we had to constantly be looking at the weather forecast. Snow and ice could put a serious kink in our plans. We never knew when a cold front was going to set in. None of us could think of a way to use the temperature to our advantage. Sometimes we could act under the cover of clouds. Not in this instance. Clouds could mean snow. Which could impact our freedom of movement.

With the frigid temperatures we couldn't be caught outside for very long. I don't know how people lived in these conditions for months on end.

Colonel was the only one used to operating in the cold. I did it in Yura Lake, but I didn't like it. Nirliq's parka helped. She insisted I take it.

It didn't matter what we talked about or what plan we discussed it all came back to one thing. What if the compound was rigged with explosives?

That's why we couldn't just storm it. We had the firepower. The manpower. The skill. Even the will. Everyone, including the Colonel, was getting impatient. But we weren't going to go charging in without knowing how to capture Mr. Z. before he could set off a bomb.

Colonel rearranged the papers on the table and put the schematic drawing of the Greenland compound on the top of the others. I'd work with someone at the CIA to come up with the layout of the buildings. As I remembered them.

"All the compounds are constructed in basically the same manner," Colonel said. "The only difference being topography. Things are moved around based on the best place to put them from a construction standpoint. Greenland is pretty much like Yura Lake."

He paused to see if anyone had anything to add. When we didn't, he continued. "The observatories are always facing north for obvious reasons. So you can see the Northern Lights. The entrances are open to the general public."

"Inside the observatories are two viewing rooms," I said. "One for the general public and one for the cult members. They are separated by a wall. There's a door, but it's locked."

Colonel nodded.

"We should go check them out," Bond said. "If they're open to the public."

I shook my head.

"There are security cameras everywhere. We can't risk blowing our cover."

"How are you coming on hacking into the security system?" Colonel asked Alex.

"I'm basically there. All I have to do now is cover my tracks, so no one knows I'm in. It doesn't do any good to hack into the system, if it alerts Mr. Z. to the fact that we're watching him. That takes away our advantage."

"I think I could wear a disguise and get into the observatory," I said.

"But you've already seen it," Colonel said. "I don't see what good that would do."

"I could go," Bond said. "Mr. Z. hasn't seen my face."

"I wish I hadn't seen your face," Alex quipped.

Colonel ignored Alex. "Jamie has already described it for us. I don't think any of us should show our faces around the compound until we're ready to act."

"I agree," Alex said.

"Let's get back to the plan. The police station is connected to the observatory," Colonel said. "Take it from there, Jamie. Walk us through how you got to the underground facility."

"You can exit the police station two ways," I said. "One leads you to the helipad. Right here."

I pointed to it on the satellite photo and then on the schematic plans.

"This is the door that leads to the elevator. That leads to the underground. That's one of two ways to get down there. That's how Leo and I got there."

"How did you get into the compound, love?" Bond said.

Bond called all the girls love. I was used to it. So was Alex although he didn't like it. Bond flirted with me so much early on, I thought he and Alex were going to come to blows. He had toned it down considerably.

"I used the Sheriff's keycard," I said. "That's how I got in."

"After you killed him, I presume," Bond said.

"Of course."

"You were inside the compound for several days," Bond asked. "Why didn't the guard at the gate or anyone else try to stop you?"

"I don't know."

I did know but didn't want to say.

Bond wouldn't drop it. "You had to be on all the security cameras. The guard at the entrance let you flash the Sheriff's keycard and didn't question it?"

"He questioned it. I talked my way around it."

"What did you say?" Bond asked.

"What does it matter?"

"You might be able to do the same thing here. Talk your way inside."

"I doubt it."

"Don't sell yourself short, love. If it worked once, it might work again."

"Just drop it, Bond!"

"I don't understand why you won't tell us what you said."

"I got inside because I told everyone I was the Sheriff's lover! There. Are you happy now?"

Alex had been leaning on the table with his elbows propping himself up. His eyes widened so much, I thought they were going to pop out of his head.

Predictably, the ribbing started. Coming from Bond. Bond was ready to kid someone at the first opportunity that presented itself. If it went too long between opportunities, he'd create one.

"You dirty dog," Bond said. "Jamie Austen. You've been a bad girl. Is that considered cheating?"

"Shut up, Bond," Alex said.

I got defensive. For Alex's benefit. "The Sheriff was dead. People saw me leave with him. I had to explain why he suddenly disappeared."

"Ahhh. You're so busted. Pretending to be a Hurdie."

A British slang term for loose woman. Bond had several to choose from. Bint. Crumpet. Essex girl. Fulham virgin. I'm glad he hadn't used scrubber or slag. Which meant slut. Of course, the worst was Toe Rag. Being around Bond, we'd heard most of the British slang words and terms over the years.

"It's not what you think," I said roughly. "The Sheriff was taking me back to Iqaluit. To the airport. Actually, he had other plans. He thought he could take advantage of me. The sweet innocent vulnerable girl that I am. I didn't give him the chance."

"How did it go down?" Alex asked. Probably wondering why I hadn't mentioned it before. He knew I killed the Sheriff. That was the extent of it.

"We were in his SUV, out on the ice. Away from the town. I killed him and sent his car plummeting to the bottom of the ocean. I went back to town and told the people that we were lovers. Had spent the afternoon together. That the Sheriff went to another town for ten days. That made everybody afraid of me. Because they were afraid of the Sheriff. That's why it won't work here. Not unless you want me to try and befriend this Sheriff."

"No!" Alex said.

"Sounds like you had a good plan, Jamie," Colonel said. "Very creative. Way to think on your feet."

"And not on your back," Bond said.

"Shut up, Bond," I said. Sometimes he got close to crossing the line. Even I wanted to slap him upside the head.

Alex's facial expression didn't give anything away. I doubted he was mad at me. Maybe slightly perturbed. Nothing happened. Other than that I took advantage of the situation and used it to further the mission. It wasn't the first time I'd used my feminine wiles to lure a man into a trap. Wouldn't be the last. Alex wasn't naïve enough to think that didn't happen.

He did the same thing. Not that we liked it. Just part of the job.

I needed to change the subject.

"That gives me an idea," I said.

"What?" Colonel asked.

"I still have the Sheriff's keycard. I wonder if it would work in Greenland."

"Alex?" Colonel said.

"It's the same system. It's based on a code. But Rikki probably changed the code. I know I would."

"Maybe not," I said. "It'd be easier to keep the same one everywhere. The password for the keypad was the word zone. Easy code to crack."

"It doesn't matter," Alex said. "Once I'm in the system, I can create a keycard that will work."

"Okay," Colonel said. "Here's the plan."

That's how the Colonel worked. He kept discussing things and asking questions. Then out of the blue, he had a plan. Usually filled with brilliance.

"Alex will hack into the security and keycard system. He'll create a keycard that will get Jamie into every part of the compound. Including the elevator which will lead to the underground area."

"I can do that," Alex said. "I'll also save some security footage, record it, then run it as a loop. That way, the security cameras are dark, but the monitors still show activity. Mr. Z. won't see Jamie coming."

"Good. Jamie will enter through the observatory. She'll use the keycard to get into the members only area."

"Who's going with her?" Bond asked.

"I'm going alone," Jamie said.

Colonel shook his head. "There needs to be two of you. You'll need backup."

That was the rule. Always go in pairs when possible.

"Like I said, who goes with her?" Bond said. "It should be me."

"Don't you think those women have been traumatized enough?" Alex said. "Without having to be subjected to you, Bond?"

"That's up to Jamie," Colonel said. "It's her rodeo."

Technically, it was my mission. I had the final say in everything pertaining to the plan.

"I'll take Kaley."

"Bollocks," Bond said.

"Good choice," Alex said. "Keep Bond as far away from the women as possible."

"Not funny, mate."

"It's kind of funny."

I didn't mind the banter. The mood was serious enough. Curly said we should always lighten it when we could.

"Jamie and Kaley will enter the police station," Colonel said. "Take out the threat. If he's there."

"If the Sheriff is there," Jamie said. "I'll take him out."

"Don't take him out on a date," Bond said. "Take him out. As in kill him."

Bond had an annoying grin on his face. I was tempted to slap it off of him.

"My date with the Sheriff was like your dates," I said. "Where the girl wants to kill the man within the first ten minutes."

"Now that's funny," Alex said.

"Why is everyone picking on me?" Bond said.

"You started it," Alex said.

"Can we get back to the plan?" Colonel said.

"Please," I said. "Kaley and I will take out the threat in the police station. If there is one. We'll exit to the helipad and then go through the door to the elevator. We'll use the keycard Alex provides. Kaley and I will ride the elevator down. If it's like last time, there'll be one guard where we exit."

"If Alex does his job, the guard won't know you're coming this time," Colonel said.

Everyone knew what happened with Leo. I needed to go over things with Kaley. To make sure the same thing didn't happen. In case the guard unloaded his weapon on us again.

"Bond and I will be over here," Colonel said.

He pointed to the area outside the compound. Mr. Z. had a house-like structure about a mile outside of it. With the same retractable roof. More than likely another helipad. We all assumed a tunnel led to it from his underground suite.

"We'll guard this area to cut off Mr. Z.'s escape route," Colonel said. "Alex will stay at the hotel to monitor the security cameras and warn us if there are any threats."

Alex was flailing away on his computer keys.

"I'm in," Alex said. "I can see all the security cameras and the archives."

"Find the elevator," I said excitedly. "There's a camera in the hall-way pointed right at the elevator."

"Just a sec."

His fingers were going a mile a minute.

"Got it."

"Go to yesterday. At three o'clock. Right around that time. That's when the giant brings the wives back from school. Assuming every-thing is the same at this compound as it was in Yura Lake."

We all gathered behind Alex and watched as he rewound the footage.

The monster appeared on the screen. Right at three o'clock.

The men led out a gasp.

"That's him!" I said. "That's the giant."

"Gordon Bennett!" Bond said.

He'd used that term before. A British expression of surprise.

"Cor Blimey, look at that!" he added.

Another expression. Kind of like our holy cow.

"That's the biggest man I've ever seen," Colonel said.

"We've found Bigfoot," Alex said.

"You're going to have to take him out," Colonel said to me.

"I'm looking forward to it."

34

If the keycard Alex made us didn't work, we'd have to abandon the mission. There were other ways into the compound. Through the guard gate. Trying to pick the locks. Small explosives would open the doors. But none would work without making our presence known.

A risk we couldn't take. We had to get to Mr. Z. before he could detonate the explosives. His escape route through the tunnel was blocked, but I wouldn't put it past him to blow the whole thing up even if he were still inside.

The man was a coward. Preying on young women and children. Hiding underground in remote parts of the world. Faced with the choice of killing himself or life in prison, he might choose to blow us all up. One last bit of satisfaction if he killed us before we could kill or capture him.

Therefore, this had to be a stealth mission. Kaley and I were tasked with getting inside and down the elevator, taking out the guards without alerting Mr. Z., and getting to him before he could push the detonator button which he probably kept nearby at all times.

Which meant everything had to go perfectly. A daunting task. How often did that happen? Rarely.

We entered the observatory through the public entrance. Reassured by Alex that the security camera feed was on a loop and Mr. Z. couldn't see us. The observatory was packed which worked to our advantage. The Northern Lights were on full display and putting on a remarkable show. We didn't have time to stop and admire them.

Mr. Z.'s familiar voice filled the room providing additional cover. We were able to walk right up to the door that led to the cult member's viewing room, without anyone even noticing.

The moment of truth came when I took the keycard and tried the door.

Yeah, Alex!

I don't know why I questioned him. His skills in this area were beyond belief.

Even so, I tamped down my elation. It didn't mean the card would work on the elevator. We also had to get by the Sheriff in the police station first. If he was there.

The second viewing room was filled with cult members, mesmerized by Mr. Z.'s words. Hearing the cult leader's voice, talking nonsense, misleading all those people, sent a fireball of rage through me. I despised the man.

He was talking about love. What did he know about love?

Nothing.

Those poor people had no idea that their so-called god would blow them to smithereens if it suited his purposes. Mr. Z. only loved himself. And would manipulate anyone and everyone for his own pleasure and survival.

He'd gotten rich off the backs of those people. Pillaged their resources. Raped their women and children. I'd encountered a lot of vile and evil people over the years. I don't think I detested any of them any more than I did Mr. Z.

The keycard worked on the second observatory door as well. A good thing since we were able to exit the observatory quietly. By that point, the anger was boiling inside of me at such a fevered pitch, I might've kicked in the door rather than abandon the mission. It would've taken a lot of self-control to walk back out of there and start over.

Fortunately, we didn't have to. We were able to sneak through the observatory with no problem and found ourselves inside the police station. Our guns were drawn now. No one was in the building. I didn't care either way. If the Sheriff had been there, he'd be dead. It made it slightly easier that he wasn't.

The configuration was the same as the layout in Yura Lake. I made a beeline for the room where I presumed the explosives were being kept.

It was empty.

Which sent a chill through my already cold bones.

We had to wait outside the observatory longer than planned. Until Colonel and Bond were in place over at the helicopter building. We couldn't wear thick clothes. We wanted freedom of movement.

We were freezing by the time we got the word to go inside. Once I was back home and this mission was over, it might take months for my body to unthaw.

The stash of weapons was there. Same as Yura Lake. Including a missile launcher. I still didn't know why Mr. Z. had those.

We exited the police station and were met by the cold air again. I already had the keycard out and ready. I didn't want to spend one minute longer in the night air than necessary. We practically ran through the helipad area, and I opened the door that led to the elevator quickly.

So far, the keycard had worked each time. I was tempted to see if the word zone worked on the keypad to the elevator but didn't bother. Time was of the essence.

We had silenced all radio communication in case Mr. Z. was monitoring the frequencies. Kaley and I were using hand signals to communicate.

It didn't do any good to darken the security cameras so Mr. Z. couldn't see us coming, if we made the mistake of letting him hear us coming.

Kaley matched my movements. She knew what to do. I'd gone over it in painstaking detail. I didn't want a repeat of Yura Lake. Leo's memory would be with me for the rest of my life. In a way, I was dedicating this mission to him.

Once inside the elevator, I took Leo's position. Kaley was on the other side with the button. That panel was wider and provided more protection. She got down on one knee like I taught her to do. If the guard started shooting when the elevator door opened, he'd shoot above her, and she could get a shot off at him.

I would stay behind the smaller panel. Careful not to make the same mistake Leo made.

Hopefully, the guard was sitting in his chair. Bored.

We'd soon know if we'd gotten that far undetected.

I motioned for Kaley to push the button. Took a deep breath and calmed my heartbeat. Clutched my weapon which was to the side.

We couldn't come out of the elevator with our guns blazing. That'd alert Mr. Z. that we were there. He'd hear the gunshots from his suite. If the guard didn't start firing when the elevator door opened, I had a different plan. One that had worked for me over and over again through the years.

"People are stupid," Curly had said in more than one training session. "Especially the bad guys. Act like you're supposed to be there, and they won't know any better."

The elevator stopped.

So did my breathing.

The door opened.

I flinched.

Nothing happened.

I placed my gun in my pocket but kept my right hand on it. Walked out of the elevator like I owned the place.

The guard reacted quickly. Raised his weapon but didn't act like he was going to fire. The reaction I expected. He was a low-level guard.

With a dull job. I couldn't imagine sitting in that chair staring at the elevator every day for hours on end.

Hopefully, he wouldn't know what to do when the unexpected happened. Like when a blonde and a red-haired woman walked out of the elevator. If Mr. Z. had circulated my picture among the guards, I couldn't tell it by his reaction. No sign of recognition on his face.

"What are you doing?" I asked sharply. "Don't point your gun at me. Mr. Z. won't be happy with you."

The imbecile lowered his weapon.

"Who are you?" he said.

"None of your concern. I'm here to move the girls."

"I don't know anything about that."

"Why would you? Gunvald doesn't have to tell you everything."

Mentioning the giant's name might disarm any concerns he had. I tried not to grin at the disarm pun in my head. As I stared at his assault weapon which thankfully was by his side now.

"Where are you taking them?" he asked.

"I wouldn't ask too many questions if I was you. If Mr. Z. wanted you to know, he would've told you."

Mentioning Mr. Z's name was even better. A look of fear flashed across his face.

I flashed my keycard in his face. He became extremely cooperative.

"Does this open the door down there?" I asked, pointing down the hallway where the girls were located. Alex had verified it when he hacked into the security cameras. We were able to see the entire layout. Except for Mr. Z's suite.

The gunman nodded.

All the information I needed.

I motioned for him to come with me.

Stupid man. Turned his back to the real threat.

Kaley came up from behind and struck the guard on the side of his neck. Knocking him unconscious. A kick to the head finished the job. He was either dead or would be out for hours.

Kaley and I hurried down the hallway. I didn't need to shoot out the cameras or the lock since Alex had the loop going. I swiped the keycard and the door swung open. My gun was hidden behind my back. I didn't want the guards to see it.

Two of them were sitting behind the desk.

Their eyes widened but they didn't reach for their weapons.

"Keep your seat," I said. "Mr. Z. wants me to take the girls to the observatory."

"Okay."

They didn't even ask why.

"How many girls are there?" I asked.

"Nine," one of them said.

"Take me to them," I said.

The two men stood to their feet and came out from behind the desks. I caught Kaley's eye and nodded slightly.

They turned their backs to us. This was easy.

For whatever reason, Kaley and I both chose the same move. A blow to the liver. The two men dropped to the floor. Then a stomp to the back of their heads. I heard vertebrae snapping.

No reason to check the men. They were dead or sufficiently incapacitated.

The girls weren't congregated in one area. They were in their rooms. Two of them per room. Kaley went to the doors on the right and I went to the ones on the left to round them up.

"Get dressed," I told the girls. "Shoes. Coats. It's cold outside."

None of them had coats.

"Dress in layers then," I said.

I took the girls back to the main foyer. Kaley was already there. I was becoming more impressed by Kaley by the minute.

I only counted eight girls.

"I'm getting you out of here," I said to them. "We're here to rescue you and take you back to your home countries."

A collective squeal filled the room.

"Is this everyone? I was told there were nine of you."

"Idelle isn't here," one of the girls said.

"She's with Mr. Z.," another one said. "Tonight was her night in the suite."

"Okay. Take the girls up the elevator," I said to Kaley. "Take them to the rendezvous point."

We had two buses outside the compound. Prepared to take the girls to the airport and put on our plane.

Fortunately, Kaley didn't ask what I was doing. Better if she simply followed orders.

Since she didn't ask, I offered an explanation. "I'm staying behind. I'm going to get Idelle. But not until these girls are safe. Radio me when you get them to the buses."

"Will do. Follow me," Kaley said.

The girls disappeared out the door and down the hall. I walked behind the desk to look at the security cameras. Alex still had the loop going. It looked like a guard was still at the elevator and the two guards were still at the desk.

Alex could see the security cameras in real time. I waved to him, then sat back in the chair. Closed my eyes. Alex would come on the radio and warn me if a threat was coming.

It took twenty agonizing minutes until Kaley said, "All clear."

I bolted up from my chair.

"Bama, can you see Private?" I asked. At this point, I had no choice but to break radio communication.

"Negative," Alex said.

Private was the Colonel's code name. Bama was Alex's. We were each given a name for radio communication. I was Dolly. As in, Dolly Parton. Because of my flat chest. I was tall and thin. The only reason my mother bought me a bra in high school was because I was embarrassed in gym class. I didn't want to be the only girl not wearing one.

I'd filled out some through the years, but I wasn't going to win any wet t-shirt contests. Not that I would enter one.

Alex didn't seem to mind. He had said many times that he was a butt-man.

The code names were supposed to be funny. Alex was Bama because he lost to Alabama in the national championship game. We all got used to them even if we hated them.

I had asked Alex if he could see Bond and Colonel hiding at the helipad. If he couldn't see them, I wanted him to turn the feed back on. So Mr. Z. would see that the girls were gone.

"Restart the feed," I told him.

"I don't think that's a good idea. Not with you still there."

"There's one more package. She's in the suite with Mr. Z."

"Why not wait until she comes back? When he's finished with her?" Alex asked.

"Who knows when that'll be?"

"Give it a few more minutes."

He was right. I needed to be patient. Mr. Z. probably didn't keep the girls around for long afterwards.

A few minutes later, I heard a noise. A door opening. It startled me.

"Somebody's coming," I said to Alex.

"Just a sec," he said.

It sounded like the door that led to Mr. Z.'s suite.

I was standing with my gun drawn within seconds.

Alex said. "You're good Dolly. It's the package."

I lowered my weapon. A figure appeared. A woman.

She jumped when she saw me.

"Are you Idelle?" I asked.

She nodded.

"Go get some warm clothes on. You're coming with me. I'm getting you out of here."

She hesitated.

"Hurry. We don't have much time. You'll be safe with me. I'm rescuing you."

Sometimes the girls were like deer in headlights. They didn't believe me.

"Bama. I've got the package. We're going to the top. As soon as I'm clear, restart the feed."

"Will do."

I wanted Mr. Z. to look at the security cameras and see that the girls were gone. Then panic. Rush out the tunnel. He would look at the helipad security cameras first. If he saw that the coast was clear, he'd make a run for it. He wouldn't blow the place up until he got away.

We had discussed this as a possible plan. Colonel and Bond would be ready if and when Mr. Z. emerged from the tunnel.

The woman was back within a minute or two. With several layers of clothes on.

We hurried to the elevators.

I pushed the button and it started upward.

We got to the top and the door opened.

The giant was standing at the door.

35

CIA Headquarters
Langley, Virginia
Five weeks later

Sometimes mission debriefings were important. Other times, they were nothing more than a formality. Today's meeting was an important formality. By every matrix, the mission to bring down Rikki and his sex trafficking organization was a huge success. A feather in Brad's cap, if he actually wore caps.

More than three hundred women and young girls were rescued in seven countries and three continents. The Chosen cult was still in existence but without a leader. Also without any money or resources. Alex had sufficiently drained all of Rikki's bank accounts. Deposited the billions of dollars into AJAX's bulging coffers.

We didn't intend for the money to stay in our accounts. We were trying to figure out a way to reimburse some of the disillusioned followers who had been duped into giving Rikki all their life's work and savings. What was left over, would go to the *Save The Girls* organization or other non-profits. Or we'd use it to fund more sex trafficking rescue operations.

The reason the debriefing was a formality was because Brad didn't really want to know what happened. He had signaled that early on. He was pretending to grill us on the details of the operation.

We were in his office, sitting at the conference table. He had a pencil in his hand. Along with the mission files and a notepad, which didn't have anything written on it, even though we'd been there for more than two hours.

We'd gotten to the point where I confronted the giant.

"When the elevator door opened, you said the giant was standing there. Is that correct?" Brad asked.

"Yes. Gunvald was there."

"Was he armed?"

"Yes."

He had arms.

Our standard answer when we killed someone who didn't have a weapon. In this case, the giant had massive arms but no knife or gun. Although, if pressed, I would've argued the point. Anyone with fists the size of sledgehammers was armed in my opinion. Nevertheless, according to the rules of engagement, we could only use deadly force if faced with an immediate threat to life or limb.

I certainly thought that was the case at the time. The giant would've killed me if he had been given the chance.

Not a rule I followed anyway. If I had an opportunity to kill a sex trafficker, I did it. Armed or not. Unless I had a reason to keep him alive.

Idelle, the last girl to be rescued from the compound, let out a scream when she saw the giant. As was often the case for me, time stood still. For whatever reason, I remembered my recurring dream. The nightmare. When I had fought the giant in the snow. Then again in the underground prison cell.

In the snow, the giant got the best of me. The second time, I won the physical confrontation. Even though it wasn't easy.

The second dream gave me a roadmap on how to beat the giant in a fight. The moves flashed across my mind.

It didn't come to that.

"Alex, you had eyes and ears on the situation," Brad said, interrupting my thoughts. "Why didn't you warn Jamie that the giant was there?"

The first probing question Brad had asked. One of the main reasons behind a debriefing was for Brad to find things we'd done wrong. Things we could improve on. Training opportunities, he called them.

"Jamie asked me the same thing," Alex said. "I tried to contact her, but she didn't have radio reception in the elevator."

That was true. Alex had seen Gunvald on the security cameras. He tried to warn me. I didn't hear him.

Nevertheless, I was prepared.

Thank you, Curly.

He had drilled in me to expect the unexpected. To never let my guard down.

When the elevator door opened, Gunvald took one look at me. The blood drained from his face. His already wide eyes widened further.

My gun was pointed right at him.

He was impossible to miss.

The first two bullets hit him in the chest. Center mass.

Gunvald didn't fall.

Most elephants would've been on the ground by then. He looked down at his chest. At first, I thought maybe he had a bullet proof vest underneath all those clothes. A spot of blood dripped from the bottom of his coat to the floor, and I knew I'd found my mark.

Tap. Tap. Tap.

The next three bullets were headshots. One to the bridge of the nose, two in the forehead. I don't remember ever needing five bullets to kill a man.

He fell to the ground with a thud. Sounded like a tree falling on a house.

Brad listened intently to my story. Every word of it was true. I didn't see a valid reason not to share the details.

A few more questions followed.

Brad still didn't write anything down. The debriefing wasn't being recorded. Sometimes it was, sometimes it wasn't.

This mission was problematic because of all the jurisdictions. The investigations were ongoing in all the countries. Brad had said he heard from them almost every day. They weren't cooperative with each other, even though they tried to compare notes.

The intelligence agencies had a lot to answer for and were getting a lot of pressure. Especially once the press got wind of it. How did they let Rikki operate such a huge operation right under their noses?

"Tell me what happened to Rikki," Brad said.

"He's dead," I said.

That wasn't a lie. Rikki was dead.

"Where's the body?"

Now was the time to lie. Another tricky part of the mission. The team had argued about it for hours.

I wanted the man dead. I had remembered something Rikki said to me in my dream. That if I killed him, I'd make a martyr out of him. I was convinced that was true. So I wanted him to disappear off the face of the earth. Never to be heard from again. With no one but us knowing what had happened to him.

The team was unanimous that Rikki had to die. If we had let him live, a trial would be problematic. Who had jurisdiction? Where would he be tried first? The trial would be a public spectacle.

All his followers would have a rallying point. Amazingly, the man had millions of followers. Politicians might give in to public pressure.

We couldn't risk him getting off.

For that matter, Rikki could continue running his cult from his prison cell.

No way we could let him live. The debate was over what to do with the body.

If we killed him and displayed his body for the world to see, we'd prove the man's mortality. That he wasn't actually a god like he had said. But that'd spark an outrage among his followers and among the liberal activists.

Brad stared deep into my eyes. I realized I hadn't answered the question. I chose my words carefully. He didn't need to know what really happened.

"Rikki came out of the tunnel," I said. "He somehow eluded Colonel and Bond. Got in his helicopter and flew off. Had engine trouble and had to land on the ice. We watched it all unfold."

Brad was stoic. His expression didn't give anything away. Although he knew the truth. No way Rikki could escape the trap Colonel and Bond had laid for him.

In reality, Rikki came out of the tunnel, with the detonator button around his neck. As soon as Colonel and Bond laid eyes on him, they opened fire. Not willing to risk giving Rikki the opportunity to push the detonator button.

They each fired one shot. Only one bullet found its mark. Rikki fell to the ground with a gunshot wound to the head.

The debate between the two had become heated once Alex and I arrived on the scene.

"I can't believe you missed, mate," Bond said to the Colonel. "You must be losing it in your old age."

"I didn't miss. My bullet hit him between the eyes. You're the one who can't shoot straight."

"Bollocks. I had him dead to rights. I was aiming right where the bullet struck him. That was my kill."

The two were equal in marksmanship. Both had experience as snipers. Hard to believe either of them missed. They were carrying handguns which did make it harder to hit a moving target.

Maybe both bullets found the same spot. No one took the time to inspect the body which was immediately loaded into the helicopter. Then flown to the helipad by the police station. It took all of us to load the giant into the helicopter.

Bond flew it to a location just off the coastline and landed on the ice. I went with him. Together we hiked over the ice to the shore. I had the missile launcher from the police station with me. I fired it from the shoreline. Striking the ice near where the helicopter was sitting. I didn't want to hit the helicopter with the missile because it would leave a debris field.

The ice gave way and the helicopter fell through immediately. To the depths of the ocean floor.

"So Rikki escaped," Brad said, skeptically.

"Nope," I said. "Like I said, the helicopter took off and landed on the ice. I guess the ice wasn't thick enough. It fell through. Rikki is at the bottom of the ocean."

No one would ever try to recover it. Very few people would even know this information. Certainly none of the other countries. All they needed to know was that Rikki was dead and we weren't able to recover the body.

"And what happened to the giant's body?" Brad asked.

"We don't know. Didn't stay around long enough to find out."

This wasn't the first time we had lied to Brad about a mission and wouldn't be the last. In this instance, the lies were sanctioned. No one was around to refute the story. It'd be buried in the archives anyway. Classified. Labeled top secret.

Everyone who counted would be beyond thrilled. A successful mission in the books.

Brad sat back in his chair. Satisfied.

"Lily's doing good," he said. "She's with a good family."

I held up my hand to stop him.

"I don't want to know any of the details. I especially don't want to know who has her."

"Understood."

"I'm glad she's in a good home," Alex said.

"The family is ecstatic," Brad answered. "She has a sister. Lily was an answer to prayer for them. The mother isn't able to have any more kids."

"I'm glad. We're working to help the other rescued girls as well. Altogether, Rikki had more than a hundred wives and more than twenty of them were expecting. Another thirty or forty of the trafficked girls were pregnant. No telling how many children Rikki actually sired."

"That's crazy," Brad said. "The investigators in all these countries are pulling their hair out. They have a huge mess on their hands. Trying to sort it all out."

"I'm not surprised," I said. "They've got all those children who were already born. Taken from their mothers and given to other families to raise. It will be hard to figure it all out."

"There will be custody battles," Alex said.

"Jamie, how did Kaley do?" Brad asked.

"Exceeded my expectations. She's good. Really good."

"I'm glad to hear it. Does she still have a thing for A-Rad?"

"Yes. And he has a thing for her. But he's afraid to act on it."

"That's A-Rad," Alex said. "He'll charge up a hill with a dozen people shooting at him. Can't drum up the courage to ask a girl out on a date."

"It's complicated," I said. "We had that same problem before we started dating. Remember Alex? We weren't sure it was a good idea to start up a relationship. I remember your feet being a little cold."

"I always wanted to be with you." Alex said.

"Hey, Brad. Do you remember when you sent Alex and I on our first mission together?"

He nodded.

Brad had an analytical mind. He probably remembered every mission he'd ever sent us on.

Alex chimed in. "You sent us to Singapore. Posing as a married couple on our honeymoon!"

"It was Curly's idea," Brad said.

"I didn't know that!" I said.

"He said you'd either kill each other or end up married for real," Brad said. "Guess he was right."

"Why don't we do the same thing with A-Rad and Kaley?" I said. Feeling a sly grin come over my face.

"What thing?" Brad asked.

"Let's send A-Rad and Kaley to Singapore. On a mission together. Posing as a married couple on their honeymoon."

"A-Rad will have a cow!" Alex said.

"It's a good idea," I said. "It'll force them to define their relationship."

Brad picked up his phone.

"Can you send A-Rad and Kaley in now, please?" he said to his secretary.

They were in the lobby of his office. Waiting for their Germany mission debriefing.

The door opened and they walked in.

I looked over at Alex and smiled. He had a wide grin on his face. Our time in Singapore had been eventful. To say the least.

"Have a seat," Brad said.

They sat down at the conference table. Both looked nervous.

"I have a mission for the two of you," Brad said. "Germany went so well, I'm going to send you to Singapore."

"What are we going to be doing there?" Kaley asked.

"You're going to pose as a married couple on your honeymoon," I blurted out.

"What!" Kaley said. Her mouth gaped open.

A-Rad turned bright red. His cheeks were the color of a tomato.

I looked over at Alex.

Their reactions were priceless.

If their mission was anything like ours was, then they were in for the shock of their lives.

Not The End

Thank you for purchasing this novel from best-selling author, Terry Toler. As an additional thank you, Terry wants to give you a free gift.

Sign up for:
Updates
New Releases
Announcements
At terrytoler.com

We'll send you a copy of *The Book Club*, a Cliff Hangers mystery, free of charge.

READ MORE BOOKS FROM TERRY TOLER

Jamie Austen Thrillers

Read all the Jamie Austen Thrillers. They must be good.
They've been number one on Amazon in ten different countries.
Click on the link below.

THE JAMIE AUSTEN THRILLERS (12 book series)
Kindle Edition (amazon.com)

https://amzn.to/3vmPUy7

Cliff Hangers Mystery Series

Who wants to read a good mystery? We've got you covered! Read the Cliff Hangers where homicide detective, Cliff Ford, solves crimes in Chicago, with help from his wife Julia. These books have everything Terry Toler is known for. Page turning suspense, a hint of romance, and an ending you won't see coming.

The Cliff Hangers Mystery Series (4 book series)
Kindle Edition (amazon.com)

https://amzn.to/36WX3go

About Terry

Terry Toler is an Amazon international # 1 best-selling and award-winning author. He writes clean fiction with a message and life-changing nonfiction. He's a public speaker, entrepreneur, and has authored more than forty books.

Sign up for his newsletter where you'll get free stuff, exclusive content, and news of releases and promotions. He can be followed at terrytoler.com.

If you like his books, please take a few minutes to leave a review on Amazon. We really appreciate it. It helps draw more readers to his books. Thanks!